This book is a
through the years that I worked undercover. To Reese, I love you
and thank you for standing strong even though I might have been
difficult to deal with at times. I know I was not there for some
pretty significant events because of my commitment to my job and
my mission to fight drug traffickers and organized crime. Thank
you for being so understanding, supportive, and for all you have
done in caring for our children while I was not at home, especially
during the six years of my overseas deployments on U.S. federal
government operations and missions. None of this would have
been possible without your love and constant support. I am truly
blessed to have you in my life, and I thank God that He brought
us together. No matter where life takes us, I will always respect
you and appreciate all that you have done for our children and me.

To my sons (Kaleb, Noah, and Hunter) and daughter
(McKenna), I love you and you are my life! All that I did was in
order to make the world a better place for the four of you. You are
my inspiration and the motivating force to do what is right even
when the odds are stacked against me. I know my contributions to
make this world a better place may seem insignificant in the larger
scheme of things but I hope I demonstrated to each of you how to
live life to the fullest, always try your best, and to do what is right
no matter the cost. I also want to thank you all for the sacrifices
you made, by allowing me to devote a significant amount of time
and energy to my work. I will love you forever!

Thank you to the rest of my family and friends for
supporting me over the years. Mom, your kindness towards others
will always be known and does not go unnoticed. Dad, your work
ethic has been a motivating and driving force in my life and made
me who I am today. Heather, I know we have disagreed at times,
especially when we were younger, but I will always love you and

be here for you. Clint, I miss the days when we were younger and use to hang out together more. I regret taking those times for granted. Kinsley, Ellory, Coleton, Teagon, Cohen, Brian J., Laura J., Anna, Angel David P. (RIP), Joan P., Tony L., Danny T., Nell T., Angel Grandma Sally, Angel Grandpa Walt, Angel Grandma Evangeline, Angel Grandpa Donald, Angel Aunt Laura G., Angel Papa Hicks, Chad, Jay, Lindsey, Uncle Max, Uncle Scott, North, Amy, Uncle Kurt, Aunt Polly, Kelley, Michelle, Ryan, Angel Scott (RIP), Uncle Paul & Aunt Kay, Aunt Debbie, Aunt Sandy, Uncle Lamar, Uncle Rick, Aunt Sara Jane, Brent, Brandy, Sallie, Nate C., Tatum, Catherine W., Cady-Nell, David K., Blake, Mary Louis, Zach, Lee, Rebecca, Clark, Ansley, Jeff P., Autumn, Christian, Jake, Carlton, and to anyone else that I unintentionally failed to mention, I love you all.

I would also like to thank my fellow narcs and other law enforcement brothers and sisters for always having my back, no matter the price. Specifically, I would like to thank two of my closest friends and the most skilled undercover partners I had the privilege of working with during these times, Lyle K. and Pat W. In addition, I would like to thank all of the other narcs that I worked with over the years, specifically: Mark W., Bobbie C., Melissa L., Doyle B., Jeff S., "AJ" H., Scott W., Tina D., Randy E., Charlie B., Jim B., Steve P., Craig M., Brad S., John G., Ed H., Neysa, Pat M., Chris M., Rob C., Will L., Ret. Capt. John G., Brian C., Scott H., Jason P., Jay R., Randy S., Mark P., Dave W., Tim M., Mike K., Jim K., Steve T., Chris I., Mike T., Michael V., James T., Scotty B., Waseel C., Sean A., Stacy G., Carlos O., Kevin G., Jorge C., "Jank", Big Rick M., Wes M., Chad B., and anyone else I forgot to mention.

I would like to recognize and thank Charlie F., Rad F., Mark W., and Tony R. (RIP brother) for your guidance, knowledge, wisdom, and advice as mentors to younger undercover officers. A special thanks goes out to Roger T., Sam H., and Jim B. for being positive mentors and role models to me at the beginning of my law enforcement career.

May God bless all of those who gave their lives fighting to make America a better and safer place for future generations. The following colleagues gave the ultimate sacrifice: Deputy Andrew M., D-38 (EOW: 08-17-2003); K-9 "Billy" RIP; Special Agent A. P. S. (B.A. # 169), S/A Corbin (B.A.T. Class #169), Tony R. (GCSO), Chester B. (SLED & Afghanistan), and Special Agent Enrique "Kiki" Camarena for giving your life to the cause, which ultimately saved many other DEA Agents who served after you. Because of you, the cartels learned the hard way not to mess with the DEA.

Although they were not narcs, the following people need to be recognized because they were some of the most assertive officers I worked with and people who prided themselves in cleaning the streets of drug dealers: Ranger Mike M., Ranger Jason L, Matt F., Waylon R., Rob C. ("Jersey"), and Arnold A. There are many other great street cops, dispatchers, and personal friends that I feel compelled to recognize, as well. Thank you, Charlie D., Jonathon E., Adam M., Brendon M., Mike E., Lance M., Kale J., Cheryl H-W., Ret. Sgt. Jim B., George M., Fred M., Margaret Q., Jennifer L., Mike T., Timmie W., Sam H., Cheryl W., George M., Jason P., Travis G., Weibel, Jeremy B., Adam S., Adam R., Darren P., Morris M., Doug N., Ben A., Jennifer L., Sandra M., Shay B., Ernie B., Dominique A., John U., Steve R., Gene D., Judge Dean F., Greg W., Jeff L., Chris M., Beamer M., Cindy M., Kevin P., Betsy P., Ron P., Janet & Chloe M., Doug N., Kathy & Mike N., Addison K., Greg W., Rick G., Adam H., Brenda O. & Angel Susan O., Patty & Guy H., Ben & Angel Stacy R., Mike & Lori T., Preacher Terry R., Mr. T. & "Wonderboy", Micha V., Jon W., Don & Sandee W., Shaun W., Jeff & Gail W., Corey B. (Simper Fi), Tre' I., Jason D., Hommando G., Sal G.,

Tee J., Randy F., Mike G., Kevin P., James K., Marc J., Rocky D., Charles B., Robbie K., Mike K., TJ K., Jeff & Tracy J., Jon & Dawn I., Kristina A-E., Mr. Holloway, Chris H., Adam M., Edgar F., Grand Master Kim, Master Wan, Sylvia & Charlie L., Sam L., Eric & Julie J., Linda & Walt L., Pat T., Joel C., Jeff & Erin C., Mark R., Ed H., Carlee & Vic S., Richard & Kay D., Jason & Jennifer J., Kylee & Robbie D., Geneva L., Taylor G., Elizabeth B., Dr. Welborn, Racheal T., Marilyn T., Coach Charlie & Shea M., Joe & Michelle L., Ben W., Zach G., John G., Byron B., Brad & Susan L., Roxy & Jim K., Jennifer & Keith T., Mike H., Joe B., Steve D., Michelle G., Dave G., Todd & Marguerite G., Kayla, Chris & April E., Roy B., Coach Van T., Taylor III, Coach Mike H., Coach Mike "The Barrell" S. (RIP), Rachel, Aaron S., and anyone else I forgot to mention.

Thank you, Retired Police Chief Harrold S. (RIP Brother), for giving me a shot when I was a young man fresh out of college. Also, a token of my appreciation goes to Retired Chief Willie J. and Retired Sheriff Steve L. for allowing me to work undercover for both of your departments. A big shout also goes out to my previous supervisor with the DEA, Steve T. ("Big Steve").

Special thank you to Bob G. and Connie G. for allowing and trusting in me to write drug education articles for the *Sentinel Newspaper*. Thank you to photojournalist Gwinn Davis, formerly of the *Tribune Times*, for the articles and photos I would like to personally recognize a special group of local, state, and federal prosecutors that were willing to take my cases and many other cases to trial, especially when the defendants were playing hard ball. Thank you specifically, Joyce M., Allen F., Tom C., JD R., Andy M., Matt W., Linda W., Regan P., Dave S., Sara D., Chet, Tony M., Walt W., Andrew C., Sloan E., George C., Jenny B., Kimberly H., Lisa B., Howard S., and Judy M. Also, I would like to thank some defense attorneys for keeping me on my toes over the years and for the learning experiences you gave me: Ryan B., Brooks D., Wes M., Wally F., Jim B., Bill B., Bruce B., Chase H. and any others I accidentally forgot to mention.

In addition, I would like to thank my law enforcement brothers that I worked with in Afghanistan, Haiti, and West Africa, specifically: Jerry B., Cliff O., Addison K., Jeff P., Mike M., Oscar D., Pat C., Tim B., Ashen "Sonny" R., Tommy P., Andy C., Donnie F., Shane J., Scott H., Mike B., Stan K., Dr. Paul Z., Varney S., and Akim. I am grateful that we all made it home safely and are back with our families again. Thank you, Patrick S. and Tony C. for being so supportive and encouraging me to finish this book; Phil K. for the advice on writing and publishing; and Heidi B. for being my editor and so much more throughout this process.

A special shout out goes to Jason Edward Fort, a friend, amazing author, mentor, and fellow law enforcement officer that guided me in getting this book published. I sincerely appreciate your help and assistance to make this dream into a reality for me. I am looking forward to reading more of your fictional adventure book series, The Knox Mission.

Finally, I would like to thank GOD for guiding me spiritually throughout my life and for bringing me home safely each night for more than twenty years in law enforcement. Thank you for my family, friends, and talents. I am truly blessed. You are my Savior and strength in everything I do.

Preface

Early in my law enforcement career, I began thinking seriously about writing my autobiography. I wanted my family, especially my children, to know what I was doing when I was not home. During my days of undercover work, it was hard and often impossible to talk about what I was going through day-to-day. So, this book is my attempt to give my family and readers a true glimpse into the physical, mental, and emotional aspect of my life as a law enforcement and undercover officer. Throughout this book series, I will describe in great detail the many triumphs and struggles that I faced on my way up the ranks from, Undercover Police Officer to County VICE & Narcotics Investigator to Special Agent with the Drug Enforcement Administration (DEA). Most law enforcement officers may only experience undercover work from one of these perspectives, but I was honored to be able to experience all three. You will learn how I had to intentionally mislead others and how I mentally prepared myself to overcome the various difficult situations I encountered in my more than two decades in law enforcement and undercover work.

Eventually, I managed to reach the highest level of drug enforcement when I was hired as a Special Agent with the DEA. Some of the things I did I would do differently if I had the second chance. It is said that, "hindsight's twenty-twenty", but looking back, I truly have no regrets, because during each situation and every step of the way, I learned so many valuable lessons. I learned that I must decide between right and wrong in a split second, while keeping my safety and that of my coworkers always in the forefront of my mind. I also was reminded, with each case, that the separation between good and evil is truly a thin line that should never be crossed.

It is my hope that my readers will enjoy these real-life undercover stories as I recount them in the pages of this four-book series. You will experience my day-to-day life through these very raw and honest accounts of my work as an Undercover Police Officer (Vol. 1), County VICE & Narcotics Investigator (Vol. 2 & 3), and DEA Special Agent (Vol. 4). The stories are broken down into various undercover investigations and operations that took place over the years, as I evolved in my career from a rookie cop into a veteran narc.

You will also learn some valuable insight into the drug underworld, about drug users, and the many effects of the different drugs they use. You will learn how undercover law enforcement officers overcome some daunting challenges such as pretending to use drugs, the constant fear of being exposed as a narc, and literally fighting for your life while gathering evidence for cases. You will see that a law enforcement officer with the right mindset, physical toughness, ethics, and faith can escape the most harrowing experiences.

A large percentage of my career has focused in the areas of drug/narcotics and gang investigations. I have a vast level of experience in undercover operations and have worked in an undercover capacity in the following types of operations: purchasing drugs/narcotics, buying automatic weapons, murder for hire, illegal gambling, prostitution stings, human trafficking, and gang infiltration, just to name a few. During my career as a law enforcement officer, I have personally been involved in over two-hundred successful undercover drug operations and over six-hundred narcotics/vice investigations. I have executed more than three-hundred and fifty search warrants and investigated more than fifty clandestine or secret criminal drug labs.

My vast amount of knowledge and diverse undercover experiences have allowed me to consult with the prosecution on major drug cases and on numerous occasions to testify on behalf of the federal and state government, as an "expert witness." In my career, I have had more than twenty newspaper articles published in the areas of drug identification, drug use, and undercover operations.

After my time as an undercover narc, I was able to achieve many great things in my career such as having the honor of serving as Chief of Police. While Chief of Police, I trained my entire department in drug enforcement tactics and increased drug arrests/drug crimes detected by more than 287%. As a result, I took my jurisdiction city from #28 Safest City in the State of South Carolina to #1, within two years' time.

Eventually, I climbed the ranks of international policing when I became the United States Contingent Commander for the United Nations on an overseas mission in Haiti and also a national commander on a U.S. federal government contract in Afghanistan. Then I became a Senior Law Enforcement and Leadership Advisor under a U.S. federal government contract in West Africa. In each of these positions, I found a drug nexus and my roots as a narc helped me to excel. When my career in law enforcement has ended, I want to be remembered as a man who "walks the walk and does not just talk the talk." With the support of community members, colleagues, friends, family, and especially God, I trust that I will.

TABLE OF CONTENTS

Disclaimer

The information in each crime fiction book is meant as a general resource book for entertainment purposes; it is not meant to provide any legal, medical or any other advice. The Publisher and the Author make no representations or warranties with respect to the accuracy or completeness of the contents of the work and specifically disclaim all warranties of fitness for a particular purpose. The advice and strategies contained therein may not be suitable for every situation. The work is sold with the understanding that the Publisher and the Author are not providing any legal, consulting, rehabilitative, medical, or other professional services. If legal, consulting, rehabilitative, medical, or other expert assistance is required, the services of competent and/or licensed professionals should be sought. All stories within these books are based upon true and actual events, but for the readers excitement and the creative fiction element of the book, to also protect actual person(s), the names, businesses, events and incidents, within the content may or may not include some information that is the product of the author's imagination, but the overall stories are intended to be true and factual to the best of the authors recollection of the events as they occurred. With that said, some events in the books may be the most accurate recollection of the Author's memory based upon facts told to him by others, so the Author shall not be held responsible for any inaccuracies as a result of information told to him by seemingly reliable sources. The Author has changed names of most, if not all, parties, omitted some specific locations and redacted facial images or identifying characteristics in photographs, as well as identifying information in public documents in order to protect the identity of parties involved. Any resemblance to an actual person(s), living or dead, may or may not be purely coincidental, and is not intended to cause any harm to the professional reputation or personal character of any individual. Neither the Publisher nor the Author shall be liable for any loss of profit or any other commercial damages, including but not limited to special, incidental, consequential, personal, medical, financial, or other damages. No part of this publication may be reproduced, stored in a retrieval system, or transmitted in any form or by any means, electronic, mechanical, photocopying, recording, reenacting, scanning, or otherwise, without the prior written permission of the author. If you do not accept these terms, please stop reading at this time.

A NARC'S TALE
VOL. 2 of 4

Based Upon A True Story
Working Undercover as a
County Narcotics Investigator

KEITH P. GROUNSELL

Chapter One

Transition from City to County Undercover

After a year working undercover, as discussed in A NARC'S TALE: Volume 1, and seeing a few ethically questionable things done by the administration of that city police department, I decided to move on to a larger, more diverse county law enforcement agency. One of the things that really tipped the scale in favor of me leaving was when our Chief of Police testified against his own officers, as a character witness for the defense in the trial of an accused criminal. Not only was this unexpected, but he kept his job after doing so. The defendant, which the Chief testified for, was a known drug dealer. Years earlier, that drug dealer assaulted several police officers from another agency, and it was all caught on video. It just so happens that when that incident occurred, I was working for that particular agency, and those law enforcement officers were my friends and colleagues who had been violently assaulted. It was alleged that the Chief of Police worked against his own officers who arrested this guy because of pressures from members of a large area church who were supporting the defendant.

After the Chief's testimony, the suspect only received house arrest instead of the ten-year prison sentence he was probably facing. I was so disappointed and disgusted. Although I respect some of the things this Chief did in his career, and I was thankful for him allowing me to work undercover, I did not want to work under his type of leadership any longer. So, I decided to put in my application with the sheriff's office. I always stand for ethical principles, and I do what I believe is right in my heart, no matter what. Therefore, once I decide on something, I do not doubt myself or ever look back. This headstrong and steadfast approach has earned me a lot of respect throughout my life but has also come with its fair share of heartache and sacrifice.

It truly was not a hard decision to make the switch, because the county had recently elected a new Sheriff who replaced the 'good ole boy' politician who had been in power for decades. Our new Sheriff was what we called a "cops' cop" and a hard-core lawman, having served in special units and with the SWAT team. He never came across as a polished politician, but more of a straight-shooting lawman. In the back of my mind, I imagined that one day I too might become Sherriff. I would want to be as equally respected and viewed in the similar light or even better than him, all while adding my own unique flair and style of leadership.

Within two to three weeks of putting in my application for employment, the sheriff's office hired me. They loved to do lateral transfers from the city because they were always competing with them to maintain experienced and certified officers. The sheriff's office was an approximately four-hundred-man department, excluding civilian employees and personnel at the jail. From day one with the sheriff's office, I let it be known that I wanted to get back into working full-time narcotics. Like anything in life, you need to make your goals known and then do what is required to achieve them. You never know who is listening and who might help you along the way. Any assistance may not come immediately, or ever, but it is worth the shot.

Although the new Sheriff was an honorable and hardworking man, sadly, it seemed that the 'good ole boy' mentality and the political system still existed among the other top officers with ties to the previous Sheriff. This meant that you had to know the right people for advancement, and one thing I refuse to do is kiss someone's ass. Also, I hated to toot my own horn or talk myself up. I figured I just needed to tell the right people that I wanted to work dope for the sheriff's office, and then let my work ethic, team-player attitude, and track record speak for itself. I was confident that I would make significant drug cases and get recognized; it was only a matter of time, so I buckled down and went to work.

This same approach is something I use today to instill values in my children. It can be applied to everyday life, but especially to athletics. All of my children are competitive athletes in their chosen sport. Sports teach many valuable lessons in life from overcoming obstacles, winning/losing, and working together as a team towards a common goal. For these reasons and plus the fact that exercise is great for you both mentally and physically, I push my children to participate in athletics. I teach my children not to talk junk when they play, but to demonstrate greatness during their games or competitions. I also teach my children to

4

play their hardest, leave it all on the field, but to also demonstrate sportsmanship along the way. Meaning, if they run someone over in a play due to extra hustle or gusto, then they should be the first to help that person up; or if someone blows a play and their team loses the game, they should be the first to lift them up and encourage them because they might be in their shoes one day with the roles reversed.

I have always lived by the biblical motto of Treat others the way you want to be treated. I let my children know that if they will do these positive things, others will do the talking for them and their successes will speak volumes without my kids having to say anything. As I have mentioned earlier, tooting your own horn, which I try to avoid because it can come across as egotistical and big-headed, is necessary sometimes. I ran into this dilemma later when I was the Chief of Police, and then again when I ran for Sheriff. In elected positions, you must sell yourself to get votes. This means you must tell everyone why you are the most qualified over others to get the job you want. For me, it was awkward and uncomfortable, but it was a fine line I had to walk, without coming across as arrogant.

All in all, I spent a little less than six months working in uniform patrol with the sheriff's office before I was promoted to an investigator position with the Vice & Narcotics Division. During those six months on the road, I made plenty of felony drug arrests and had to transition back into the openly-tactical-cop mode and mindset. When working undercover, you had to be tactical, but had to do so with more subtlety. If you appear to be 'blading' a suspect with your strong side back to protect your weapon every time you speak to someone, you would not last long undercover. You have to behave and think like a cop continually, but while undercover, this can never be obvious to targets, or you will blow your cover and possibly get hurt or killed.

During those six months on uniformed patrol, I was able to make the "Mad Dog 20/20 Club" every month. This was a special award given out to deputies on the Delta Platoon, of which I was Delta Forty-Nine (D-49). This meant that I made over twenty arrests and served over twenty warrants each month while working twelve-hour shifts over only a fifteen-day span, which makes these numbers even more commendable. Never one to accept the status quo, and always being a hard worker, I would clear close to forty in each of these areas; warrants and arrests, in each month. These arrests and citations were accomplished above and beyond my regular duties (i.e., monitoring traffic and non-stop service calls) as a beat-cop.

While in uniform patrol, I surrounded myself with like-minded and assertive cops, such as Ranger Mike, Will L., Drew M., J. Lopez, and several others. We were borderline too aggressive for some, and tough to supervise at times. But we were the go-to guys to hunt down gang members, violent felons, and drug traffickers in our area. We were the guys that asked forgiveness later instead of permission first when told to track down a suspect. We patrolled the west side of the county that bordered the city limits and extended to the mountains. This area did not lack action and excitement, which was only compounded by our "shit magnet" personalities. Always making big cases and calling the vice and narcotics unit to pass on intelligence gathered, is what built the trust of some members that were already investigators in the unit. I never kept things to myself and had no issues sharing intelligence, so that vice and narcotics investigators could take their work to the next level. The fact that I never sought recognition for any of this earned me a reputation as a team player.

Also, this exceptional work ethic got my name out there as being precisely the type of guy they wanted in the Vice & Narcotics Unit with the sheriff's office. This was a very close-knit unit, and if they did not think you would be a good fit, you were not accepted. Earning their respect was especially important, and that was done by being part of the team, supporting others, and not acting like a know-it-all. They did not give a damn how much experience I had, or what I knew from my time working undercover in another agency, until they realized how much I cared for and assisted my colleagues in this unit. When an opening came up, the Sheriff accepted my application. Although I had not yet reached the minimum one-year requirement to work uniform patrol before entering the Vice & Narcotics Unit, because of my experience working undercover for the city and positive track record, I was considered for the position anyway. I was also interviewed by several of the officers in the narcotics unit to ensure I was a good fit for them. Like I said, this was an extremely close group of people that worked in a hazardous environment on sensitive cases, so they had to know I was someone they could trust with their lives before they gave the green light on my approval.

I was greatly appreciative that after only six-months the Sheriff waived the one-year requirement and put me into Vice & Narcotics. I was never able to thank him personally. Not long after my promotion he died in a car accident while leaving his gym. It was later determined that the Sheriff had a heart attack while driving and was dead before impact. Losing a "cops' cop" as your leader sucked, to say the least. I had finally gotten to a good place in my career with a great leader and now he was gone. Not being deterred, I never let it affect me at the worker-bee level. His death only served to remind me how precious and short life can be, so we should live it to the best of our abilities for as long as we can.

(BELOW) My first patrol car with the sheriff's office was a 2001 Crown Vic. I was unit D-49, covering area 9.

(BELOW) This is one sample of the Mad Dog 20/20 Club commendation letters I received each month on delta platoon.

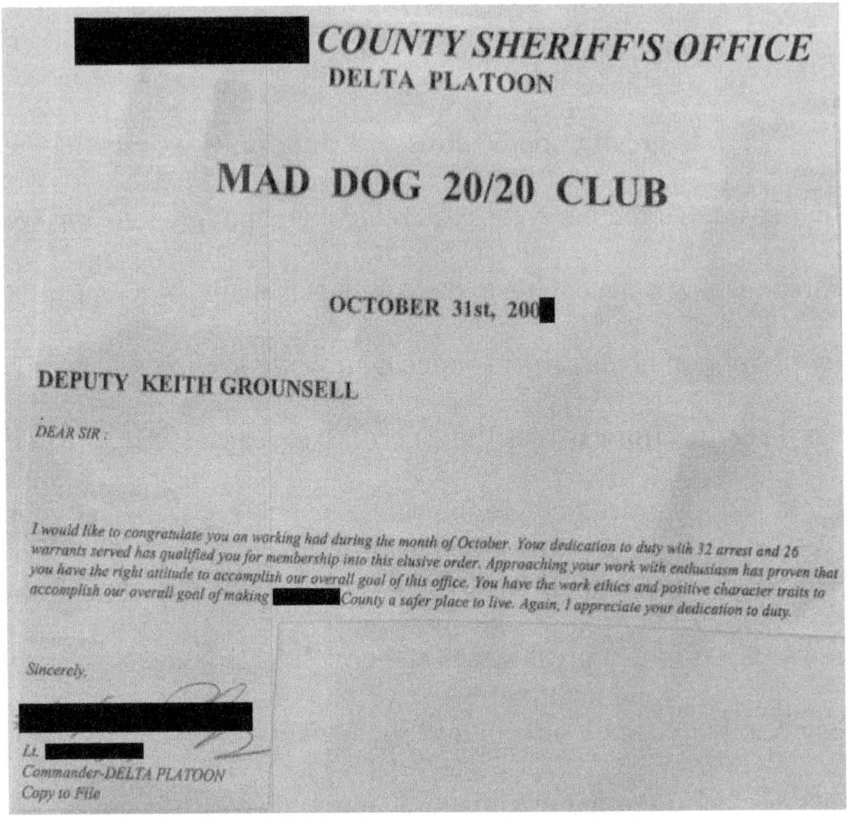

█████████ COUNTY SHERIFF'S OFFICE
DELTA PLATOON

MAD DOG 20/20 CLUB

OCTOBER 31st, 200█

DEPUTY KEITH GROUNSELL

DEAR SIR :

I would like to congratulate you on working hard during the month of October. Your dedication to duty with 32 arrest and 26 warrants served has qualified you for membership into this elusive order. Approaching your work with enthusiasm has proven that you have the right attitude to accomplish our overall goal of this office. You have the work ethics and positive character traits to accomplish our overall goal of making ███████ County a safer place to live. Again, I appreciate your dedication to duty.

Sincerely,

████████████

Lt. ████████
Commander-DELTA PLATOON
Copy to File

(RIGHT) This is one of the only pictures of me in uniform while with the sheriff's office

10

(BELOW) Newspaper article when the Sheriff passed away.

The Difference Between City Vice & Narcotics and County Vice & Narcotics

The city police department covered an area that was about twenty-five square miles and had over two-hundred uniformed police officers. The sheriff's office covered an area that was about seven-hundred-fifty square miles and had over four-hundred uniformed deputies. Clearly, there was a big difference in jurisdiction size and workforce, but the City and County Vice and Narcotics Units, were both fifteen-man units. This made no sense to me. One of the most common mistakes that I see among law enforcement administrations is, they fail to give adequate numbers of personnel for the investigations of drug and vice-related crimes. This is common however because the primary emphasis is on what citizens can see: uniform patrol, not what they cannot see (i.e. Undercover or Vice & Narcotics Investigators).

My estimate is that more than ninety percent of all crimes can be linked to drugs and alcohol in some way, shape, or form. This can be anything from the burglar breaking into a house and stealing to pawn some items to get money to purchase drugs, to the domestic violence perpetrator who beats his wife while under the influence of drugs or alcohol. No matter what crime you analyze, it can more than likely be traced back to drugs or alcohol, abuse, sales, or trafficking. With that said, for a sheriff's office or police department to devote less than five

12

percent of its total manpower specifically to drug and vice crimes is somewhat unimaginable. Still, it is something that goes on across the country. This makes me ask myself, *Are we truly serious about putting a dent in the drug problem?*

In the past, there had always been a bad working relationship between the county and city vice and narcotics units in my area. Since I worked for both the city and county, I knew there was not a lot of difference in the actual investigators themselves. Over time, I tried my best to mend that strained relationship but felt I was talking to deaf ears. Since I had worked for both the city and county units and knew all the investigators/detectives, I felt like I may be the right person to do this.

For some reason, the county looks at the city as though they are stepping on the county's feet each time they call for assistance with something that they have in the county. On the other hand, the city looks at the county as untrustworthy, because they always get pissed off or are given the shaft, because the county officers cannot always be there to help out any time when the city initiates something outside of their jurisdiction and in the county. This division was partly due to our supervisors, who said, "If it comes in the county, it is our case, and we don't need the city's help."

The city needs the county because its jurisdiction is limited, but the county looks at it as though they do not need the city because the city limits lie within the jurisdiction of the county. In other words, we did not want to work together because nobody wanted to give up what they were doing to help the other unit because they would not get any credit. The city and county units did not share seizure or arrest stats. This is where I think a metro narcotics unit would have indeed benefited both the county and city units. Then the problem comes up of who would control it, the Sheriff, the Chief of Police, or the Solicitor? None of these individuals would want to come in and allow someone else to run something that operates in a law enforcement capacity within their jurisdiction, without their oversight. Maybe a board consisting of these persons would be the answer. Who knows? I am often thinking of these problem-solution scenarios.

Fast forward twenty years, and this is what happened when they formed a Drug Enforcement Task Force that consisted of six police departments and the sheriff's office. The leadership from each agency voted on the task force commander, so it quickly became political. In these situations, guys like me that are hard-chargers and do not play politics are never given a shot. It did not matter if I was ten times more qualified and the right guy for the position. They were not going to pick me because I was not a guy that could be controlled like a political puppet. A few of my law enforcement character traits are dedication, innovation, and a non-conformist. If you want drug dealers, gang

14

members, and other violent criminals locked up aggressively, then I was your guy, but if you want a figure-head type to hold the position and merely do the status quo or the bare minimum, then that's not me. As I was once told by a supervisor years later about my work *little cases, little problems; big cases, big problems* and he said, "You are causing me big problems." It is a sad reality, but this is how some leadership views people like me and others, the workhorses that fear nothing to get the job done.

One of the most significant differences between the county and city units is that because the sheriff's office was so much larger than the city, a person could work undercover for a lot longer in the county before they got burned. This meant I could spend years working undercover. Whereas with the city, after a couple of years, I might easily be identified by previous targets or their associates. The limited city jurisdiction causes an undercover to run into the same people repeatedly, which could become dangerous over time and after several arrests.

At the vice and narcotics investigator level, there was little to no difference in the city and county units. The difference was at the top with the supervisors and older personnel that had *bad blood* and held grudges. As a narc, I knew that collaborating with other local agencies on cases increased our numbers and gave us access to additional equipment and resources. Increasing our numbers and sharing intelligence improved our chances of identifying and apprehending more high-level drug traffickers, which should be the goal of any vice & narcotics unit.

Unfortunately, I never fully mended the relationship between the city and county narcotics units. Still, I know I helped a little by assisting the city whenever they needed to work in the county on a case, that initially started in the city limits. I often had to do this on the down-low because my supervisor was not keen on taking me off assignment to help the city, which was part of that 'old school' mindset. It was like a reunion each time I went back to the city vice and narcotics unit to help, so I never minded. The city wanted the relationship because they needed the county for jurisdiction purposes. The problem was that the county did not need the city, and because they felt that they had no incentive to do so, they failed to help on numerous occasions. This is a typical and on-going battle between city police and county sheriffs all over the United States. However, the more efficient vice and narcotics agencies, are those who finally realize that they are more powerful working together.

(BELOW) This is a copy of my sheriff's office identification card approximately 1 year prior to the new one (above) being issued. During this time, the Sheriff died and a new digital ID card was one of the first changes, which is why they look so different.

(BELOW) This is a copy of my sheriff's office identification card, also known as my credentials. After constantly getting stopped by the uniformed patrol officers working the front desk/entrance when I went to the main law enforcement building, I had the records personnel get me a new police id with a photo that looked like me now. My old photo was with me looking like a cop on the road, not an undercover cop. The new id helped officers to not give me as much of a hassle when I showed my police credentials to enter a private area restricted to police personnel only.

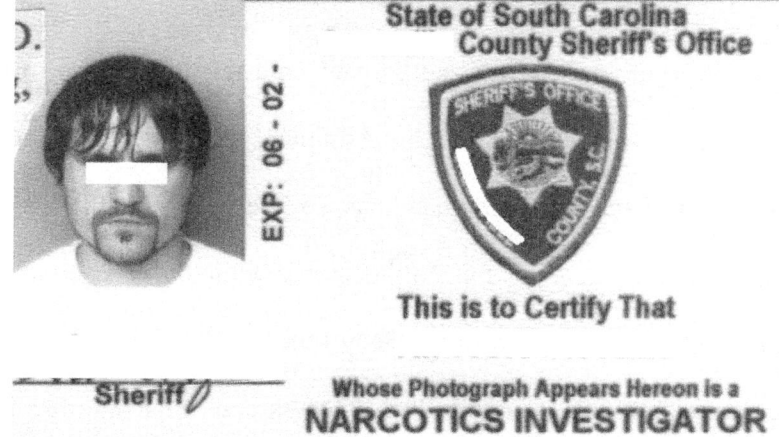

(BELOW) *This is an image of me with city narcs and members of the local DEA office posing with drugs and cash we seized in a joint operation. This was one case that started when we helped the city and it subsequently involved the DEA, so jurisdiction was not a problem. It only goes to show how much can be accomplished working together.*

Dating & Marrying a Narc and
the Mental Effects of Undercover Work

Working undercover can be hard on a relationship, no matter how strong the relationship may be. As a narc, I needed to hang out at the local clubs and other drug hangouts, so I became a familiar face in the drug game. Of course, this only occurred while on duty, but a true UC narc is never really off duty. Many times, people might not know who I was, but they recognized my face as somewhat familiar in a particular environment; that opened up doors for me in the drug game. I needed to be patient and realize that the deals did not happen immediately; unless I fit in with the crowd and did not appear to be a suspicious outsider. This meant looking and acting like the 'target' or a drug dealer. To stay mentally grounded, I always tried to remember that this was only role-playing, and I was not one of them. I needed to learn to turn it on at work and off at home. Unfortunately, this is much easier said than done.

A couple of months before I started working my first fulltime undercover assignment, I met the woman who later became my wife. When we first met, I was still in uniform patrol, working for the city police department. She was a corporate trainer and waitress at a worldwide restaurant chain. As with most people, when you first start seeing someone, you like to show each other off to your friends, especially if you have a good-looking woman that you are proud of like I was. Dating and going out in public was not a problem when I was in uniform patrol, and I did not care if anyone knew I was a police officer, but it was something I could not do when I worked undercover.

When we first got together, we were both a little wild, and neither of us was looking for a serious relationship. At least, we both acted like we were not ready to settle down, but we both knew we wanted to find that right person that we could trust and with whom we could spend our life. A mutual friend introduced us; a fellow cop (Rob C., a/k/a "Jersey"). She lived in Georgia at the time and traveled to SC every day to work as a corporate trainer for her employer.

For us, it was never your traditional story-book romance; it was much harder than that, and always seemed to be. It was not love at first sight with us. As a matter of fact, she did not like me much at first. She would later say, it was not until she saw me dancing that she started liking me or was really interested in me. One thing is for sure; I do like to have a good time and cut loose on the dance floor. This is not to say I am a great dancer, by any means, but maybe she felt sorry for me or thought my dancing was cute or sexy. Who knows?

After that, we started hanging out a lot, then fate took over when she had a vehicle accident. Thank God she was not injured, but her vehicle was totaled, leaving her without a car. It made it difficult to commute to work each day. We already got along very well, and she seemed like a sweet enough girl, so I asked her if she wanted to stay with me until she got her vehicle situation worked out. At first, I was reluctant to ask, and I am sure she was also hesitant to accept. But for some reason, we both did what we felt was right at the time, and it felt natural for us. The rest, as they say, is history. She moved in with me, and we started dating each other exclusively after that. This was a big step for me since I had never lived with a woman or at least not one in which I was romantically interested.

After a month or so of dating, I was given my first fulltime undercover assignment. As part of my new undercover role, my girlfriend agreed and had to tell all her friends that I got fired and was no longer a cop. This was done for my safety and to protect her. That is not to say it was an easy thing to do. It did not take long for the rumors about me to make their way back to my girlfriend. Her friends told her what a *dirtbag* I was and that they saw me out at the night clubs talking to and hanging around with drug dealers and other women.

Since she was my girlfriend at the time, she held her tongue and listened as her friends spoke negatively about me. Her not revealing my undercover status contributed to a deep trust between us and is one of the main reasons our relationship developed quickly. She was mentally tough and endured a lot from others as they told her how dumb she was for staying with a guy like me who was probably going to end up in prison. She was committed to keeping my secrets, and she never let all this negativity from others and her emotions overcome her. Little did we know at the time, but the enormous mental stresses of my working undercover were hardening and changing both of us as people. That eventually had considerable adverse effects on our relationship.

Nevertheless, I attribute much of my success in working undercover to her, because as it is said, "Behind every good man is an even greater woman." With us, this was undoubtedly true. Not divulging my secrets, fending off her friends' negativity about me, and ignoring her own needs to set the record straight about me showed me how strong she truly was. I will be eternally grateful to her for setting aside her image, which was temporarily tarnished by being involved with me in order for me to be successful in undercover work.

I am also glad that she did not let her pride in front of her friends stand in her way of protecting me, and my position as an undercover. She understood the potentially deadly consequences for me if she did leak my identity. By being able to trust her, it made the stress of the job much easier to bear. This relationship proved to me that I had found my future wife, even though I had not been looking to find her. God's timing is perfect, and everything happens for a reason.

After dating for more than a year and living together, we were engaged and married rather quickly. Again, things were not your typical story-book romance for us, but that was alright. It suited us and our lifestyles. We rented out a large banquet hall and had our ceremony and reception in the same place, surrounded by family, friends, and fellow narcs.

We were older when we married, and we were more independent. So, we paid for the wedding in large part ourselves. However, our family and friends volunteered catering and support at every turn. It really helped us out a lot since we were just beginning our lives together, and money was tight. Thankfully, I was able to shave and clean up for our wedding. I looked more like your typical groom, although we did not get married in a church. We took a week-long honeymoon to Daytona Beach and Disney World. We had a great time, but then it was quickly back to work for me, which meant returning to my undercover persona and looks.

Being married did not change the way I saw myself or work; it solidified my ethics. I am a very loyal person, whether it is in my marriage or on the job. A man who cheats on his spouse is not cut-out for undercover work. You must have the strongest of ethics and morals in order *not* to cross the line. If I had crossed the line and stolen money or done anything unethical or illegal during these years, I would have been a hypocrite, and no better than the people I sent to prison. You are given many opportunities to compromise your ethics and are tested daily while doing undercover work, but you must always be faithful to the job and yourself, just as you would be to your family.

I think at first, my wife thought it was pretty cool what I was doing as an undercover narcotics agent, despite the stresses previously mentioned. Some women are attracted to the *bad-guy* vibe, even if they never admit it out loud. Many women want the *bad-boy* image, but not the negative side of a real-life *bad boy* (i.e., jail, drugs, violence, etc.). She told me after I stopped working undercover that some, not all, of my different personas were sexy. It was like sleeping with a different person on a rotating basis since I looked so different all the time. It definitely helped to keep some extra spice in our love life, but eventually, things got mentally and emotionally tough on both of us, and there is nothing sexy about that.

I honestly had an awesome job, but the reality was that nobody knew what I did. Imagine doing something really cool every day, but nobody knew about it, and you could not tell anyone. There were tons of excitement, close calls, constant adrenaline dumps, but I could not tell anyone. Also, I would get so into my undercover personas that I would have a hard time turning them off when I got home. I would often speak in street slang, or unintentionally lash out at my wife as if she were a common thug I had faced that night.

I did so many crazy things that I would not tell my wife about because it would have caused her to worry about me more than she already did. She did not need that added stress. Sharing my deep undercover life with her would have been comparable to someone watching the daily news with reports about drug busts, crime, murder, prostitution, and danger twenty-four hours a day. It would have been too much. If I had told her everything, this knowledge might have forever changed her emotionally and her views on society and people in general. I was not immune to the negative consequences of seeing so much evil in the world, so working undercover changed me over time.

Not being able to talk about my day-to-day life made my job a little less cool and exciting. Also, since my wife and I had personal struggles, we were not always able to talk about them because we wanted to protect each other. I kept things from her to protect her psyche, and she kept things from me so as not to burden me with worries as soon as I walked through the door. Years later, after I was finished working undercover, I found out that she had a lot of things going on with the kids and other stressors about which she never told me. She held all these things in because she loved me and was trying to shield me from extra stress and distractions.

At the time, this allowed me to maintain focus for my mission, working undercover. I am grateful that my wife decided to withhold those stresses from me at the time. Sadly, we both sacrificed and suffered quite a bit alone, adding more strain on our marriage. Furthermore, I am not sure that if she had told me about problems during those days, I would have been there for her emotionally because I was deeply committed to my career and undercover work. This is not to say

I did not love my wife and the kids, but I knew this was my livelihood and what paid our bills. Plus, I truly knew that I was making a difference in this world. I believed in my mission and felt it was a calling from God, so I would let nothing get in my way or hold me back from being successful.

There were many mental obstacles I dealt with not only in my UC role but at home. One of the things that bothered me the most was that I felt like my wife was not as attracted to me when I looked like a drug addict because she was used to the clean-cut man she fell in love with. I later realized that much of this was just in my head and was part of the overall mental struggles of working UC. I think it helped when I tried to see things from her perspective. I know it had to have been tough on a good-looking woman like my wife, especially when we went out, to look nice and put together while I looked a little rough and like a *dirtbag* compared to her.

As a couple, when we went out, it was common for us to receive some pretty weird looks. I could only imagine how uncomfortable she felt with me at times. Some of the discomforts may have been that she did not know who I was dealing with at work, or what they looked like, so she could not have her guard up to look out for certain people. These cases were active and confidential, so my wife did not even know who my targets were.

It depended on the UC role I was playing at the time, whether or not I looked halfway decent or presentable. When posing as a crack addict, I did not shave for months, or cut my hair or fingernails. However, when posing as a high-level dealer, I would clean up, which at least made me feel better about myself while at home. This constant change in identity mentally affected my confidence and that trickled down into our relationship. Yes, it was a job, but I had to look the part, on and off duty, to be successful and survive in this undercover drug world. It was not like I could shave, cut my hair and nails, and then quickly grow it all back the day I returned to work. Sometimes it took months to get the look I wanted to achieve for a particular role: longer hair, full-length beard, long nails, and skinny or more muscular, etc. Without saying anything, I could see people thinking, *What in the Hell is she doing with him?*

I am sure we sometimes looked like a scene from *Beauty and the Beast*. None of this mattered to her, or if it did, she did not let it show, and she never complained. She was great at rolling with the punches and adapting to any situation. My wife was a country girl and was raised around guns. This was a good thing because I always wore anywhere from one to three on me.

People often asked why I had so many guns, and why I did not just carry one with an extra magazine. I often thought that if I had guns located on many different parts of my body, that I would always be able to reach one, no matter what position I was in (i.e. standing, squatting, lying down, hands behind my back, etc.). I also thought it would be quicker to keep shooting with one hand while retrieving the other gun with the other hand, so I could just continue shooting without having to stop for reloading if it ever came to that. This also gave me the added option to emergency deputize a citizen and hand him/her a gun if it was an actual life and death situation. You never know what you would face working undercover, so I prepared for the extreme worst. Maybe this was obsessive, but it was almost like my comfort blanket, to go into some of the situations that I did where I was often out-manned, and what the suspects thought was out-gunned.

Despite not being a drug user, I was paranoid like one at times. If I heard a noise outside my house at night, I grabbed the gun and went running outside. Having no hesitation, I was ready to kill anyone if I felt they came to my house to harm my family or me. I lived fearlessly and thought I was invincible at times, which is actually scary. I think this made me take more risks. I was not afraid to die either. I felt that if it was my time, then I wanted to go out heroically in a gun battle, taking out criminals at the same time.

This mindset was dangerous to not only me but others. I remember one day on the way to work, some punk rode my bumper and almost hit my UC car. He looked like a drug target I was dealing with, and I believed it was him. He kept revving the engine and almost rear-ended me intentionally three different times. I took a couple of turns, and I could not shake him, so I believed he was a threat. I finally had had enough and was not going to wait to be assaulted, so I slammed on the brakes in the middle of the road and ran up to his window and pulled him halfway out of his car before I knew what I was doing.

Just as I was about to beat the shit out of him, I came to my senses and caught myself. I let go of him as he fell the rest of the way out the window. I walked back up to my car, and drove away. If he had reported me to the police and had run my tags, they would have come back clear; as 'not on file.' After I let him go, that guy turned off the next street, and I continued driving. At this point, I knew I better get a grip on my paranoia and check myself, or I would end up getting in trouble. Even though I could have arrested him for the traffic violations, that would have been pushing it, and I was wrong in how I responded. I turned to exercise (i.e., weightlifting and boxing) as my natural-stress reliever. The job's stresses finally caught up to me, but my pride and love for the job never allowed me to tell anyone. I never told anyone about that incident on the road, until this book. At the time, I feared being pulled from doing UC if I said I needed to talk to someone, so I covered up my stress. I also felt that asking for help made me look weak, and I was known for my toughness, both physically and mentally. I know that all this bottled up stress contributed to me being quite difficult to deal with at home sometimes.

Years went by working undercover when I had a memorable conversation with my wife's gynecologist. He told me how he remembered meeting me for the first time at his office. He said he came into the room and saw my wife, an attractive woman who always was dressed classy, and then he met me during one of her visits while she was pregnant with our first child. He said he remembered thinking to himself after leaving the room, *to each his own,* meaning that he was confused why an attractive woman like my wife would be married to a guy who looked like me.

After a few visits, I felt almost compelled to tell the doctor who I was, so he would not perceive me as a *dirtbag.* After all, if you cannot trust your doctor or patient/physician privileged conversations, that is a problem. Once I told him about what I did, I noticed he immediately relaxed in his manner, and he became more personable in his demeanor towards me when I went with my wife to her appointments. Not that he was ever rude before, but he was not as talkative and personable before discovering what I did for a living.

Each doctor's visit from then on, he was very curious and would ask me questions about my work. Frequently, the doctor would stay in the room after my wife's exam and talk to me even longer than the examination had taken. I am sure this upset the next patient waiting but was glad that I finally had someone I could talk to without repercussions. When given an opportunity, I loved to share what little I could of the cases already adjudicated, while still withholding names and other specific details.

His enthusiasm for these thrilling stories was a common reaction for someone who found out I worked undercover. It was fascinating to most people, but it was also depressing, because before him, I did not have anyone besides my wife at home with whom to share my stories. As stated before, even with my wife, I could not tell her everything that went down on each deal. When I did share some about undercover, I at least downplayed the danger factor. I knew she had enough on her plate, and I did not want to worry her any more than was necessary. This was one of the reasons I initially started writing this book. I wanted to finally share the real and whole stories of what my work was like for her and my children to be able to read one day.

Living on the edge and always being hypervigilant added others stresses to my marriage. Still, I was so focused on my mission that I became somewhat insensitive to how it affected my wife. Like I have said, and despite it all, I never heard her complain about it. Over time, with me working longer and longer undercover, my wife and I started to become somewhat reclusive. It came to the point that we isolated ourselves and did not get to know or associate with our neighbors out of fear that they may find out who I was and tell someone. Occasionally, we found good neighbors that knew me before like Jon and Dawn, so it was easier to hang out with them off duty. They never asked any crazy questions, and I felt I could be myself around them because they knew what my job was. The other issue was when I was home, many times, I just did not want to talk much, and this shut down communications in my marriage. If my wife wanted to talk and I was not in the mood because of something shocking or traumatic I just did at work, I would not tell the reason, but I might snap at her or ignore her. Over time, this caused her to shut down, and our lines of communication continued to suffer as a result.

We also lived in constant fear that we may run into a drug target of mine if we went out for a night on the town or were out with the kids. I did not worry about myself but did not want any dealer to know I had a wife and kids. I thought it was better to prevent this from happening than deal with it if it came up, so we stopped going out except for when absolutely necessary, for things like groceries or doctor's appointments, etc. We tried to do our shopping late at night, or anytime we felt we would not run into someone I did not want to see. Additionally, I was on duty all the time because I regularly got calls throughout the day and night, from different people trying to set up deals. The problem was that this reclusive behavior did not give us an outlet or freedom away from the job on my days off.

What made undercover work the most difficult was that it was more of a lifestyle change than a nine-to-five job. In a regular job, you can go to work eight to twelve hours and be professional, and then go home at the end of your shift and be yourself. As an undercover, I received phone calls at all hours of the night from targets and informants. I always looked for new opportunities for a dope deal and bust but could never let my guard down, not even for a split second. This caused me to stay in 'undercover mode continually,' and I would often forget who I really was or how I was supposed to act in a given situation.

I remember being more than a little paranoid during the days when I was working deep undercover for the DEA, and a large Mexican cartel we were trying to take down (which you will read about in A Narc's Tale: Volume 4) had beheaded two informants. To say I was a bit jumpy, and continuously looking over my shoulder would be an understatement. I was always ready for a gunfight with anyone, but one evening, I almost made a costly mistake when I heard a noise in my house. I am a very light sleeper, and I quickly jumped out of bed when I heard a *thud*. I grabbed my pistol from the nightstand and silently walked in the direction of the noise. My oldest son's bedroom was across the house, and he was about two years old at the time. I wanted to make sure that if someone was in my house, I confronted them before they got to my wife or son. Coming around the corner like I was clearing a drug house with my pistol, I pointed my gun at a movement I saw. I quickly noticed it was my son; he had fallen out of the bed, woke up, and was coming down the hallway with his blanket to get in bed with us. Thankfully, I did not have my finger on the trigger, which is a safety precaution most cops are taught, but I pointed my gun at my two-year-old child and was ready to shoot, so that bothered me deeply. I quickly grabbed him up, comforted him, and took him back to bed with me. I could not have imagined what I would have done if I had shot my son due to my paranoia.

Outside of work, while driving, even with my family in the car, if a vehicle followed us for long, I would take alternate routes and lose them before going to my intended destination. I would pull out my pistol and hold it in my hand while driving, if it appeared, they were following me turn for turn, so I could get the first shot if needed. My mindset was never to be a victim. I became paranoid that I was being followed and did anything to protect my family's identity and where we lived. I know this took its toll on my wife, but she stood by and supported me without saying anything. Many years later, she told me that one of my most exceptional qualities is that of a protector. She knew that as long as I was around, I would lay down my life before anyone got to my family. Many people say they would do this, but the reality is not everyone has what it takes to aggressively fight any threat. The sad truth in life is that about three percent of the population or less will actually fight when it comes down to it. Most people are passive and avoid confrontation or freeze in the eyes of evil. This is why you have to have a sheepdog mentality to protect the flock (i.e. people) from the wolves (i.e. criminals/predators) of the world.

I often did these evasive driving tactics without saying a word, but I know that she knew what I was doing. All these things played a crucial role in developing my tendency to be an excessive thinker. This could be both a positive and negative thing. I started to *what if* everything in my mind. I did this to constantly run plans through my head on how to react to unknown situations. I know this could slowly drive a person crazy. Many years after undercover work, I still find myself doing this, and I try hard to shake the habit, but it is almost impossible after it has saved my ass on many occasions. I mentally justify doing this today by saying that it prepares me for anything. Sometimes paranoia and planning go hand and hand. However helpful, a little paranoia may be, I could not let it take over.

As I stated, the last thing I wanted was for a drug target to know that I had a wife and kids. These people are ruthless when you threaten their livelihood or freedom, and I would not put it past any of them to harm my family. This is why I chose never to wear my wedding band. This also meant no one except really close friends and family knew that I was married, as it was not apparent to strangers, including women. As an undercover, if you have an insecure or jealous woman in your life, this could escalate into a huge problem.

My wife and I have an understanding about the cheating thing; we just did not do it. It was a non-negotiable deal-breaker. Likewise, if you love and respect a person, but fall out of love with them, then you would let them know you are no longer happy with the relationship, and you should go your separate ways, especially if you feel the need to be with someone else. It is this mutual trust and shared understanding that got us through many challenges in our marriage.

I do not know how she put up with not being able to go places with me because I was always afraid that someone would try and do her harm to get back at me. I still have this fear to a degree; I have put a lot of people away in prison for a long time, and one day they will be released back into society. Some people have been released over the years, and I have run into them. Thankfully, most have been respectful when we cross paths, or are more bark than bite. It is the ones that I may not see coming that I worry about the most. The ultimate question is, "Will they hold a grudge for me doing my job, or will they let it go, knowing they got caught for doing something illegal?" Only time will answer that question.

Once while out with my boys at Walmart, I ran into a target who I had put in prison years ago. It was Benji (referenced as the "stick-up boy" in some of my undercover cop operations in A Narc's Tale: Volume 1). We saw each other from a distance. I took the corner around the isle and handed my boys the key to my truck. I pointed to a side exit and told them to head out, get inside the truck, and not to come back inside for anything. I told them that if I do not come back out in thirty minutes, ask for help and call their mother. My boys were trained for this type of situation. We often discussed how to react if something like this were to happen. I sent them on their way and kept an eye on Benji to make sure he did not see my boys leaving or try to follow them. He did not, and I made sure we had a chat, giving the boys time to get safely out to the parking lot first.

I did not want a physical confrontation, but if he wanted one, I was ready for anything, even a gunfight. At this point, Benji looked more like a hardened ex-con than the street punk I purchased drugs off a decade earlier. At one point, he plotted to rob and kill me, but we busted him before he could do it. I walked towards him, and we made eye contact.

As we got closer, I nodded and said, "What's up, B?" B was the old street name he used to go by back in the days.

He said, "Nothing much, Keith." He definitely remembered me.

I asked him, "Are we good?"

He nodded and said, "Yes, we're good." He went onto say something that floored me.

He said, "That was a long time ago, and you probably saved my life because the path I was going down would have led to my death."

That is precisely the type of thing I always wanted to hear out of criminals that I put away. I shook his hand and wished him luck and walked away. This run-in with a former target went better than I could have imagined. Benji was a guy that served his debt to society and changed as a result. Shame on me for judging him for his new look, which included a shaved head and tattoos all over, including his head. When I went outside, my boys asked if everything was ok. Noah, who is the most like me when it comes to protection and attitude, wanted to know what Benji had said. I told him everything. I had a new level of respect for Benji after that and was happy to see him doing well.

These types of incidents must have stressed out my children, as well. Living in fear and the paranoia of always having to look over your shoulder takes its toll on the whole family, over time. I never wanted to put this on them, and I do not yet know the full extent of the consequences of being raised as children of an uncover narc, but I pray they are not too bad.

Speaking of the kids, when I worked undercover, things got a little more nerve-racking when we threw children into the mix. Suddenly, I was concerned not only for the safety of my wife and me; now, I was worried about my children's safety. Like I have said, drug dealers are ruthless, and some would go after my family instead of me because they were easy targets. They also know that this would hurt me much more emotionally than to simply harm me. This is the sick and twisted mindset of drug traffickers. Revenge and greed trump all else in the multi-billion-dollar drug game. There is often the *Get them before they can get me* mentality.

I have always tried to follow the law, but one thing that would ultimately push me over the edge would be if someone was to harm my family. I am fair game if you want to attempt to kill me, but if you cowardly go after innocent children or my family, then be prepared for the consequences. I would gladly go to the grave or prison, protecting them at all costs. If someone got the upper hand and killed me first, I would ask God to let me come back and haunt them before going to Heaven. I say that tongue and cheek, but my point is I never give up a fight and will die for my beliefs and especially my family.

To ensure my family could also protect themselves, I trained them in gun safety and shooting tactics. My boys were given custom built AR15 rifles after they proved they could safely handle guns. Of course, I keep them locked up when not target practicing or doing dry runs on clearing the house or preparing for a burglar entering the house. A *no-victim* mindset is carried on by the others in my family.

(BELOW) These are images of my two oldest boys with their AR15 rifles.

One of the great things about the relationship I had with my wife is that no matter what, she knew the old me, the one before I ever worked undercover. That always kept me grounded. It is amazing to love someone who gets you and knows who you are deep down inside. She did not know exactly what she was getting into when dating a guy who worked exclusively undercover, but she quickly learned and adapted nicely. If you speak with her, she will openly tell you that those were some tough times in our marriage, but it also made our relationship even stronger in a lot of ways. Working undercover was not just an assignment for me; it was one that my wife and kids had to endure

40

twenty-four hours a day. My wife never talked about it at the time, but she later told me that every day she used to fear when I was working deep undercover, that I would get hurt or even worse, killed. Every police officer's spouse fears for their lives, but the spouse of a narc, has this fear even more so, whether they verbalize it or not.

This reality and fear hit us especially hard when one of my old partners was killed in the line of duty. He was shot in the head by a drug addict. If this bothered her as bad as she later explained to me, then she somehow miraculously never let it affect our relationship back then. We were close to this deputy and his wife, so we went out on double dates with them before he was murdered. I am thankful to my wife for not wearing her emotions on her sleeve during those hard times, for everyone's sake. I needed her to be strong, and she was. If she had decided to nitpick at every little issue it could have easily been a distraction and caused me to slip up in my work and to get hurt, or it could have hindered my success on the police force. Emotional distractions could have caused me to overlook something important at work because I thought about my wife or kids when I should have been concentrating on the deal at hand.

In addition to suppressing fear, my wife often had to suppress her irritations or anger against me. To be successful at undercover work, your life outside of work must be as happy and care-free as possible. I honestly do not think that a deep undercover narc could be successful if his marriage were a train wreck, with constant bickering and anxiety. An undercover narc spouse must be willing to hold in some thoughts and keep their frustrations in check. It is essential for a spouse not to start fights over little issues, which could later be a big distraction to you.

My wife's strength and ability to put up with my mood swings, because of slight stages of depression I went through, was the primary reason I was able to hold myself together in tough times. I am not going to say we never fought because we had our share of arguments. However, any disputes that we had never got physical because hitting a woman is just wrong. Also, when I asked my father-in-law's permission for her hand in marriage, he had me promise never to hit his daughter. That was an easy promise for me to keep, and being a man of my word, I honored his request until he was laid to rest. I will continue to keep my promise for the rest of my life because of the respect I had for him, the fact that I do not believe in hitting women, and the love I have for my wife.

Another rule that my wife and I maintained over the years, which kept things in perspective and our priorities straight, was never to let me leave for work with us mad at each other. No matter what, we told each other that we loved one another like it was the last time we

42

would see each other because that could have easily been the case. This was sometimes difficult to do but we both knew that it was important if something were to happen to me. Death is too much of a common-place reality for police officers, especially narcs.

Working deep undercover is comparable to the military going into battle. Calling narcotics work the 'war on drugs' is appropriate for more than one reason. However, the difference between war and undercover work is, with war, you have weapons ready, body armor, other protective equipment, and rules of engagement. In an undercover deal, you hide your weapons, have no body armor, and no radio to call for backup. Also, you do not know when things will go from good to bad in a split second. You can be mentally prepared, but your actions as an undercover are more reactive when it comes to using force.

I think my hypervigilance and edgy personality prevented many gunfights over the years. Criminals want an easy fight, not one in which they may lose their life. If they know you have multiple guns and are not afraid to use them, plus they think you are a little crazy, most of the time, they will not try to do you harm. Again, these are great traits for an undercover narc, but not that of a husband, especially when you get to the point when you cannot switch between your cover persona and your real self that quickly.

As mentioned, deep undercover work wreaks havoc on a couple's level of communication. Since we both held things in and avoided subjects to protect each other, this created an emotional barrier. Eventually, that type of distance would take its toll on any relationship, no matter how strong the foundation. It was not her fault or mine, but it was a result of the decisions I had to make, and the mentality I developed to stay alive. One main issue with us was that even after my days with deep undercover work, my wife and I stayed in that protective mode of keeping things to ourselves thus not communicating well, which created even more distance between us. This hurt our relationship a lot. Looking back, we could have done a better job of sharing our feelings and talking things out.

If not for one major thing, we might not have been married as long as we were. Even though we did not always communicate as well as we could have, we did get one thing right. We always had an unfailing trust in each other and God. Over the years, we did not dwell on the dangers of my job, because we both felt that if it were my time to be taken from this earth, God would take me, regardless of what I was doing or what career I happened to have. Also, my wife proved to me early in our relationship that no matter what we endured, she was trustworthy and would help me maintain my cover. Regardless of my keeping irregular hours, negative talk about me from her friends, facing life's

44

stressors alone, or living in constant fear for my safety, she was always loyal to me. I knew that I could trust her with my life. My wife is my best friend, and I am beyond appreciative for the love and support she showed me during these trying times, and for giving me wonderful and beautiful children.

Not only does working deep undercover place a huge emotional burden on family life, but it is also a massive time commitment for both an officer and his/her family. Undercovers may miss out on many things such as a traditional wedding, socializing with family and friends, vacations close to home, ballgames, and even attending church regularly. Even though so much was sacrificed, I know that at the end of the day, all of it was worth it to make the world a better and safer place for my children and those I was sworn to serve and protect.

In the end, it was not my undercover work that caused major issues in our marriage, but many other life stressors, and something that happened almost twenty years after we met. A career in law enforcement can wrap you up, consume you, and destroy you if you stand up against corruption and the "good ole boys" system that seems to rule most towns. That almost happened to me, but I have come out on the other side of this battle stronger, and I am a more emotionally mature and grounded person. I know who I am and where I am going, and nothing nor anyone will hold me back.

Having high ethical standards and a never-quit attitude was a must for many successes in my career, but it also hurt me tremendously as I climbed the ranks in law enforcement. As a Chief of Police, I took a stand against decades of corruption, which led to criminal convictions of our city Mayor and the former head of investigations in my police department. They were charged and convicted of misconduct related offenses by public/elected officials. The former head of police investigations pled guilty to public corruption-related crimes, which included a charge of tampering with evidence to cover up a murder. As Chief of Police, my predecessor was also indicted for extortion, but the charges were dismissed during trial preparations. Unlike being an undercover narc, the fight was very public this time, but I did not for a second think of backing down. This staunch approach and being a fighter at heart cost me a great deal. Regardless, I would never change the fact that I stood up against corruption and evil. The only thing I do regret is the emotional toll that this battle took on my family life. I was forced out of my position as Chief of Police and ended up needing to seek employment overseas to stay in law enforcement and to fight the war on drugs. In the States I found myself essentially unhireable because of the lies told about my character and job performance, by people related to these corrupt officials that I helped expose. Again, this was a *Get them before they get me* mentality that I was used to from those in the drug game. I never thought I would have to face this *dog-eat-dog* reality outside of vice and narcotics. This time the guilty parties were corrupt city leaders who simply would not let me do my job.

After leaving my position as Chief of Police, I submitted literally hundreds of job applications to law enforcement agencies across the South East. All of them were essentially ignored because of the negative image created about me during the very ugly and public corruption battle. However, the United States Federal Government seemed to disagree with these skewed and biased opinions about me and seemed to find value in my track record in law enforcement at the county, city, and federal levels spoke for itself and was greatly respected. I had integrity and a passion for my career, which was unsurpassed, and those in charge of my future employment realized this.

Therefore, I found myself in Haiti, and eventually Liberia, working as a Senior Law Enforcement Advisor. I train and advise other police officers in developing and maintaining their police forces and necessary policies. I have spent the past four years, separated from my wife and children, all because I refused to be a *'yes man'* to those in local power, and I refused to do anything illegal or unethical.

I have enjoyed the work overseas but being forced away from my family for taking a stand against evil and corruption was a hard pill to swallow. It was like I was somehow being punished for doing the right thing. I am incredibly saddened, yet appreciative for what my family endured during these dark days. They handled everything we faced with grace and dignity, and they showed others how they walked with God through their actions. Unfortunately the stresses were too much on my marriage and it came to an end as a result. Like I said, this job can consume you at times and have long lasting consequences, both good and bad. Fortunately, we are still friends and co-parent together. I will always love and respect her for the things mentioned and many others.

Regardless of how bad it got; I knew it was not my job to punish all those corrupt people. I always prayed for them and still do, because one day they will meet their maker and will have to answer for their wicked ways. It will be at that point that they will finally 'pay the piper' and be held accountable for the lives that they wreaked havoc on by their actions. Looking back, I can see now how all of my experiences and time working undercover hardened and prepared me to endure my time as a chief of police and the years that followed working overseas.

(BELOW) This photo was taken after I completed Operation New Year's. My family and I went on one of our first vacations to the museums in Washington, DC. We did not feel that we could safely go on vacation anywhere locally since over 100 drug dealers were all recently arrested due to my undercover work (that equals a lot of enemies if you count their friends and families), so we went out of the state to be able to relax and be ourselves.

(BELOW) This is a photo of me and my wife when we were dating. We did not follow the traditional path in our relationship. We lived together and purchased a house together before we were married. We knew it would all work out, so we just did what we wanted and let it flow naturally. I was clean shaven in this picture with my hair cut short, because this was during the short 6-month window that I went to work for the sheriff's office and was on uniform patrol before becoming a narcotics investigator.

(RIGHT) This is a photo of me when I was growing my hair long. It was one of my many looks while working undercover. Of course I got a haircut for my wedding day.

(BELOW) This is a photo of me and my new bride with some of my fellow narcs and their wives at our wedding reception.

51

(BELOW) This is a photo of my groom's cake at our wedding. The center of the marijuana leaf cake was my sheriff's office patch. My wife ordered this cake for me as a surprise. It was the perfect fit for my groom's cake, but it drew many questions for the guests of our wedding, which was quite funny considering many had no clue I was an undercover police officer.

My Grooms Cake

The Birth of a Baby Narc

The birth of my first son was one of the greatest and most memorable days ever but of course, like everything in my life, it came with its drama and excitement, fitting perfectly into the undercover lifestyle. During this birth, my wife spent thirty-six hours in labor before finally delivering our son by an emergency C-section. At around the twelve-hour mark, I went to McDonald's to get us some food. We had already been in the hospital for two days because my wife was having complications with her pregnancy, so it was not like I left to eat right after she got there and had gone into labor.

We also had numerous family members and close friends there to support my wife since this was our first child. It was kind of crowded in the hospital room, and my wife had insisted that I get her something other than hospital food to eat, so I gladly honored her request. It was nice to get out of the hospital for a few minutes, even if I did not plan to be gone for very long.

I drove quickly through the McDonald's drive-through across the street from the hospital. I got the food and went quickly back to the hospital and made my way to the top of the parking garage. I decided to sit in the car and enjoy my meal, away from all the craziness in the delivery room. Being the son of a career U.S. Marine born in the Beaufort Naval Hospital on Parris Island, SC, I learned over the years how to eat all my food quickly and get back to the task at hand.

While eating my hamburger, I saw two white guys driving around the parking lot in an older model F-250 pickup truck with an extended bed. They stopped behind another truck, and both of them jumped out. They appeared to be carrying something in their hands, but at that moment, I could not make out the object. They had caught my attention now, so I watched closely to see what they were doing. They approached what looked like a construction worker's truck that had a large toolbox and ladder rack. They unbolted the toolbox in a jiffy by using the long tools they had in their hands. I later determined that these were home-made bolt cutters. They each had one, and the heads on the cutters were filed down so that they could be turned sideways and slid between the toolbox and the rails of the truck bed. This allowed them to reach the bolts holding down the toolbox, which they managed to cut within a few seconds. Once they had the bolts cut, the toolbox was quickly lifted out of one truck bed and thrown into theirs.

I could see that they had at least five or six other toolboxes piled in their truck's bed. It would seem that they were having a pretty good day for a bunch of thieves. They quickly jumped back in their vehicle and drove a short distance and stopped behind another truck with a toolbox in the back. They jumped out and repeated the same process in about thirty seconds or less. There was no doubt that these guys had done this many times in the past because of the speedy and polished procedures they used. At that moment, I had a dilemma. I asked myself, *Do I just call 911 and let the local officers handle it, because my wife was in labor? Or "Will my wife understand if I get involved?*

54

Of course, I called 911 and wanted to let the *on-duty* officers do their due diligence because my wife had a baby to deliver. However, I told the 911 dispatcher who I was and what was going on. This was in the city limits, and I worked for the sheriff's office at the time, so I did not know the dispatcher. I told her my location, and she said they had some units on the way to me.

I told dispatch I was in my personal vehicle and would likely not be able to follow them for very long without being spotted, because these guys were constantly looking around to see if anyone noticed them. To me, they looked like two tweaked out meth heads on a theft rampage. I knew that people high on meth were extremely paranoid and had a propensity for violence, so I wanted uniformed officers present to handle this situation.

It came to the point where I could no longer sit in my parking space and still see them, so I decided to follow them by driving parallel to them in the parking garage. I was about four rows away, paralleling them at an angle, and trying my best not to let them see me watching. The way I looked at it, I was not going to let them get away without at least trying to stay with them. It was clear their truck bed was almost to its maximum capacity, and they would be leaving the area soon. I followed them around the parking garage until they inevitably noticed me watching them. This was one of those sizeable top-story parking garages where you can see across the entire parking garage, not to mention that I was driving a larger and taller SUV. In a split-second, they took off at a high rate of speed. So much for letting the on-duty guys handle it.

Winding down and out of the parking garage, we went, and I followed them through several residential and business streets that ran around the hospital campus. They tried to lose me and slid around a corner, striking a curb, and almost caused one of the toolboxes to come out of the truck bed. The whole time I thought, *Where are the police?* It all happened so quickly that I did not have time to get out my phone and dial 911 dispatchers to give an update.

Next thing I knew, they pulled down a dead-end street. I do not think they knew this at the time, but I did because I knew that area. It was not a cul-de-sac, but more of a dead-end without any signs indicating the road ended. They approached the end of the street at a high rate of speed and managed to slam on breaks and prevent going over the curb and into a group of large trees. As they got to the end of the narrow road, I pulled sideways across the road, attempting to block their escape. The problem was that I was about forty-to-fifty yards away from their truck. Suddenly, the driver threw his truck in reverse and gunned the accelerator. With the rear tires spinning, they eventually gained traction, and he proceeded to drive towards me, and my wife's

56

SUV. All I could think was, *Oh, Shit. They are going to hit my wife's car, and she is not going to be happy.*

Instead of trying to drive away, I jumped out. Running, I got the heck out of the way. Just as they were about to strike my vehicle, they slammed on brakes and came to a sliding stop. I pulled out my gun that I always carried in my waistband, a nickel-plated .38-caliber Smith and Wesson revolver with a pearl handle. This was not exactly your typical cop gun. It was signed out of evidence after it cleared what it was initially seized for on an unrelated case. UCs used something like this instead of purchasing brand new guns with taxpayer's money or using a more standard cop gun, which would be too obvious.

I am right-handed, and my wallet, with my badge and credentials, is usually in my right rear pocket. I had been trying to get in the habit of having those items on my left side, so I could draw my gun with one hand and retrieve my badge with the other, but I forgot on this day. I honestly thought about getting out my credentials but could not reach them while I had them at gunpoint. With just my gun drawn, and no police ID or badge showing, I told the driver to get out of the car and get down on the ground; then he complied. The passenger was not as cooperative. So, I grabbed him by the hair and pulled him out of the driver's side door and onto the ground. This was not a time to play around and pull on his shirt to try to remove him. I learned a long time ago that where the head goes, the body usually follows; this day was no exception. Businesses lined the dead-end street along one side. These were mainly smaller doctors' offices, with patients coming and going on a routine basis. At this point, some of the bystanders had dialed 911, and others were watching in shock. I later found out that one of the 911 callers had reported this as a carjacking in progress, and I was described as the perpetrator.

I was able to control my adrenaline and collected my senses about me once I had them both face-down on the asphalt at gunpoint. I realized I might need to pull out my badge and police credentials, so everyone would know I was friendly and *not* mugging them. I switched my revolver to my weak or left hand and pulled out my badge and police identification. As I did, a patrol car pulled up and skidded to a stop. He came in hot, and the officer nearly ran over one of the suspects that I had prone out on the ground.

When I say he almost ran over the suspect, I am not exaggerating. As the officer skidded to a stop into the parking lot, I jumped up and moved out of the way while the front end of the police car hovered inches over the suspect. The vehicle never touched him, because it stopped with the suspect just under the front end/bumper of the patrol car. It was a very close call and scared the suspect so much that he literally pissed himself.

Later on, when I was told that one of the citizens in the parking lot who witnessed the whole thing called 911 and reported a carjacking in progress, I started to think about my actions. At the time, I had long hair and a pin-stripe beard, so they thought I was just a common street thug. Thank God the city police officers who first pulled up on-scene were some of my buddies from my old uniform patrol days, and they remembered me from working undercover for the city where they currently worked. If it had been some rookie cop who did not know me, it might have ended badly for me or the cop. It did not occur to me when telling the dispatcher, that I was an undercover cop. So, I did not mention that I did not look like an average police officer. I just told her that I was an investigator with the sheriff's office, and she probably assumed I looked like all other police with the high and tight haircut and was clean-shaven.

I managed to help the police handcuff the two thieves and quickly made it back to the hospital room before my son was born. I told the police I had to get back to the hospital and asked them to come up to my wife's hospital room if they needed to interview me for further facts on the case or to give a statement. They told me to hurry up and get back to my wife. Eventually, one of the officers made their way up to my wife's hospital room, where they interviewed me about what happened. As my wife's contractions got more intense, the police quickly left the hospital room. Several hours later, we had a healthy baby boy. While in the hospital for the first few days after his birth, I used my free time to type up a police report/statement regarding the whole incident.

(BELOW) This is a picture of me holding and kissing my oldest son in the hospital when he was a day or two old. As you can see, I looked nothing like a cop, so it must have scared the guys I went to arrest when I pulled out a pistol and put it in their faces.

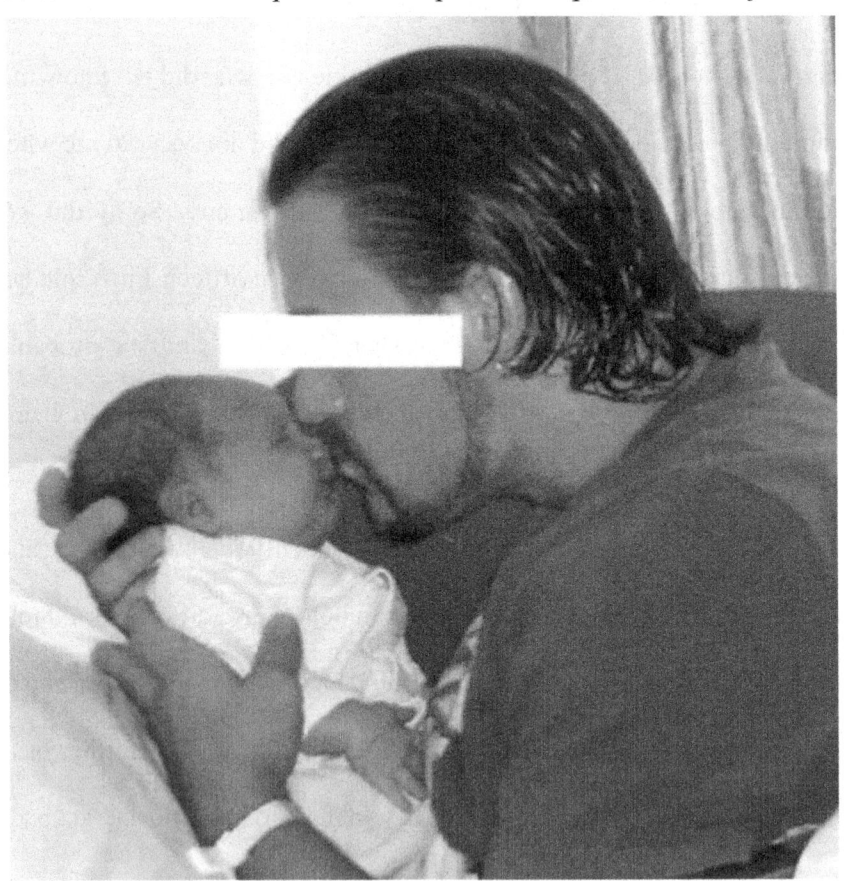

(BELOW) This is a photo of my oldest son and me before I went out to do the round up for one of the many undercover operations we did.

(RIGHT) This is a photo of my oldest son and I with a fellow police officer (Brendan M.) at his wedding.

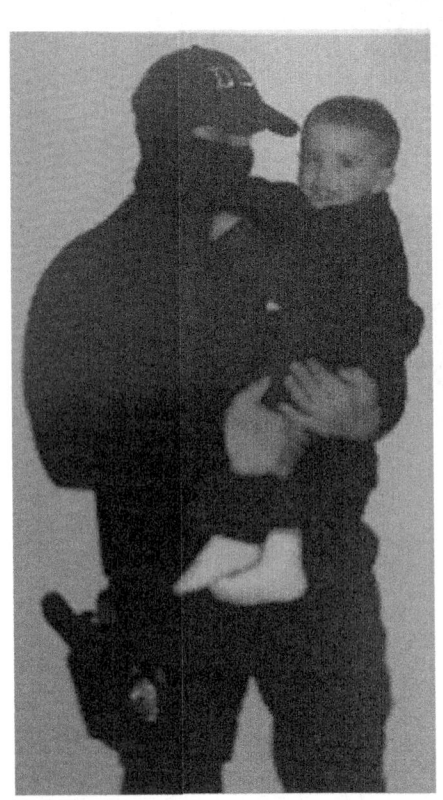

(LEFT) This is a photo of my oldest son and I before I went out to do a raid with the DEA when I was a Special Agent.

As a new father, I used my child and later children as a motivation to keep driving me on, doing what I was doing to rid the streets of illegal drugs and criminals. During my career, one of the most haunting things that I saw working undercover at the federal level, which I will never forget, was a video of a child used to smuggle drugs. This case involved an unsuspecting family who went to a foreign country for a vacation. Their small child, whom they brought with them, could barely walk. At some point, when the parents were not paying close enough attention, the child was abducted. The parents immediately got a hold of the local authorities to report the missing child. The authorities responded and told the parents to go to the closest border crossing to assist law enforcement in seeing if someone tried to cross the border with their child.

Some past child abductions have been done in such a way that babies could be quickly carried across the border and sold on the black market. Unbeknownst to the parents at the time, this kidnapping was part of a much larger and even more sinister drug-smuggling organization's plan towards overall organized crime. I know you might ask what this child has to do with drug smuggling because that was my first thought, too.

However, to my horror, within an hour of the abduction they took the child to a different location where he was cut open from his neck down to his groin. Then they removed all his insides, gutting him like a deer. I am uncertain if they sold certain body parts on the black market or not. They then stuffed the small child with prepackaged sized bundles of heroin and sewed him back together, cleaned him up, and redressed him in the same clothes he was wearing at the time of the abduction. Sadly, I can absolutely assure you that all of this was started while the child was still alive.

The child was then passed off to a "*mule.*" *Mule* is street slang for someone who smuggles drugs. The mule's job was to walk across the border with the child in his arms as if he were a sleeping baby. In this case when the mule stepped up to the border crossing, the child's parents and authorities immediately approached the person holding the child to investigate if it was the abducted child. The mule freaked out and threw the child's lifeless body down to the ground and attempted to flee. Some of the authorities went immediately to render aid to the child and discovered that it was too late. The child had been murdered in this gruesome fashion.

I do not tell this story to sensationalize or glorify crime in any way, but to remind parents to be ever vigilant when watching their children. Unfortunately, many people in this world, especially drug dealers, will stop at nothing to smuggle drugs and to make a profit. These parents' lives were forever ruined, and their child was brutally murdered to smuggle about one kilogram, or 2.2 pounds, of heroin across a border.

This incident motivated me to be even more relentless in my pursuit of drug traffickers. Whenever I felt down about my job and wondered why I put in the countless hours I did and missed so many significant family events, I would watch the evidence video of this case (i.e., the autopsy of them removing the heroin from inside the child) to remind myself. It quickly set my priorities in order and got me hyper-motivated again to do what I did best; put away suspects. This video also angered me, but I channeled that anger into working even harder.

These are the types of incidents that people without top-secret government clearances hear about and brush off as urban legends. I cannot speak to other crimes like this, but the autopsy images of this child are forever ingrained in my mind. I tried to better understand why someone would take these risks such as murder and kidnapping to aid drug trafficking, but nothing logical comes to mind. I also learned that small children's organs were sometimes sold on the black market and used in rituals that represented sacrifices to some idols or gods in which the traffickers believed. Unfortunately, it was not the last time in my career where I worked in an area that ruthless, callous, horrific killings of children or adults happened, and not surprising each time the suspects had a substantial drug nexus.

Many years after undercover work, while in Liberia (West Africa) as a Senior Law Enforcement Advisor to the federal government, I learned of cannibalistic rituals done during a civil war. There was one specific general in Liberia that would kill small children in order to drink virgin blood before going into battle. This was done while fighting buck-naked, and high on cocaine, marijuana, and palm wine.

While in Haiti, working on another federal contract, we encountered a female voodoo witch doctor that did the ritualistic killing of humans and served human meat at the local market to unsuspecting customers. The gang that this lady was affiliated with ran kilogram quantities of cocaine, working directly with Columbian drug cartels. Again, to the average person, these stories may sound unfathomable, but they are all real and linked in some way, shape, or form to drug sales or use. If you ever wonder if the war on drugs is worth fighting or not, just remember these stories.

(BELOW) These are images from Haiti of the body parts in a drum and human stew being served to the public.

 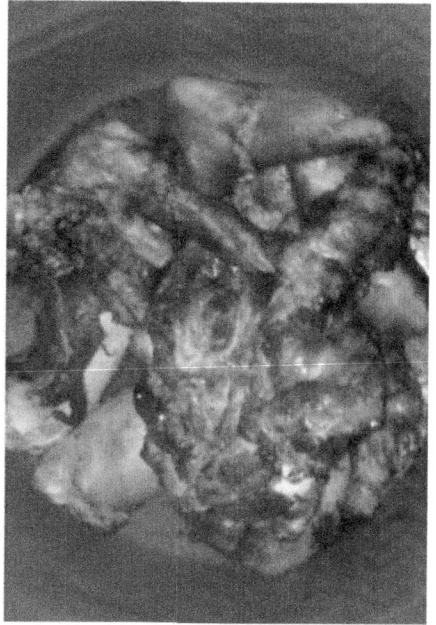

Getting Certified as an Expert Witness
in Street-Level Narcotics

Becoming an expert witness in street-level narcotics was a big accomplishment in my profession. This was something that I knew would be great for my career as a narc; plus, I really enjoyed giving an opinionated testimony in court. For those not familiar with courtroom testimony by witnesses, only expert witnesses can give an opinionated testimony, and all others must stick to facts that they have direct knowledge of. Imagine the impact your testimony could have on influencing a jury on the innocence or guilt of a suspect. Therefore, it was not easy for just anyone to become an expert witness. Being able to answer the following type of question clearly made a jury lean one way or the other.

Solicitor: "Investigator Grounsell, in your expert opinion, if a person is found in possession of $2,000 in small bills, a bag containing small individual user quantities of crack cocaine, a scale, and a gun; What are they up to?"

Me: "These items are consistent with or indicative of someone involved in street-level sales of crack cocaine."

Of course, I could also elaborate and give my opinion on the meaning/significance of the gun, scale, possession of that quantity of drugs, packaging of the drugs, small denomination of currency, and other evidence in the case. All of this is after-the-fact testimony; not based upon my direct knowledge of being there in the field during the incident, but based upon my expert opinion formed by countless hours of experience, training, and participation in drug investigations.

It is that simple, but very impactful on the jury when trying to determine if the suspects possessed drugs with intent to sell or for personal use, which is usually the difference in being sentenced to probation or prison. To the average person, this may seem like a common-sense thing, but that is not always the case to a juror who may have never been around drugs, or been in any type of trouble in their life. The credibility of the expert witness is established, and the weight of their testimony is to be determined by the individual jurors.

Becoming an expert witness for the first time all started when my Vice and Narcotics Sergeant asked me if I would go help the local solicitor's office with a case. For those of you from other parts of the United States or abroad, a solicitor is the same as what many refer to as a County Prosecutor or District Attorney. A solicitor is elected as the "chief prosecutor" to cover a jurisdiction, and has a group of assistant solicitors or attorneys, investigators, paralegals, and other personnel working for him/her.

This solicitor's office happened to cover two large counties, and a population of more than a half a million people. It was the largest and one of the busiest solicitor's offices in the state of SC, which processed about fourteen-thousand warrants annually. Interestingly enough, many years later, I became the Investigator to the Solicitor/Lead Investigator for this very same office.

In this specific matter, the Assistant Solicitor needed someone to testify about the manufacturing and street-level sales of crack cocaine. Prior to court, I was given a heads up and had been warned of the types of questions that I needed to be able to answer. Approximately five minutes before I got on the stand, I met with the Assistant Solicitor and was told some of the additional facts of the case. By then, I had already worked more than one hundred hand-to-hand undercover drug/narcotic buys. This sounded good in court, when the defense asked how many undercover buys I had made in order to get myself qualified as an expert. After this initial certification in state court as an expert witness, I got certified in state and federal court on numerous occasions, covering undercover tactics and other areas of drug investigations.

One of the highlights of testifying as an expert was in a case where I was referred to as Frank Serpico in the courtroom by a defense attorney. During this trial, I sat in the back of the courtroom, on the defendant's side of court, until it was my turn to testify. I usually did this to blend in with the criminals who may be present in the courtroom. My undercover identity was never revealed until I actually took the stand. Just prior to giving my testimony, the Judge granted a short recess. I approached the prosecutor's table, where he was speaking with the defense attorney. The prosecutor introduced me to the defense attorney, and I could tell I caught him off guard.

He told me that he thought I was one of his client's or the defendant's friends, coming in to testify as a character witness on behalf of the defendant. This showed me this defense attorney was not prepared, because you usually sit down with a witness to discuss their

70

testimony before trial. Therefore, he should have known what all of his witnesses looked like, unless he conducted a phone interview with them. He was also given a witness list by the prosecutor before the trial and would have known my name before I was to testify before him.

That day in court, I wore a double-breasted mafia-style suit, which I would not wear today, but it was the only one I owned at the time. I had my long hair pulled back in a small, tight ponytail. I used a men's facial hair wax stick to slick down my beard and smooth it down into almost a point at the bottom. I had a scruffy beard at the time, and this beard wax stick was the only way I could tame my beard and feel cleaned up enough in court to match the way I was dressed. It gave my beard a damp sheen. I still looked rough, but I was well-dressed. I looked like any criminal who temporarily cleans themselves up for their big day in court. The defense attorney spoke to his client and pointed at me while saying, "And the Solicitor brings in 'Serpico' to testify today." Most people who do not know the story of Frank Serpico might see this as an insult, but for me I took it as a high-level compliment.

Frank Serpico was one of two police officers who stood up against police corruption in the New York City Police Department during the 1970's. His fortitude and integrity, which never faltered, led to the *Knapp Commission* being formed, which revealed a substantial amount of NYPD officers as being corrupt, and partaking in crimes ranging from murder to the taking of bribes/payoffs. Frank Serpico was hated at the time by the corrupt officers, who tried to take his life, but he remained steadfast and stood for honesty and had integrity beyond that of the norm. So, as you can see, being called Frank Serpico was a huge compliment in my book.

One of the obstacles that I encountered all too often with defense attorneys, who could find no other way to counter my testimony, was when they called me a liar. If the defendant did not have a true defense, defense attorneys attacked the character of the witnesses in order to impeach them and their testimony, making it sound untrustworthy. Oftentimes, the defense must only put the slightest bit of doubt in the mind of one of twelve jurors to be successful.

I recall one time when I testified, the defense attorney kept talking about how I was lying to his client, and that I *lied* for a living working undercover. He wanted me to admit that I *lied*, as if to insinuate that I may be lying on the stand in court that day. He asked me several times if I ever lied to his client, and each time I responded with a simple *no* answer. This frustrated the defense attorney; especially when he would ask me about any specific situation, and I would explain it. He then repeated his question about if I had lied to his client or not, and I would say, "No," again. I then stated how I was not lying, but merely role playing; quite like how an actor does in the movies. The fact that I

72

can say that I was not lying made it more appealing to the jury, and made me more believable and credible. Once a defense attorney saw that I was too smart to be trapped into his/her little game of calling me a liar, he/she normally moved on to a normal line of questioning.

In a separate memorable case, when I was testifying as an expert witness in federal court, something happened that I never saw again in my career. After a lengthy discussion and all-out fight to try to not get me qualified again in federal court as an expert witness, I was granted expert witness status and my testimony was limited to only certain things. The defense attorney was not happy with the Judge's ruling, and put different objections on the record many times; but constantly got overruled. While testifying, the defense attorney kept approaching me and getting slightly aggressive with encroaching on my personal space in the witness stand. The Judge warned him not to do this, twice. One time he had a pair of scissors in his hand, which had been used to open and present a piece of evidence. He waved them in front of me in an almost slashing motion. It was to the point that I moved my head backwards a few inches as he raised his voice doing this. When the defense attorney did this, the Judge stopped court and had the bailiff escort the jury out of the courtroom.

It was towards the end of a long day of testifying when this happened. Nerves were raw and everyone was tired. We knew this was not going to be pretty. The defense attorney tucked his tail between his legs, and walked back to the defense table where he should have been standing all along while asking me questions. Once the jury left the courtroom, without hesitation, the Judge held the defense attorney in contempt of court and ordered the US Marshals to take him into custody. They placed him in handcuffs right there in the courtroom in front of his client. They detained him overnight, and the trial proceeded the next day. He was not given the option to pay a fine, which could have happened. I think the Judge was flexing his muscles to show this attorney who was boss, and it worked. Federal judges are appointed for life, and they do not play games. Of course, my testimony had to stop and proceeded the next day. This Judge had me nervous that if I said something wrong, or looked the wrong way, I might get locked up also. Thankfully, I made it through my testimony in that case and got another expert witness certification under my belt in federal court.

Another one of the most memorable moments for me testifying as an expert witness in a case started after my testimony. During this case, I was asked by a local solicitor/prosecutor to take a look at the evidence in one of their cases. I did not have any knowledge of the case during the time that it happened, but I was brought in after the fact to explain certain facts to the jury. Prior to the trial I reviewed the evidence and drew up my conclusions based upon what I read, the evidence collected, and my experience dealing with drug dealers/traffickers. I testified as to the street value of drugs and their potential for profit when sold retail (street level) versus wholesale (in bulk). When I came to court that day, I was fortunate enough to have gotten certified again as an expert witness in the field of street-level narcotics; more specifically crack cocaine and cocaine, as well as to explain wholesale versus retail prices of each. Showing the potential value of drugs is incredibly significant to educate the average citizen juror, who might have no idea about the potential value in drug sales. The following is a condensed version of the case showing what I testified to, and the arguments about my testimony.

Below is a copy of the case law printed on the following public website: www.judicial.state.sc.us.com

South Carolina

JUDICIAL DEPARTMENT

4229 - State v. ███████

THE STATE OF SOUTH CAROLINA
In The Court of Appeals

The State, Respondent,

v.

████████████,

Appellant.

Appeal From ████████ County
████████████, *Circuit Court Judge*

Opinion No. ████

Submitted March 1, 2007 – Filed April 2, 2007

AFFIRMED

Appellate Defender ██████████, *of Columbia, for Appellant.*

Attorney General ██████████ ████████, *Chief Deputy Attorney General* ████████ ████████, *Assistant Deputy Attorney General,* ████████ ██████ *Senior Assistant Attorney General* ████████ ████████████, *all of Columbia; and Solicitor* ████████ █████, *of* ████████, *for Respondent.*

████████: ████████████████ *appeals his convictions for trafficking cocaine, trafficking crack cocaine, resisting arrest, failure to stop for a blue light, and possession of a firearm during the commission of a violent crime. We affirm.[1]*

FACTS

On the night of ▓▓▓▓▓▓, 2004, the ▓▓▓▓▓▓ County Sheriff's Office dispatched Deputy ▓▓▓▓▓ ▓▓▓ to investigate a suspicious vehicle parked in the middle of a dead-end road located in a cul-de-sac. He found the vehicle, a Chevrolet pickup truck, parked without any lights on. ▓▓▓ shone his patrol vehicle's exterior spotlight into the truck as he was driving by, did not see anyone inside, and believed the truck was abandoned. He positioned his patrol car behind the truck and called in the truck's license plate to his dispatcher.

While waiting for the dispatcher to respond, ▓▓▓ saw an individual, later identified as ▓▓▓▓, suddenly sit up in the driver's seat of the truck. ▓▓▓▓ immediately put the truck into motion and began driving away. ▓▓▓ turned on his blue lights and pursued the truck. The truck stopped several times during the chase, but never long enough for ▓▓▓ to approach the truck on foot. ▓▓▓ radioed for backup; Deputy ▓▓▓▓▓ and Deputy ▓▓▓▓▓ quickly joined the pursuit.

Once the truck stopped long enough for the deputies to approach, ▓▓▓ and ▓▓ advanced towards the vehicle on foot. ▓▓▓ ordered ▓▓▓▓ to exit the *vehicle and he slowly complied. The deputies searched* ████████ *and placed him into one of the patrol vehicles. Upon searching* ████████ *truck, the deputies discovered a loaded .45 caliber pistol and a bag from a fast-food restaurant containing four, clear plastic bags with drugs inside. Two of the four bags contained cocaine and the other two contained crack cocaine. Altogether the bags contained 54.77 grams of cocaine and 19.21 grams of crack cocaine.*

The ████████ *County Grand Jury indicted* ████████ *for trafficking cocaine, trafficking crack cocaine, resisting arrest, failure to stop for a blue light, and possession of a firearm during the commission of a violent crime. A jury found* ████████ *guilty on all charges and the trial court sentenced him to concurrent terms of confinement totaling ten years plus three years probation.*

LAW/ANALYSIS

████████ *argues the trial court abused its discretion by allowing the State to present expert testimony about the dollar value of cocaine and crack cocaine. We disagree.*

The qualification of a witness as an expert and the

admissibility of his or her testimony are matters left to the sound discretion of the trial judge, whose decision will not be reversed on appeal absent an abuse of that discretion and prejudice to the opposing party. *Nelson v. Taylor*, 347 S.C. 210, 214, 553 S.E.2d 488, 490 (Ct. App. 2001). An abuse of discretion occurs when the conclusions of the trial court either lack evidentiary support or are controlled by an error of law. *State v. Wise*, 359 S.C. 14, 21, 596 S.E.2d 475, 478 (2004).

During █████████ trial, the State sought to call Investigator Grounsell of the █████████ County Sheriff's Office as an expert on the street value of cocaine and crack cocaine. █████████ objected, arguing testimony about the value of cocaine and crack cocaine was irrelevant and prejudicial because there was no evidence he committed or attempted a drug transaction. The trial court allowed Grounsell to testify as an expert, but limited his testimony to the "wholesale" and "retail" values of cocaine and crack cocaine for the general area.

The trial court allowed Grounsell's testimony based on several cases from the United States Court of Appeals, Fourth Circuit. The trial court reasoned *that jurors typically do not have knowledge about the illegal drug industry.[2] Grounsell testified that the drugs found in █████████ truck had a street value of between $2,750.00 and $9,319.00, depending on the quantities sold.*

In his defense, █████████ claimed the drugs belonged to someone else, possibly one of his employees who also had access to the truck.

We agree with the trial court that jurors typically do not know the current street prices of illegal drugs. Grounsell's valuation of the drugs, based on his years of law enforcement experience, allowed the jury to better determine whether a person would reasonably leave expensive narcotics unguarded and disguised as trash in a truck allegedly used by numerous people.

If the jury did not believe █████████ assertion that an unknown individual left thousands of dollars worth of drugs disguised as garbage in an area where other people had access to the drugs and might even throw them away, it reinforced the State's case that █████████ was knowingly in actual or constructive possession of the drugs at the time of his arrest, a key element of the trafficking charges. We therefore hold the trial court did not err by allowing

Grounsell to testify about the street value of the drugs found in ███████████ *truck.[3]*

AFFIRMED.

██████████*., and* ████████████████ *concur.*

---

[1]   We decide this case without oral argument pursuant to Rule 215, SCACR.

[2]   See, e.g., U.S. v. Gastiaburo, 16 F.3d 582, 589 (4th Cir. 1994) (noting the court has "repeatedly upheld the admission of law enforcement officers' expert opinion testimony in drug trafficking cases."); U.S. v. Johnson, 54 F.3d 1150, 1156-57 (4th Cir. 1995) (holding the district court did not err in qualifying a detective as an expert and allowing the detective to testify about the current street price of illegal drugs).

[3]   See State v. Matthews, 720 So. 2d 153 (La. Ct. App. 1998) (holding an agent from the Drug Enforcement Agency could testify regarding the street value of cocaine where the agent was testifying regarding matters within his personal knowledge and experience as a narcotics officer);

State v. McCoy, 414 S.E.2d 392, 395 (N.C. Ct. App. 1992) (ruling a law enforcement officer's testimony on the street value of cocaine was properly admitted in defendant's trial for trafficking cocaine because the testimony was both helpful and relevant in showing the defendant's intent); *Martin v. State*, 823 S.W.2d 726, 728 (Tex. Crim. App. 1992) (ruling a sheriff's testimony on the price of marijuana was admissible and relevant because it allowed the jury to comprehend the quantity of illegal drugs recovered in terms that are easily understood); *cf. State v. Lawrence*, 264 S.C. 3, 16, 212 S.E.2d 52, 58 (1975) (ruling that testimony as to the black market resale value of prescription drugs when sold without a prescription was relevant to prove motive for the charge of conspiracy).

The accomplishment of having state case law established, based upon my testimony, meant a lot to me. This was one of those things where you just had to be at the right place at the right time for it to work out for you. This was not a goal I set for myself or anything I could have anticipated, but it is something that I am proud to have accomplished. I testified as to a wholesale price when the drugs (cocaine and crack cocaine) are purchased in bulk, versus street-level retail prices when the drugs are resold in small quantities. Keeping my testimony as simple as possible for jury understanding, I did not go into details on my charts about the fact that drugs would probably be diluted, commonly referred to as "cut-up" or "stepped on", before being sold. This meant that dealers commonly added ingredients or some cutting agents to increase the quantity of drugs that could be sold to potential customers, thus doubling or possibly tripling profits. I mentioned it in my testimony, but it was not part of my presentation materials on the drug weights and values since it is impossible to know the purity of a drug unless it is sent off to a lab for quantitative analysis.

On the following page is a copy of the chart that I use to testify in court about wholesale versus retail prices of drugs. This was enlarged and displayed on a three-foot by four-foot board so that the jury could see it clearly. They even took the chart back in the jury room during deliberations. I used this chart to testify in many other cases after this one and allowed other narcs and prosecutors to use it as often as they needed. When viewing these prices, keep in mind that they are subject to change and are estimated according to this region of the United States (i.e. Southeastern). From personal experience, purchasing these quantities of drugs working in an undercover capacity in other parts of the United States, I know prices vary according to different geographic regions and supply/demand.

After the trial, on the jury feedback/comment cards, there were numerous compliments about how impactful this chart was for my testimony. Not everyone grasps things and learns through verbal communications or testimony alone. Personally, I am a visual learner, so I knew this would appeal to like-minded jurors. It worked, and in that very first case, the defendant was found guilty.

*(**BELOW**) This is a condensed version of the chart used to testify as to the wholesale vs. retail prices and values of cocaine and crack cocaine.*

Cocaine Wholesale Prices	Cocaine Retail Prices
½ gram = $30	½ gram = $50
1 gram = $60	1 gram = $100
½ Eight Ball (1.75 grams) = $115 - $150	½ Eight Ball (1.75 grams) = $175
Eight-Ball (3.5 grams) = $175 - $250	Eight-Ball (3.5 grams) = $350
Quarter Spoon (7 grams) = $350	Quarter Spoon (7 grams) = $700
½ ounce (14.1 grams) = $400 - $600	½ ounce (14.1 grams) = $1,410
1 ounce (28.35 grams) = $800 - $1,200	1 ounce (28.35 grams) = $2,835
Quarter Pound (113.4 grams or 4 oz.) = $3,200 - $4,800	Quarter Pound (113.4 grams or 4 oz.) = $11,340
Kilo (1,000 grams or 35.27 oz.) = $18,000 to $25,000	Kilo (1,000 grams or 35.27 oz) = $100,000
Present Case:	
504.48g= approx. $9,000 to $12,500	504.48g= approx. $50,448 (excluding the use of cutting agents)
**Potential Profit Range- $37,948 to $41,448	

Crack Cocaine: Wholesale Prices	Crack Cocaine: Retail Prices
Crumbs or Beebies (0.05grams or less) = $3	Crumbs or Beebies (0.05grams or less) = $5
Twenty (0.1grams or 1/10th of a gram) = $10	Twenty (0.1grams or 1/10th of a gram) = $20
Forty (0.2grams or 2/10th of a gram) = $20	Forty (0.2grams or 2/10th of a gram) = $40
Quarter spoon (7 grams) = $350	Quarter spoon (7 grams) = $1,400
1/2 Cookie (1/2 oz. or 14.1grams) = $400 - $500	1/2 Cookie (1/2 oz. or 14.1grams) = $2,820
Cookie (1 oz. or 28.35grams) = $800 - $1,000	Cookie (1 oz. or 28.35grams) = $5,670
Quarter Pound (113.4 grams or 4 oz.) = $3,200 - $4,000	Quarter Pound (113.4 grams or 4 oz.) = $22,680
Kilo (1,000 grams or 35.27 oz.) = $15,000 to $25,000	Kilo (1,000 grams or 35.27 oz.) = $200,000
Present Case:	
39.18g= approx. $1,500 to $1,800	39.18g= approx. $7,836
**Potential Profit Range- $6,036 to $6,336	

In another unrelated case where I testified as an expert witness for an Assistant Solicitor, I created a display case showing different cutting agents, representing the same consistency of powder cocaine, in individually wrapped bags for all the different quantities and weights of the given drug commonly found on the street. I did this to exhibit to the jury what a gram of cocaine looked like compared to an eight ball (one-eighth an ounce), to an ounce, to a quarter pound, and eventually a kilo. These are common drug weights, and the jury needed to see what they looked like, versus just hearing how many grams they weighed. I knew that the average person in America uses the Standard Measurement System rather than the Metric System of Measurement. Therefore, the jurors would more than likely know only ounces and pounds; grams and kilograms may be completely foreign. We got a conviction in that case, with the jury returning a verdict in less than an hour. This tactic was so successful that the prosecutor asked for my display to be used for future cases. Many years later, I found out that the prosecutor kept this display in her office for the rest of her career as a drug prosecutor. This same prosecutor later became the Chief of the Drug Prosecution Unit, and we worked closely together on many cases.

Undercover School & The Changes It Made in Me

If I had to summarize one of the most significant attributes for making successful undercover buys in one word, it would be confidence.

Without the proper form of training in narcotics/undercover work, you can only draw knowledge from life's experiences and your street smarts. As a guy who was never around hard-core drugs as a youth, I was out of luck as far as experience goes. I did have natural street smarts and a survival mindset from fighting, but I needed more than that to take my work to another level. I was not satisfied with just being an average or even a good investigator; I wanted greatness and to be the best. Getting to the point that you realize, *You do not know, what you do not know,* seeking outside guidance and training to evolve and take my career to the next level, was the key which was paramount to my future success.

Prior to ever receiving any type of formal training in undercover work, I had made over one hundred hand-to-hand narcotics buys. It was not until my second undercover narcotics assignment that I received the opportunity to finally attend undercover training at the Regional Counterdrug Training Academy (RCTA) in Meridian, Mississippi. I probably should have gone to this school before I started working undercover, but that opportunity never presented itself. I finally attended this training with a fellow narcotics investigator, Lyle K., from the sheriff's office, who was my undercover partner at the time. The school was two weeks long, and it consisted of ninety-two hours of scheduled instruction. It was there that I gained a newfound respect for undercover work and learned how to do things I really wanted to try but did not know how to do it.

I was trained by some of the best undercover instructors in the nation at this school (i.e., Charlie, Rad, Pat, etc.). I learned how undercover officers were a dying breed, because of the high risk involved and how we are misunderstood as undercovers. Charlie F. was the lead instructor in this class. Charlie is a retired ATF agent who spent the majority of his career working or teaching undercover work. I looked up to Charlie and his successes in the undercover world. He was like an older brother to me. I have asked him for advice throughout my undercover career and respect his opinion tremendously. He also has published an undercover book and does public speaking around the world.

Prior to attending this training, I made what I would call nickel-and-dime buys, with occasional ounce deals or larger. Almost immediately after the training, I made kilo buys and also posed as a hitman in a Solicitation of a Murder case. The difference in me before and after the training spoke for itself in my level of cases. No matter what problem was brought in front of me, I felt like I had the answer because now I was ready for it.

This training focused on practical problems, where you posed as the undercover making cases against trained role players. In this school, I learned how to do large-scale dope deals safely, buy illegal guns and bombs, pose as a hitman, and when to come out of my undercover role, etc. If I had the opportunity to speak to any person who was interested in doing undercover work, I suggested that they get this type of formal training before they began their work. It could prevent them from making some of the mistakes that I have made, and it most certainly could save their life. I feel that my street smarts are what allowed me to be successful and stay safe, even though I did not have any formal training when I first started working undercover.

One of the things that really stuck out in my mind which was done in this UC school was they had a city built like an elaborate movie set. Furthermore, actors played roles like they were living and working there in different scenarios. There were cameras and microphones on every inch of the compound, it seemed. When you were given an undercover scenario, everything was recorded (audio and video) from your entry into the city, to the drug transaction, and finally, your departure.

After the transaction took place, you went into a private room with two instructors and watched your video. Each instructor had extensive undercover experience in the real world, so their input was valuable. It was here that you learned so much about yourself and your body language. I learned some nervous habits I had that I never realized. Having this knowledge was key to my awareness as an undercover, so I could make sure I did not do them at the wrong times in the future.

The actors also pushed the envelope concerning touching you, from a sexual perspective to aggressive attempts to search you during undercover deals. They tested how you warded off these advancements, stayed in your undercover role, did not expose your body wire or undercover identity, and how you handled the pressure of the situation in general. Everyone is different, so this was an eye-opening experience to learn about myself in general, not just in regard to working undercover. What was discussed behind closed doors was not for the class to know, or for a grade. It was done to create awareness and allow you to prevent these things from happening in real-life. The knowledge gained undoubtedly had the potential to help save my life. This course was real and raw. It went into every aspect of undercover work and how to execute it properly and safely.

(BELOW) My class ID and class photo from the two-week-long undercover investigations school I attended. This school changed me as an undercover and taught me so much.

Shortly after attending the two-week long undercover school, I was invited back as a paid-guest instructor. This was a huge compliment to me, indicating the impression I must have made on the instructors, and it was an offer that I could not refuse. My undercover partner Lyle and I were both invited back to be instructors. We went to teach at this school and thoroughly enjoyed ourselves. We worked from 7:30 am until almost midnight each night for two weeks during the course. We learned so much, ourselves, by critiquing other undercover narcotics agents from across the county. Seeing other people's ideas or mistakes was more of a learning experience than going through the class as a student.

As an instructor, you had better know your curriculum because students will ask questions. Anyone who has ever taught an instructional class knows that it is hard to teach to a bunch of cops. Cops analyze every word of what you say and are not afraid to call you on something if they think it is bullshit. I enjoyed teaching and wanted to go back to teach on other occasions. This training was great at making me more marketable as an undercover narc, wanting to assist any agency with undercover work. It was a huge deal to having our sheriff's office investigators teaching narcs across the nation, putting our unit on the map with positive recognition.

The instructors who wrote the curriculum that we taught are retired ATF agents and others, who took it upon themselves to teach aspects of undercover work that the federal government did not allow them to teach when they were employed with ATF (known today as the Bureau of Alcohol Tobacco Firearms and Explosives, or BATFE). For example, they taught the psychological aspects of UC work, which was forbidden to talk about at one time. I believe that attitude has changed more recently, but then again, there are not that many true long-term undercover agents in America today, so it may not be of a priority for discussion. Eliminating undercovers because it is too dangerous, and only depending upon unreliable criminal informants, is not the answer. But rather it is imperative to continuously train the new yet dying-breed of undercovers for the future.

On one occasion, when I was asked to be a paid instructor, I had one particularly memorable experience. It did not happen in the school or after school, but on my way there. I remember that Lyle and I were running behind, and we were going to be late for the start of the Sunday preparation session before the start of school. I cannot stand to be late for something, and I usually arrive early when I can. So, being late to school when you were one of the instructors was not an option. I liked to lead by example and practiced what I preached, so I did not look like a hypocrite.

I tend to have a lead foot anyway, and on this occasion, I used the excuse of running late in order to speed. I remember going well in excess of the speed limit. Let us just say my speed was into the triple digits, without divulging exactly how fast I was going or what the posted speed limit was. I looked ahead of me and saw what looked like a patrol car on the side of the road running radar. I immediately broke it down and reduced my speed much closer to the speed limit. It was too late because he had already clocked me at my peak. Even though I was caught, I thought that *maybe he would let me go; maybe chase after someone else,* but that was wishful thinking.

The deputy pulled in behind me and initiated his blue lights and siren. I pulled to the side of the road and sat by, waiting for the ass-chewing I was about to receive, once he found out I was a *cop.* I sat in my car for several minutes, waiting for the deputy to approach. He never did. The next thing I know, I am being commanded to throw my keys outside of the window and step out of the car with my hands up, facing away from the officer. At that moment, I thought that this was a little excessive for a speeding violation, even though I was going really fast.

As I exited the car, I could see that the deputy had his gun pointed at me, and he kept telling me to face the other direction. I knew this deputy meant business, and there was no time for explaining who I was at that very moment. I followed all his commands, all the way down to the point where I was lying face down on the shoulder of the road. Once he had me in handcuffs, I tried to explain that I was a law enforcement officer. He was having none of it, and I sure as heck did not look the part with the long beard and hair. Of course, I was so deep in working undercover that I kept my police ID in my car, well hidden in the bottom of my center console under multiple items. I did this to protect my true identity, in case one of my targets was to get in the car with me, but I still wanted to have my credentials for situations like this. I kept telling the deputy that I was a cop, but he avoided my attempts to speak to him. Eventually, he called me out and said, "A cop would not be riding around in a stolen vehicle." This dumbfounded me but was also a very concerning statement. The next section details more and completes the story of what happened next.

*(**BELOW**) UC Class after hours social function*

*(**BELOW**) Student gift given to the Undercover Instructors.*

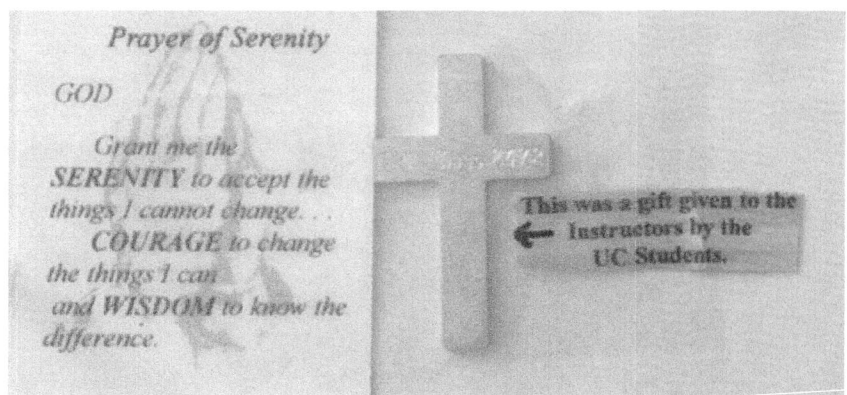

*(**BELOW**) My UC Instructor ID Card for Federal Undercover School*

(BELOW) Three UC instructors and one UC Student (red hat) take a picture after completion of UC scenario training.

Felony Stop on Me

On my undercover vehicle, I frequently would change out the vehicle license plates to keep people guessing who I was, just in case they noted my plate in the past. I had about seven different license plates from different states that I kept in my trunk. On one occasion, I displayed a Tennessee license plate, which happened to come back to a stolen vehicle. This was done if a dealer had access to a corrupt cop, and they ran my license plate in a law enforcement database. If they noticed it was stolen, it would most likely eliminate any thought that I may be a cop.

During this time, I was working on multiple undercover cases, and we were busy almost seven days a week. As I was describing previously that Sunday I was set to travel to Meridian, Mississippi, to teach a class as a guest instructor at the RCTA's Federal Undercover School with my undercover partner Lyle. I worked late the night before and forgot to change out my license plate and put the proper license plate on my vehicle before I left the state to go to Mississippi. As I was describing, I was also running late and wanted to try and make up time, so I was speeding. As I entered Mississippi and into a small country town, with only one exit off the interstate and not even a stoplight, when I was pulled over by a deputy sheriff.

I knew I was speeding excessively when the deputy was attempting to catch up on the interstate. Once he got behind me, he just followed closely for a few miles, so I began to wonder if he were contemplating stopping me, or if he may just be seeing how I would react. I set the cruise control on the speed limit and prayed I was not going to get stopped. Never once did it occur to me that I still had the stolen vehicle license plate on the rear of my vehicle and that he was behind me running my tag.

After a few miles, the deputy turned on his flashing lights and siren to signal for me to pull over. I immediately complied, rolled down my driver's side window, and put my hands on the steering wheel for the deputy. My UC partner Lyle put his hands on the dashboard on his side. This was a courtesy from one cop to another, so he did not fear where our hands were. Instead of seeing a deputy walk up to my window to introduce himself, I hear the deputy come over his vehicle's public address system, telling me to put the car in park, turn off the car, throw the keys out the window, slowly unlock and open the door from the outside with my left hand, and to step out and walk backward to the sound of his voice. I knew this was not a regular stop; the deputy was conducting a felony car stop on us.

I did not make any sudden movements and complied with the deputy. I stepped out of the car, and he switched from speaking to me on the PA system to yelling commands. I walked backward to the sound of his voice, got down on my knees facing away from him, and lifted my shirt with my weak hand as instructed. He could clearly see I had a gun on my hip, which was nothing like a standard-issue police weapon (i.e., Glock or something similar). As discussed before, I carried a nickel-plated with pearl handle .38 snub-nosed revolver on this day. This was a gun that was seized off a drug dealer and forfeited in an older drug case. (Instead of selling them at public auction, we used weapons we felt could help us further our drug investigations. I needed a reliable gun that looked flashy like something a drug dealer may have and was the last thing you may expect a cop to carry if you were stereotyping.)

The deputy ordered me not to go for the gun, cross my legs, and lay face down with my hands out at my side. This was summertime in Mississippi, and the outside temperature was about 95 degrees Fahrenheit, but the asphalt I was laying on had to have been over 140 degrees. The deputy made it clear that if I moved towards my gun that he would "blow my fucking brains out." I laid there for what seemed like several minutes when suddenly, I felt a heavy knee in my back and the full-body weight of the deputy on top of me. It took my breath away, and I could not speak. He handcuffed me and secured my weapon. After he rolled me over and sat me up, I had caught my breath enough to start talking.

I explained that I was an undercover police officer, but he did not believe me because of the stolen tag. He then pulled his gun back out and ordered my partner out of the car also. He secured us both quickly. Hell, I was actually impressed by how well he handled himself alone when most city cops would wait for backup before handcuffing or asking us to exit the vehicle. This may be true for city cops, but not county deputies or state troopers that are used to working alone and putting themselves at higher risks.

He asked where my credentials (i.e., badge and police ID card) were located. It was then that I realized I had placed my credentials in the hidden compartment inside the bottom of my center console. I did this because I usually worked deep undercover and never had to use them, but I kept them available if I needed them for an emergency. The only issue was the deputy was alone in the middle of a long stretch of interstate, so he did not take any unnecessary chances, leaving us alone to search the car, not to mention how we both looked like very rough characters. My partner was all tattooed up and had a shaved head with a long goatee. He looked more like a neo-Nazi white supremacist than a cop. This alone was bad enough, but the deputy was black, and I was not sure what was going through his mind seeing both of us questionable ruffians in what he believed was a stolen car. So, we shut up and complied.

He patted me down again for weapons, removed my two knives (one on the boot and one in my pocket), double-locked my handcuffs, and put me in the back seat of his patrol car. He missed the handcuff key I always kept in my back pants pocket, just in case I was ever kidnapped and handcuffed behind my back. I carried this key with me for years but never had to use it, thankfully. He did the same thing to my UC partner and put him in handcuffs in the rear of his patrol car.

As we watched from the back seat of his patrol car, the deputy walked up to my car and began to search where I told him my credentials would be located. It took him a minute, but he did locate them. Since my sheriff's office ID picture did not match how I currently looked, he called my agency to confirm that I was currently employed with them. Once it was confirmed, he un-handcuffed my partner and me. He issued me a warning for speeding, and then we proceeded to stand on the side of the road talking for the next hour. We were already late, so it did not matter at this point if we were another hour late since he cut me a break on the speeding. It was not like we were teaching a class that night, but we were doing some Sunday introductions in preparation for Monday's class.

There was a valuable lesson learned here for an undercover; always be aware of your vehicle's license plate, especially when traveling out of state. Also, if not working directly in an undercover capacity have my badge and credentials readily available. Moreover, if I were not speeding in the first place, the deputy would not have noticed me or ran my license plate to discover it was stolen. This makes me reflect on all the interdiction cases I have been involved in over the years, with persons transporting large multi-million dollar loads of drugs for cartels. In just about every case, the person was speeding or committed some other violation. Criminals make it easy because they are human and become complacent, just like I did with speeding that day.

If we acted stupid during the stop, demanding some professional courtesy while he thought we were criminals in a stolen vehicle, this could have ended badly. The key is to comply with all commands and never argue with a law enforcement officer on the roadside. If you disagree with an officer's actions, file a complaint or a lawsuit, but never argue on the side of the road. An officer is trained to stay in control, and as long as you are arguing, they will stay one level above your actions, just to ensure that they do not lose control. This is where you see many videos over the years of idiots arguing the legality of a stop or arrest on the side of the road when a regular traffic stop escalates into a deadly force situation. As cops, we knew better and had no issues, despite all of the above factors.

Chapter Two

Slain Comrade

(ABOVE) This is a photo of a plaque that hangs on the SC Criminal Justice Academy memorial wall. This was my former beat partner and a friend who was killed in the line of duty. RIP Drew. You are greatly missed brother!

I worked in uniform patrol as a member of the Delta Platoon for the six months prior to being assigned to the county Vice & Narcotics Unit. This was a forty-person platoon that covered the entire county. I was assigned to patrol area nine (Unit

D-49), and my good friend Drew was assigned to area eight (Unit # D-38), which were both considered the west side of town. The west side was the roughest side of town, with no lack of action for a lawman. Drugs and violence ran rampant in this older section of town. As adjacent beat partners, we always backed each other up and overlapped patrols in one another's beat areas. This allowed us to spend many hours working together, and we built a close bond.

Drew was a graduate of the Citadel, Charleston South Carolina's elite military college. Part of the Citadel's mission, which included a "sense of camaraderie produced through teamwork and service to others while following a military lifestyle," helped mold and define Drew as a fantastic police officer. Drew and I worked many shifts together, always getting into anything and everything along with other like-minded deputies. Drew was fearless and would do whatever it took to rid his area of criminals. We were a lot alike in our diligence with fighting crime and work ethic. He was exactly the type of cop that I liked to have in my corner and by my side. I never had to second guess whether he would be there when *shit hit the fan,* and the fight was on. Drew and I were close friends on and off duty. He, his wife, my wife, and I would sometimes double date on the weekends. He was completely devoted to his wife, his friends, and his career. He was the quintessential "cops' cop." Most importantly, Drew was a man of God and had a high conviction in his beliefs.

Shortly after I left Delta Platoon and went to work in vice and narcotics full time with the sheriff's office, the following happened. On the day of this incident, Deputy Drew conducted a stop of some suspicious characters in a high crime area that fit the description of a group suspected of harassing a local ice cream truck driver for money. He was by himself when he approached these unknown men, which is not uncommon for county deputies. When he asked them to present their identification cards or driver's licenses, the situation quickly went from routine to a nightmare. Two of the guys complied, but one did not. The guy who did not comply, hereafter referred to as Chris, stated he did not have any identification. Chris told Deputy Drew that his ID was inside a trailer down the road. Chris started to back-step while telling Deputy Drew he would get it. Deputy Drew, knowing this was a person with something to hide, grabbed Chris by the arm. Chris immediately tried to pull away and flee the area. At this point, Drew took him to the ground so that he could control the situation. The other two guys who were with the suspect fled the area on foot, not wanting anything to do with the scuffle. Deputy Drew managed to get one handcuff on Chris. Drew shifted his weight forward while he had him in a full mount, trying to get the other cuff on Chris when Chris was able to buck Deputy Drew off him. That gave Chris the time to get up and start running. Drew got up, called out on the radio, and chased after him. They rounded a house and approached a hill with a small fence at the top of it. At that point, he pulled out his service weapon, pointed it at the suspect, and yelled out commands for the suspect to stop, while still chasing after him. What happened next is unclear because the only living witness is a 5-year-old, and it was hard to get details without re-traumatizing the child with repeated interviews.

Based upon a forensic reconstruction of the crime scene, what appeared to have happened was Chris was running up the embankment and about to hurdle a fence at the top of it when Drew caught up with him. Drew's foot/boot got caught on a tree root,

106

and he tripped. When he hit the ground face first, he tried to break his fall with his hands. This would have been a natural reaction for anyone. This caused the hand carrying his gun to strike the ground first. Perhaps the bottom of the magazine well hit a rock or the ground first, taking all the force of the fall at one time. However, it happened, he lost his grip on his gun, and it landed on the ground in front of him. Before Drew could retrieve his gun, the suspect immediately noticed the weapon and picked it up. Without hesitation, Chris placed the gun to the back of Drew's head and pulled the trigger once. Drew died immediately when the bullet severed his spinal cord at the base of his skull. Chris then fled the area like the coward he was, with Deputy Drew's service weapon.

The last radio communications with Deputy Drew were that he was fighting the suspect, and he needed some help. All units were immediately paged and dispatched to the same area. The county is approximately seven hundred fifty square miles, and pulling all officers together like this leaves other areas open and vulnerable to crime, unprotected without any law enforcement presence. It was the first time in my career that I had seen this. So, I knew something was terribly wrong.

I was off work that day, but remember it very clearly. I was sitting in my recliner at home, watching the news and eating a plate of spaghetti that my wife had just prepared, when the page came out. We had alphanumeric pagers, which allowed for long text messages to be received. The pager message stated *deputy 10-89...All units respond...* to a specific area; *10-89 was the 10 code for deceased.* The message gave an intersection and numeric address where this occurred. Within three years, five law enforcement officers were killed in the line of duty in our county. So, I was not completely surprised by the call or the area indicated, since violence against police officers was the now worse that I had seen it so far in my career.

Within two minutes, I was dressed and armed with several guns, extra ammunition, three flashlights, and headed to the designated area. I also had a special "bug-out bag" in my vehicle, with many more magazines fully loaded, knives, more handcuffs, tactical clothing, and extra flashlight batteries, among other things like protein bars and bottles of water. I was in an unmarked undercover vehicle, so it was not equipped with lights and a siren-like a regular patrol car or special surveillance vehicle. On the way there, I was going fast while my mind raced wondering who it could have been that was killed.

I put two and two together, and knew that my old platoon, Delta Platoon, was on duty that day; the area where this occurred was also my old beat area. I narrowed it down to about five different guys that would have been working that area. Furthermore, I could narrow it down to about three guys who commonly apprehended drug dealers and other violent felons on that specific street regularly. At that point, I knew it was either Deputy Will L., Ranger Mike or Deputy Drew. This was already tough because I was friends with everyone on the Delta Platoon, but especially those three guys. Whether you are close friends with another officer or not, they are a brother or sister in blue, fighting for the same cause you were, so there was that sacred bond between everyone.

It seemed like it was taking forever to get to the scene, although I was 'hauling ass.' I noticed two marked patrol vehicles come by me in traffic, so I took advantage of it and got in-between them. I could not let them know who I was on the radio because it was closed to only emergency traffic at the murder scene. I guess they recognized my car and proceeded with me towards the area. Now it looked like I had a police escort with guys in the front and rear of my car, blue lights, and sirens blazing.

When I pulled up close to the scene, which was already being roped off and off-limits by that time, I immediately saw a buddy of mine, Deputy Will. Deputy Will is the one that told me that it was Drew and that he was dead. That was the first close friend I had lost in the line of duty, and I did not know how to react. Understandably, teary-eyed, and emotionally distraught, I knew that I had to hold my emotions in check because the suspect was still on the loose. I re-channeled my sadness and turned it into energy, drive, and motivation to catch the suspect, Chris.

When put in a stressful incident like this, the camaraderie of a department shows their true colors. The entire law enforcement community came together for this manhunt, and it did not matter who you were; as long as you had a badge and gun, you were out there doing what needed to be done. Even concerned citizens were diligent in calling if they saw anything out of the ordinary. I left my vehicle, which was running low on gas. I jumped into an unmarked Ford Taurus with several other plain-clothes investigators, some from a street-level narcotics unit and others from my Vice & Narcotics Unit. While searching the area, an alert came over the radio, notifying all units of several white male suspects in the area of the crime scene, which was seen brandishing a sawed-off shotgun at a motorist. We did not know the details of the crime regarding Deputy Drew at that moment, other than knowing the suspect had Deputy Drew's gun, so we assumed the man with the shotgun might be the suspect(s) or at least linked to the crime.

Almost immediately after getting the call, we spotted the vehicle coming off a side street. We approached it in our vehicle, and they sped off quickly. We came in behind them and called it out on the radio. We did not have any blue lights on the vehicle because it was an unmarked surveillance vehicle without the lights package, so it was hard to get their attention and conduct a traffic stop. What we did next might seem unprofessional, but we did not want to allow the possible suspects the opportunity to kill again. We pulled up beside the suspect vehicle with deputies hanging out both the front and rear passenger's side windows, pointing pistols and shotguns at the vehicle and motioning for them to pull over.

All of us were in clearly marked police raid gear, so they knew what was going on. Fortunately, a marked vehicle pulled up behind us just as we pulled up on the vehicle. The deputy in the patrol car turned on its blue lights and activated the siren to make sure they knew it was law enforcement. The vehicle did not even try to pull over with our guns pointed at them. So, they came to an abrupt stop in the middle of a four-lane highway.

We aggressively approached the car on foot to catch them off guard before they had a chance to go on the offensive. We extracted all four guys from the vehicle. The sawed-off shotgun lay on the floorboard in the backseat area of the vehicle. Before the occupants knew it, they were all handcuffed and lying face down in the middle of the highway. We did not realize the adrenaline rush we had from this; later, we found out that one of the deputies, when he applied pressure to the back of the head of a suspect, he was trying to handcuff, gave the suspect a severe concussion and laceration. This was not intentional, of course, but it happened and needed to be dealt with. Once we found out that these guys were not responsible for murdering Deputy Drew, nobody wanted anything to do with the new crime scene.

Nevertheless, one of the deputies took over the scene. The suspects were taken to jail for the unlawful possession of the sawed-off shotgun and possession of Cocaine, found in a common area of the vehicle. Of course, nobody claimed the drugs or gun, and they were all charged because they all were in an area where they had access to it, having at least some form of control over the drugs and gun. This is known legally as constructive possession under SC laws. The suspect who was injured ended up not suing the county once he found out why we were so aggressive. Also, since his father used to be a cop, he understood and did not want to pursue legal action. The bag of drugs and shotgun were forensically processed for latent prints. The prints came back to only one of the suspects out of the four in the vehicle. He pled guilty to Unlawful Possession of a sawed-off shotgun, and Possession with Intent to Distribute Cocaine. The charges were dismissed on the other three suspects.

Nightfall came several hours into the manhunt for Chris, the cop killer. The Sheriff called a meeting at the temporary command post set up for the incident. The Sheriff started to set us up in shifts to work around the clock for the long haul. This was an excellent strategic move, because we did not know if we would catch him within the hour, or several weeks later. We believed that we had him isolated to a specific area because he fled on foot, and we did not think he had a car or access to one. Unfortunately, in these situations, you never know if someone picked the suspect up or if he was hiding nearby. I volunteered to continue to work and stay on the first twelve-hour rotation, while some officers went to rest and prepare for their upcoming shift. I had no intention of going home after my 12-hour shift. I was determined to stay out until the suspect was located and arrested. Deputy Drew was a good friend and law enforcement brother of mine, so I was willing to do what was needed to catch his killer. I know Drew would have done the same thing if I was the one who was killed. I was given an assignment with others in my narc unit, to conduct surveillance on Chris' girlfriend's trailer, where we knew he called one time, due to emergency phone records we received. We believed that he might show up at this location, and the Sheriff did not want deputies in marked cars or uniforms around to spook him. We stayed up all night watching this residence. There was not so much as a light turned off or on the entire time.

When the first signs of daylight came, we were called on the radio about a possible sighting of the suspect in a wooded area. A construction worker arriving at work for his shift that morning was approached by a man fitting the description of Chris, asking for water. My group entered one side of the woods to attempt to flush the subject towards the other side, where the SWAT team waited on standby. Once it was confirmed that someone was in the woods, we were told to back off and get out of the area, so we were not caught in any potential crossfire. We understood and followed the orders without any hesitation. Suddenly, we heard one shot, then a barrage of gunshots and eventually silence. It sounded like a war zone of automatic weapons, which is highly unusual in civilian law enforcement.

Chris had taken a shot at some of the members of the SWAT team standing on the wood line. The SWAT team laid down gunfire into the general area of the suspect's shot. This was done because the area was all woods, without any houses for a great distance. Not to mention, this was the area we were just in and confirmed nobody else was there as we got out of the possible line of fire ourselves. The vegetation was dense, and you could not see very far ahead of you. Instead of sending in a team to be shot at upon entry, they returned fire. After the first rounds of shots were taken, a police K-9 was sent in, and yet another shot rang out. After that, the K-9 handler called the dog back so he would not be shot. Thinking they were being fired upon, the SWAT team laid down fire again. Then there was complete silence. After what seemed like an eternity, they sent the dog back in. They could hear the dog gnawing on something, so the team went in and found the suspect, deceased. The first shot fired by Chris was believed to be directed at the SWAT team. Then when they laid down fire, the suspect was struck in the throat with one bullet. The second shot that we initially believed was him shooting at the K-9, was actually Chris shooting himself in the head. The coroner later pronounced Chris' cause of death as a self-inflicted gunshot wound to the head, and not the shot to the throat. Since it was ruled a suicide, his family could not blame his death directly on law enforcement and sue the department.

Chris' death was bittersweet; at least now, Deputy Drew's widow would not have to endure a long, drawn-out trial that could potentially end in a 'not guilty' verdict, due to a technicality and the fact that there would be no other witnesses besides the suspect. This is the frustrating reality of our criminal justice system today. It is called the "criminal" justice system because it was designed to protect criminals, not the police. Unfortunately, this system does not always find justice for friends or family members of victims of violent crimes.

I tell this story because Deputy Drew was a casualty of the war on drugs that will never be forgotten. He died because a crack head would not allow anyone or anything to prevent him from getting his next high. Facing jail time, the suspect made the eventually fatal decision to kill a police officer. Instead of merely losing his freedom, he lost his life, which is often a sad reality of the war on drugs. The final police report revealed that the only drug paraphernalia found on the suspect's body was a straight shooter crack pipe. He was high on crack cocaine when he killed my friend Deputy Drew.

(BELOW) Memorial Service Bulletin

A Service Honoring and Remembering
Deputy Andrew ██████

August 30, 19██   August 17, 20██

August 23, 20██
ten o'clock
██████ First Baptist Church
██████, South Carolina

(BELOW) Newspaper Article online about Deputy Drew's murder and the manhunt that ended in the death of the suspect.

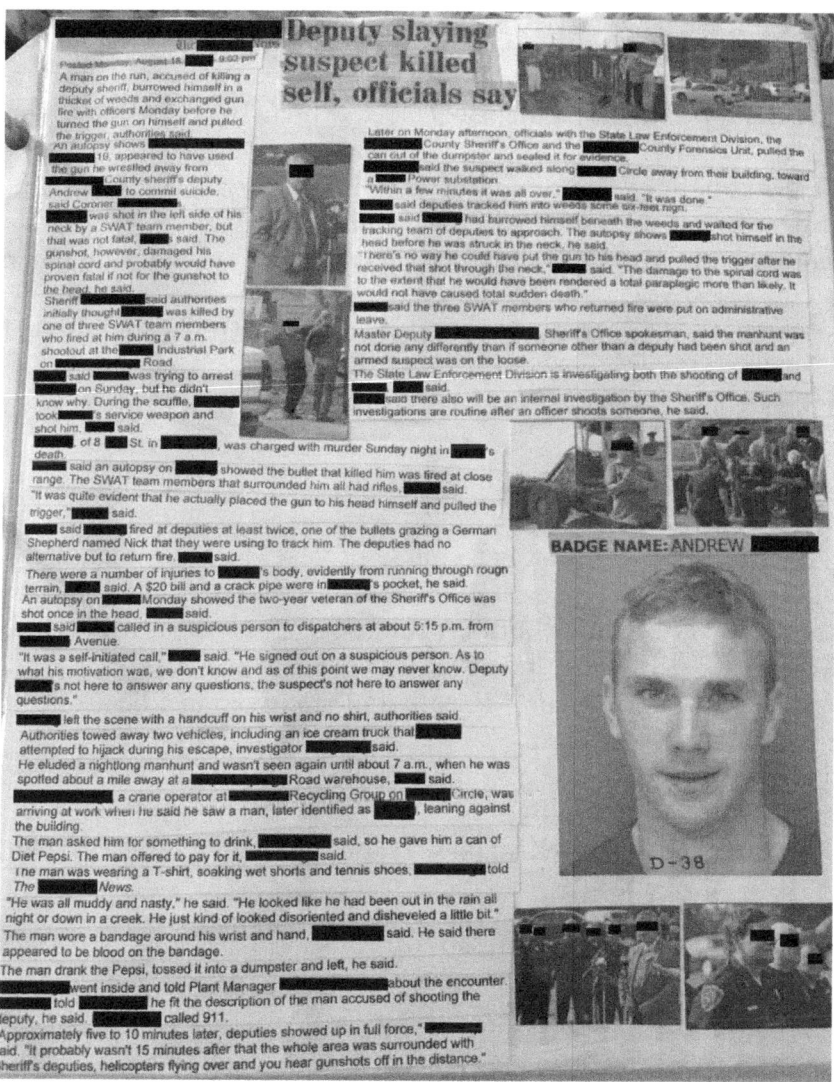

Deputy slaying suspect killed self, officials say

Posted Monday, August 18, ███ 9:00 pm

A man on the run, accused of killing a deputy sheriff, burrowed himself in a thicket of weeds and exchanged gun fire with officers Monday before he turned the gun on himself and pulled the trigger, authorities said.

An autopsy shows ███ 18, appeared to have used the gun he wrestled away from ███ County sheriff's deputy Andrew ███ to commit suicide, said Coroner ███.

███ was shot in the left side of his neck by a SWAT team member, but that was not fatal, ███ said. The gunshot, however, damaged his spinal cord and probably would have proven fatal if not for the gunshot to the head, he said.

Sheriff ███ said authorities initially thought ███ was killed by one of three SWAT team members who fired at him during a 7 a.m. shootout at the ███ Industrial Park on ███ Road.

███ said ███ was trying to arrest ███ on Sunday, but he didn't know why. During the scuffle, ███ took ███'s service weapon and shot him, ███ said.

███, of 8 ███ St. in ███, was charged with murder Sunday night in ███'s death.

███ said an autopsy on ███ showed the bullet that killed him was fired at close range. The SWAT team members that surrounded him all had rifles, ███ said.

"It was quite evident that he actually placed the gun to his head himself and pulled the trigger," ███ said.

███ said ███ fired at deputies at least twice, one of the bullets grazing a German Shepherd named Nick that they were using to track him. The deputies had no alternative but to return fire, ███ said.

There were a number of injuries to ███'s body, evidently from running through rough terrain, ███ said. A $20 bill and a crack pipe were in ███'s pocket, he said.

An autopsy on ███ Monday showed the two-year veteran of the Sheriff's Office was shot once in the head, ███ said.

███ said ███ called in a suspicious person to dispatchers at about 5:15 p.m. from ███ Avenue.

"It was a self-initiated call," ███ said. "He signed out on a suspicious person. As to what his motivation was, we don't know and as of this point we may never know. Deputy ███'s not here to answer any questions, the suspect's not here to answer any questions."

███ left the scene with a handcuff on his wrist and no shirt, authorities said. Authorities towed away two vehicles, including an ice cream truck that ███ attempted to hijack during his escape, investigator ███ said.

He eluded a nightlong manhunt and wasn't seen again until about 7 a.m., when he was spotted about a mile away at a ███ Road warehouse, ███ said.

███, a crane operator at ███ Recycling Group on ███ Circle, was arriving at work when he said he saw a man, later identified as ███, leaning against the building.

The man asked him for something to drink, ███ said, so he gave him a can of Diet Pepsi. The man offered to pay for it, ███ said.

The man was wearing a T-shirt, soaking wet shorts and tennis shoes, ███ told The ███ News.

"He was all muddy and nasty," he said. "He looked like he had been out in the rain all night or down in a creek. He just kind of looked disoriented and disheveled a little bit."

The man wore a bandage around his wrist and hand, ███ said. He said there appeared to be blood on the bandage.

The man drank the Pepsi, tossed it into a dumpster and left, he said.

███ went inside and told Plant Manager ███ about the encounter. ███ told ███ he fit the description of the man accused of shooting the deputy, he said. ███ called 911.

Approximately five to 10 minutes later, deputies showed up in full force," ███ said. "It probably wasn't 15 minutes after that the whole area was surrounded with sheriff's deputies, helicopters flying over and you hear gunshots off in the distance."

Later on Monday afternoon, officials with the State Law Enforcement Division, the ███ County Sheriff's Office and the ███ County Forensics Unit, pulled the can out of the dumpster and sealed it for evidence.

███ said the suspect walked along ███ Circle away from their building, toward a ███ Power substation.

"Within a few minutes it was all over," ███ said. "It was done."

███ said deputies tracked him into weeds some six feet high.

███ said ███ had burrowed himself beneath the weeds and waited for the tracking team of deputies to approach. The autopsy shows ███ shot himself in the head before he was struck in the neck, he said.

"There's no way he could have put the gun to his head and pulled the trigger after he received that shot through the neck," ███ said. "The damage to the spinal cord was to the extent that he would have been rendered a total paraplegic more than likely. It would not have caused total sudden death."

███ said the three SWAT members who returned fire were put on administrative leave.

Master Deputy ███, Sheriff's Office spokesman, said the manhunt was not done any differently than if someone other than a deputy had been shot and an armed suspect was on the loose.

The State Law Enforcement Division is investigating both the shooting of ███ and ███, ███ said.

███ said there also will be an internal investigation by the Sheriff's Office. Such investigations are routine after an officer shoots someone, he said.

BADGE NAME: ANDREW ███

D-38

Significant Incident Months Prior to Deputy Drew's Death

It was about three months before Deputy Drew's murder that a very similar incident occurred which I will never forget. This was before I got promoted back into Vice & Narcotics, and I worked in uniform patrol with Deputy Drew and other members of the Delta Platoon. On this night, I had just arrested a guy with ten outstanding armed robbery warrants on him. This was an unusual arrest because I knew the guy and went to high school with him, although he was a couple of years younger than me. A good friend of mine, whom I mentored since he was fifteen and I was a rookie cop, Adam M., called me to give me a heads-up on this guy. The guy was over at his house on the west side of town. This was a house where Adam was housesitting while it was going through probate court after the death of a family member.

I do not remember this suspect being a troublemaker back in school, but apparently, after high school, he got in with the wrong crowd and had joined a gang. Part of his gang initiation was to commit multiple armed robberies in one night. He and another suspect hit ten stores in one night, county-wide. After the other suspect was later identified and snitched him out, warrants were issued for his arrest. He had been on the run for more than two years at this point.

My buddy, Adam, told me that this guy showed up at his house to try to talk to a girl with whom he was close friends. He got a bad vibe that he was not upstanding. Through some questioning, Adam extracted casual personal information, such as what school he went to, his approximate age, and his full name. Adam called me, and I did the research and found a guy fitting that description with ten active Felony Armed Robbery warrants, but I needed to confirm in person this was the same guy. The police department said that they did have the warrants in-hand, and I got a picture sent to me of the suspect's current driver's license. I recognized him immediately as the same guy I went to school with, and I started driving towards Adam's location to determine if this was indeed our guy.

When I arrived on the scene, I ran into the suspect out in the driveway. He was all hugged up against the female he came to see. I was in a marked patrol car and uniform, but he did not run for some reason. When I got out of my car, he recognized me and was friendly. We talked for a second, and then I let him know about the active warrants. He almost seemed relieved he did not have to run anymore, and voluntarily turned around and placed his hands behind his back to be cuffed. The female got upset with me because Adam never told her that he called me. The reality was she thought I was just coming to see Adam on a break, and just so happened to recognize the suspect and know he had warrants. I never tried to explain the whole situation to her, because it worked out better this way, and protected Adam for giving me a tip.

I put the suspect in the back of my patrol car after searching him for weapons and started to transport him to the detention center to be processed and arraigned by a judge. While en route, Deputy Drew came over the radio, and in a high-pitched and excited voice stating he was "getting out on foot with a suspicious (10-88) black male at Cot..." Then the transmission went silent. The dispatcher asked Deputy Drew to repeat himself and give his location several times. There was no response, so I immediately assumed the worst. Without an exact location, it is hard to determine where he was at that moment. The dispatcher kept trying to reach Deputy Drew on the radio but was unsuccessful. I was one of Drew's beat partners, but our beat area was huge and covered several square miles in a densely populated and impoverished area, so this was no easy task to figure out where Drew was. I also knew Drew pretty well, and just had a gut feeling he was searching for drug dealers in a known "honey hole" at Cotton Street, close to Rutherford Road. I prayed I was right, and that "Cot" was the beginning of Cotton Street.

Despite having a prisoner in custody inside my patrol car and being a policy violation, I knew I had to get to that area quickly because something was wrong. I turned on my blue lights and siren and quickly drove to that area. The funniest thing was my arrestee, whom I had known since high school, got into the drama, and called out anything he saw, such as cars approaching an intersection. Hell, he was almost like having a partner in the car, calling "clear right" or "clear left" as we approached intersections. He was enjoying the last moments of freedom he may have for many years, so I just went with it. At that moment, he was not my number one priority; my brother in blue was.

Within about five to eight minutes, I arrived at the intersection where my gut feeling had sent me. Sure enough, I located Deputy Drew's patrol vehicle in the middle of the road with the driver's side door open, spotlight on, and pointed down. There were no blue lights on, and Deputy Drew was nowhere in sight. I relayed my findings over the radio to have other units head that way and assist because I had no clue what I was going to find next. I pulled past his patrol car and noticed his police radio in the middle of the roadway about fifty feet in front of his patrol car, with the lapel mic separated from the base another ten feet away. I looked further down the road and saw Deputy Drew's ASP baton lying off the road against the curb. At that point, my heart almost stopped. I relayed this over the radio, so that other units knew to step it up.

I looked around frantically and felt like I was failing Deputy Drew because I still had no clue where he was. I even commanded my prisoner to look the opposite side of where I was looking as I drove around. Suddenly, out of the corner of my eye, I saw a guy at the edge of a wood line, pointing down the hill at something. I noticed this guy was very excited, and I relayed that over my radio, along with another cross-street. I drove down that roadway, shining my spotlight and alley lights, and still could not find Deputy Drew. The road was a circle, and I drove the entire thing. On my way back to where I entered that street, I saw movement at the end of a driveway, partially behind a house.

I called the location out on the radio, pulled up, and tried to make out what was happening. I could see Deputy Drew on his back, with the suspect on top of him, tugging at his gun while still in the holster. Deputy Drew held the suspect's hands against his own body to prevent him from pulling his gun out of the holster. I came flying down the driveway and skidded to a stop. I jumped out, and without hesitating, I ran towards them and gave a flying-knee strike to the suspect's head. This was one of those "knees" that would have made my soccer coaches from the past very proud. This instantly knocked the suspect unconscious, and he flipped over and rolled onto his side. As this happened, Deputy Drew's gun flew into the air and landed a few feet away. As I handcuffed the suspect before he came to, I looked over and saw how out of breath Deputy Drew was from the fight. He was on his back and trying to catch his breath. I later found out that they fought hardcore for nearly ten minutes. That is an eternity when fighting for your life.

Drew got to his knees, crawled over, and picked up his gun and holstered it. About that time, one of my shift sergeants arrived on the scene. He came in hot because I had not given any updates since stating the suspect was on top of Deputy Drew. My radio was silent in the heat of the confrontation, and I had no clue they had tried repeatedly to reach me to make sure I was alright. When I jumped out of the car to assist Deputy Drew, I never turned on my hand-held radio. I had tunnel vision, and honestly would have had no clue of any radio communications at that moment even if my radio was on. The sergeant grabbed one of the suspect's arms, and I grabbed the other. We lifted him and began to escort him towards the patrol car. He was still dazed and partially pulling away, not fully realizing what was happening. The more he came to, the more he resisted; most likely because of the drugs he had used; later found to be crack cocaine.

As we approached the sergeant's patrol car to place the suspect in the back seat, the sergeant pulled, and I pushed, and the suspect leaned in that same direction. The momentum of all three of us going the same way caused the suspect to strike his head so hard against the patrol car's side mirror that it fell off. The mirror did not hit the ground and break, because it was hanging on by the wires that allowed it to be adjusted automatically. Thankfully, that injury did not draw blood; we already knew we would have some explaining to do either way. It is acceptable to whip a man fighting you, but once they are restrained, it is never okay to take cheap shots at them, and this could have easily seemed to be how he sustained his injuries.

After it was all said and done, Deputy Drew told me what happened. When he spotted this guy leaving a known crack house in the area, he went to stop him and talk to him. As Deputy Drew was transmitting out on his radio, things with the suspect got aggressive quickly, which caused the radio to get cut off. The fight was on after that, and he had no time to call out on the radio. After the initial fight in the roadway, the suspect broke away and ran. Drew tried to update the radio, but he did not know that his lapel mic and radio had come loose from one another, and transmissions were not going out. Deputy Drew caught up to the suspect and tackled him in the roadway. This is where his radio fell out, and the suspect ripped his lapel mic off because he was calling for help. Deputy Drew was trying to call out on the radio when all of this happened. At some point, Deputy Drew pulled out his ASP baton and struck the suspect repeatedly in his legs and arms, but it did not phase the suspect because he was high on crack cocaine.

It was later determined that he even fractured the suspect's arm, but the suspect kept fighting un-phased due to being high. The suspect took the ASP baton out of Deputy Drew's hands, and they locked up in a physical fight. They then rolled off the roadway and fell down the embankment at the wood line. They continued to fight as the suspect occasionally broke loose and tried to flee. Deputy Drew, a man that never gave up, continued to fight and pepper-sprayed the suspect. The spray did not hit the suspect where intended and was, therefore, useless. They grappled with each other again, and Deputy Drew was getting the upper hand when he went to handcuff the suspect. That was the moment I found the two of them fighting. The suspect then grabbed for Deputy Drew's gun. To prevent this, Deputy Drew dropped his pepper spray, and all his focus was to make sure that the gun did not come out of its holster.

Deputy Drew said that he knew he was getting tired at that point, and the suspect seemed to have superhuman strength, even though he was skinnier than Deputy Drew, with less muscle mass. This is what drugs like crack cocaine can do to someone. They cause a person to fight with excessive aggression and unimaginable strength. Just as Deputy Drew felt himself losing his grip and being overpowered, I managed to knee the suspect in the head and knocked him out cold; talk about perfect timing. I thank God for putting me at the right place and the right time to help my brother, who would have certainly done the same thing for me. Deputy Drew was fearless and never slowed down in his pursuit of criminals, even after this incident. It was this hard-nosed tactical approach to law enforcement that eventually led to his untimely death.

As for the armed robbery suspect in my patrol car, I transported him to the detention center. The rest of the way there, he was so excited after seeing everything take place, and could not get over it. It really was an amazing takedown, but I just acted like it was another day on the job. After Deputy Drew was killed, I had this overwhelming sense of guilt that I was not there for my brother. I had that guilt for many years, thinking *'what if I hadn't pushed so hard to go into Vice and Narcotics, and I had been there that day instead to help Deputy Drew?'*

I know that was not a fair thing to do to myself, but it bothered me, and probably always will. I know that Drew died at peace with God, his family, and his career. We had a very poignant and memorable discussion on duty one night just before I went into Vice & Narcotics, where we talked about the possibility of dying in the line of duty and how he accepted the risks that came with being in law enforcement. I was able to use that conversation to write a letter to his widow and parents. To assure them he died doing exactly what he wanted to be doing and that he loved them very much. I loved Drew like a brother, and his legacy will never be forgotten. He and his wife never had any children, but his memory will live on in this book and my heart, as I tell my family and friends about him.

Revenge Deal... No, Just Plain Old Principle

After Deputy Drew was murdered, and while the manhunt was underway, Chris' girlfriend went live on the local news stations. This lady, who I will refer to as Martha for the sake of telling the story, bad-mouthed Deputy Drew. She stated how Deputy Drew was picking on Chris, who was 'just a scared young boy.' Chris had a prior Escape charge on his criminal history from a previous arrest and was addicted to crack cocaine, so he was no saint. That live interview rubbed me wrong. Based on conversations with my informants, I knew that Martha was involved in using and selling drugs, so I took it upon myself to investigate those allegations further.

I knew where Martha lived but did not have an 'in'; someone who could introduce me so I could purchase drugs off her. Another undercover investigator and I went over to this area and started hanging out and drinking beer with some locals. We dressed like drug addicts and day laborers/construction workers. We wore dirty and raggedy-looking clothes. Some of these new contacts were addicted to more potent drugs than alcohol. It just-so-happened that one of the guys knew and introduced me to

Martha. I found her to be repulsive and unattractive. She is what you might think of if someone said to picture a 'toothless redneck.' I noticed that she was flirting with me, so I decided to lay the charm on her when we first met, and she took the bait. I only acted friendly; I made sure not to talk of sex or sexual acts and avoided any type of a potential entrapment defense.

After seeing her on more than one occasion, she invited us over to her house. I sat out on the front porch of her trailer house and talked to Martha, who was sick with the flu. I remember her, all bundled up in a winter jacket over top of her sweat suit. I acted like I cared about her well-being, which made her friendlier towards me. I knew that I did not want to lose the deal, so I did not force a buy on her. During the conversation, we talked about doing a crack cocaine deal in the future, when she got well and was feeling better. She gave me her phone number and told me to call her in a few days if I needed anything. Things were going in the right direction, and that was where the conversation ended.

On a different day, I called Martha and arranged to meet her at her trailer to purchase crack cocaine. We did not discuss the amount or other details over the phone, because I did not want to

132

make her suspicious, seeming too much like a cop gathering evidence. Since we did not discuss the details of the quantity or price for the crack cocaine, we had something to discuss when we met up. My strategy was to intentionally order up a little larger amount than I believed that she would typically have on her. I did this so that she would be forced to call her supplier and have him deliver more drugs. Then we could get him identified, as well.

In addition, if I ordered up an unusually large amount for a user and she had it readily available, it would show me that she was a larger dealer than I first suspected. The quantity of drugs that a person normally has available for sale can give a buyer an accurate gauge of what level of drug dealer they are doing business with (i.e. grams, ounces, or kilograms). This is not an absolute science, but one more tool used to determine the capabilities of a dealer. Knowing that I was going to try and order more drugs than she would most likely have with her, she would be forced to re-supply. This would allow us to get phone toll records and identify the drug dealer's number that she called at that exact time. If she had to call her dealer to get more drugs, it would allow the surveillance team to stop him and get a positive identification. Of course, the traffic stop would have to take place away from our location, and not draw any suspicion on Martha or me.

An experienced undercover, John, and I went out to Martha's residence. As we arrived at the trailer park, we walked up on the front porch carrying full cans of beer, which we often did for our cover. People do not suspect you as being a cop if they see you openly drinking alcohol, especially if you get out of a car with an open beer, which is a violation of the open container law.

I knocked on the door, and Martha shouted, "Who is it?"

I announced myself, and she said, "Come in. I will be right out."

Apparently, she was in a back room doing something. I walked into the trailer, which put me in the open living room/kitchen area divided by a bar-style countertop. An unknown male subject sat on the couch. As I walked in, he jumped up and approached us. I stood in front because I entered the residence first, and the other undercover was behind me. The guy walked up and got up in my face and immediately said, while grabbing my shirt, "Where I come from, police wear shit like this!"

This guy went from relaxed to confrontational immediately. I could tell this guy was high on crack or some other stimulant. I did not want a confrontation while working undercover, but you need to have rules, and touching me is off-limits. I did not allow anyone to touch me because I had multiple guns, knives, and a body wire. I had to react fast before he thought he could punk me out. I reversed what he said back on him and said the same thing back at him while grabbing his shirt.

My UC partner could tell that things were about to go bad in a hurry, so he casually walked around behind the guy. Now we had an advantage; one of us in the front, and the other in the back. I saw that my partner had his hand in his jacket pocket, where I knew he commonly concealed his hammerless .38cal revolver. It appeared as though he had the bead on the suspect and was ready to shoot, should he produce a gun or other type of weapon.

At that point, the suspect went to try and pat me down and search me for a body wire, or whatever else he was looking for, maybe a gun.

I shoved him off me and asked him, "What the Hell are you doing?"

He then asked if I was a cop or not. I redirected his question and stated that he was the one acting like a cop, and he needed to step off. The argument started to escalate from there, until Martha came running out of the back-hallway area, yelling, "He's cool. He's cool; I've been dealing with him for a while now." She was referring to me. The funny thing was I had never purchased drugs from her in the past, but I had hung out with her. For some reason, she vouched for me not being a cop or police informant to avoid a confrontation. I never found out why she did this, but I can only think it was for one of two reasons. She may not have wanted to lose the potential sale we were about to do, which meant she would lose money, or she may have really liked me and felt that she did not want any trouble in her house.

Afterward, we found out that this guy was from New York and had come down here for unknown reasons, possibly to avoid an arrest warrant back home. The guy walked back over to the couch and sat down, and so did we. Things settled down, but there was still some tension in the air. As a man, when two males confront each other and neither backs down, they find a certain level of street respect for one another. I think that is what this little incident did for us.

The next thing I knew, this guy, John, and I got into a conversation about shooting, girls, and fights, you know, manly stuff. I gave him one of the beers that I had, and we started to hit it off. During the conversation, the topic of murder came up. Martha instantly spoke about her ex-man, who killed a deputy. She told me her version of the story, which was insulting to Deputy Drew, and a bit one-sided. I knew the real story, so this enraged me. However, I knew that I could not let it be known that I was upset, so I engaged them farther. I figured if this case ever went to trial, they would hate it if the jury heard how they were involved in drug sales and the murder of a cop. For this reason, I let her keep talking badly about Deputy Drew, and all law enforcement in general.

During our conversation, I asked Martha for a couple hundred dollars' worth of crack, which she did not have readily available. She told me that she could call her dealer and have him deliver some. Just as we thought she would do, she picked up her cell phone and called him. Now I knew that when the phone call was made at that specific moment, it was to call her supplier. After the undercover investigation was over, I ordered up phone toll records on her cell phone and identified the dealer's number. I got the subscriber information for that phone through a subpoena and identified the dealer and his address. We used cell tower locations of the calls to identify that he was near his listed residence when she called him that day. In addition, he was identified in a traffic stop after dropping off the drugs at Martha's house. After her supplier left, Martha sold the requested drugs to me. Not wanting to purchase the drugs and then leave too quickly and raise suspicion, I decided to hang around for a few more minutes. I knew that I did not want to stay too long, because as an 'addict,' I would be craving to use the drugs. We all stepped outside while Martha went back into the house to do something. I think she went to smoke some of the crack cocaine that she just got from the dealer. She had most likely already spent any money she made off our transaction.

The guy from NY, John, and I stood outside. We continued to tell old war stories to boost our street cred with one another. We tried to top each other with each story, stating how we did something worse than the other guy. I believe this was also to try and show how tough we were. 'New York' started to tell me about an incident where he got into a fight with a guy, and when they went outside to the rear of the club to finish fighting, he stabbed him. He said exactly where he stabbed him, and that he left him there to bleed. At the time, I just figured that he was blowing smoke to make himself look tough. To make the story more believable, he reenacted the stabbing, with me posing as the victim. It was crazy because when he did the stabbing motion, he struck my body wire with his hand. I sure as hell felt it, and almost panicked inside, but he never batted an eye or questioned anything. That was a close call because he touched the battery pack to my body wire but did not say a thing. After some more conversation, we said our goodbyes and went about our business.

Case Conclusion: Martha received five years in prison for the Distribution of Crack Cocaine. This was a result of a plea bargain, where they lumped several other charges together, stemming from unrelated incidents. As for the guy from NY, the confession ended up being an unsolved night club murder in the area. When he was arrested for his involvement in the Distribution of Crack Cocaine charges (i.e., he was security for Martha and posed as her muscle in case any trouble came around while she sold drugs), he was questioned about the murder. At first, he denied it, but when the investigators played a portion of the audio recording of his confession to us during the undercover deal, he folded like a paper airplane. He tried to tell a completely different story of self-defense and how the guy had a knife, which he took from him and used against him. He ended up taking a plea for Involuntary Manslaughter and received twelve years in state prison. This deal goes to show that you never know what a small dope deal can or will turn into; this one became a murder confession while we went after a drug dealer associated with a cop killer. We ended up getting a search warrant on Martha's trailer, and of course, I gave it to the deputies of the Delta Platoon to serve. Additional drugs were found, but nothing large. I believe this gave some of the deputies some sense of closure in the death of Deputy Drew. Just like me, they were all very upset about the negative things Martha told the news about Deputy Drew. If this had been a high-level drug dealer, I would have never allowed Delta Platoon to execute the search warrant. Regardless, we maintained professional standards, and it all worked out in the end.

Chapter Three

Informants

Dealing with Confidential Informants (CIs), or what the feds call Confidential Sources (CS), is a necessary part of the job when doing narcotics investigations. As an undercover (UC), the ultimate goal is to infiltrate the organization and cut out the informant who may have given you the introduction. When it is time to arrest suspects, the further the informant is away from the deal(s), the stronger the case is when it comes to trial. The undercover, a law enforcement officer, is far more trustworthy to testify in court than someone off the streets. One thing that must always be remembered is that informants are people who are currently involved in criminal activities. Otherwise, they would not be able to introduce you to people they know who are currently dealing drugs, other illegal items (i.e. guns or stolen property), or involved in other crimes. Most of the time, informants are forced to cooperate because they face a lengthy prison sentence if they do not. Avoiding prison time seems to be a motivating force that makes just about anyone talk. On rare occasions, you may have the informant who just does it for the money. Contrary to popular belief, the local police departments and sheriff's offices cannot afford to pay informants much money and a lot less than the Feds. A federal informant who infiltrates a major drug trafficking organization can negotiate a percentage of total assets seized at the case's conclusion.

Hypothetically speaking, if an informant is responsible for taking down an organization where $20,000,000 in assets are seized, then they could stand to make a small fortune in the deal when they receive their agreed-upon cut of the assets. The assets are the combined value of money, land, and property that was seized, and how much money it is sold for in a public government auction. Conversely, just because the property is valued at $1,000,000, does not mean it will sell for that same amount. In this same scenario (i.e., $20,000,000 seized), if the informant negotiated 5% of total assets seized during an investigation as to their payment, they would get a check from the government for one million dollars. Of course, they would have to pay taxes on this money, which would cause them to lose a large chunk of it.

Either way, if an informant is not scared of getting killed by a major drug cartel, then being a CI could be lucrative. However, a CI probably would not have the chance to do that many deals with law enforcement, without eventually paying the price of their life for being a snitch. With that said, most informants do not make anything near the above example. The local police departments usually use an informant to take down and apprehend all of the persons that they know in the drug game. After they help take down all their drug contacts, the police move on to the next person who wants to cooperate. It is a never-ending cycle of people telling or snitching on one another to avoid going to prison. The people that you least expect to cooperate with the police after they get busted, become some of the best and most unsuspected informants. This causes a culture of paranoia in the drug business and increases the danger level for undercovers trying to infiltrate a drug trafficking organization.

Another major advantage of using informants was that they could vouch for an undercover they introduced to potential suspects. The catch to this was that the undercover was only as good as the informant's word on the street. If the informant was respected, then the undercover had instant street cred. This can also backfire; if the informant painted a picture, they were bigger than they really were in the streets, and the UC did not look into this first. Meaning, if the informant owed the dealer money, the UC is often looked at as part of that debt, and they may take it out of your first drug deal without you asking. That is a whole different issue in and of itself. With that said, it was a process where undercovers had to determine what they thought the level of street cred was for the informant before working with him/her. This was hard to judge, but sometimes by just talking to a person, I could tell if they were full of shit or not. This trick enabled me to handpick a group of strong informants that I tried to work with the most.

Different people are motivated to cooperate with law enforcement for different reasons. The motivation can be anywhere from purely monetary, to trying to avoid a jail sentence, to revenge for getting a loved one addicted to drugs, to being a wannabe cop, to the good Samaritan or anything in-between. Throughout this chapter, you will read a few of the most memorable informant stories during my narcotics career.

CI Buy Gone Bad

This buy was a prime reason why I would rather do a UC buy or a UC introduction with a CI than just a CI buy without a UC present. CIs have and always will be unreliable and incompetent to some degree. Some are more trustworthy than others, and once in a blue moon, you will meet a good CI that doesn't screw you over or mess up the case. However, that type of CI is like finding a needle in a haystack. No matter what, they must all be kept on a tight leash and never be allowed to control things or roam very far. Determining who is a good or bad informant is only learned through working with them. With that said, just about every narcotics unit in the country uses informants on a daily basis. The main reason that informants are a necessary part of an investigation is that their information is usually fresh. This is because they are actively involved in criminal activities, primarily drug use and sales, and they know the most recent scuttlebutt on what is happening on the streets.

This specific investigation started when our narcotics unit received a phone call from an adjacent county law enforcement agency, asking for our assistance. They had just busted a guy with a small amount of crack cocaine, and he said that he wanted to cooperate in consideration for reducing or dismissing his charges. This CI told the investigators that he knew some guys in our county that he could go in on and purchase crack cocaine. He also said that the crack cocaine in his possession when he was arrested came from these guys. Since we wanted to assist the neighboring county and maintain a good working relationship, we met up with some of their narcs. We were not very busy that day, so the entire unit showed up. It was a good gesture to show that we were willing to assist our fellow law enforcement brothers/sisters from neighboring counties.

We met at some old state fairgrounds out in the middle of their jurisdiction, close to the county line separating our two counties. It was the perfect place; it was secluded from the general public, where undercover officers could meet without the fear of being seen by members of the criminal element. The CI they introduced to me was only around nineteen years old. I remember him being a tall, skinny, lanky-looking country boy. To understand this individual better and make sure we could form a connection with him, we sat down and interviewed him for about an hour. We spoke to him about people that he had purchased drugs from in the past. We also discussed the primary guys that he dealt with who lived in the downtown area of a city within our county. We obtained some details about these guys in an attempt to identify them before doing anything with this informant. We went into details about how they conducted their drug deals in the past. We wanted to make sure that whatever went down when we used this informant was consistent with their normal drug transactions. This helped prevent the informant from getting burned or identified as working with the police.

Ultimately, a successful drug transaction with an informant involves a drug purchase, the suspect being identified, and the informant's status as a heling law enforcement remaining unknown to the suspect. The informant told us that he normally called the targets, two black males, and told them he was on his way over to them. He said it was normal for him not to talk about drugs on the phone because they knew why he was coming over, and he always got $50 worth of crack cocaine, never more or less on every past purchase. Based on this information, we decided to stick with his normal $50 crack purchase.

We decided to have the CI place a phone call to the suspects from a payphone with a phone number they would recognize. We drove to a payphone that the informant used on many of his past deals with these two targets. During the call, the suspects asked the CI if he had gotten arrested. News traveled fast on the streets because this guy was just arrested hours earlier. Without trying to hide anything, the CI said, "Yeah, they busted me. But I'm out now and need to get high because the police took my shit."

This was probably the only way the informant would have been able to go back over to that same location and purchase crack twice in one day, without drawing suspicion. The informant answered to the best of his ability at the time. I do not know that if he had lied about being arrested, whether it would have been any better for him when he went to do the buy. This conversation was one of our first red flags of how this transaction might not go as planned.

We discussed our expectations about the crack purchase with the informant. Since we were going to allow the CI to drive out to the target location, we placed a body wire on him. We taped it to his chest area because he wore baggy clothes, and said he felt comfortable wearing it. We asked him if any one of these guys had ever tried to search him in the past, and he said, "Absolutely not." He said this with confidence, so we had no reason to think otherwise.

We searched him and his vehicle to make sure that there were no drugs or other contraband. We always searched an informant and his/her vehicle before and after a buy. We did this to ensure that they did not have anything illegal on them, such as more drugs or a gun. This must be done to make a more solid case if this case went to a trial at a later date. Enough doubt can be put in a juror's mind if a defense attorney says that the CI probably had the drugs on him before he left to do the purchase and that the drugs did not come from his/her client. A search can eliminate this conspiracy theory and is a good safety practice to get into when dealing with untrustworthy people. An even better practice is to have a police K-9 trained in narcotics detection to search the vehicle and any items inside it. This eliminates the human error factor.

After we searched his minivan, I slid the side door shut. As I attempted this, it got stuck and would not close all the way. I opened the door again and went to slam it shut. When I did, the large side glass window on the sliding door shattered completely and fell out. Glass fell to the ground and inside of the vehicle. I was kind of in shock because I did not expect this and felt bad for a minute. Looking back, I should have taken that as an omen that this deal was not meant to go well.

As if the glass breaking was not a bad enough sign, right after the phone call, I already had a bad feeling about how things were going at the time. The feeling was strong enough to convince me to call the deal if I had been in charge. What bothered me the most was that, during the phone call, they questioned the informant about being arrested. This showed me that they had their guard up in case he was cooperating with the police. Looking back, I think we really should have called off the deal at the time.

I voiced my thoughts to our supervisors, but they were in

the predicament of trying to appease and cooperate with our neighboring sheriff's office. Politics of police relationships interfered with the ability to do our jobs properly, but it was something above my pay grade, and out of my control. If I were the UC, I would have called it off, but this was not a UC deal; it was an informant deal. Also, since I was not the case agent, I did not have the final say-so on this deal, and therefore I was going to back them up on whatever they wanted to do. I just assisted on surveillance during the deal, and anything else needed. Since I worked undercover, it was easy for me to get closer than some of the other plain-clothes investigators, whose vehicles may have been burned on past surveillance operations in the same area. I knew my vehicle was not one of those since I used it for undercover deals. Initially, I wanted to be the UC during this deal, but he said that he had never brought anyone with him in the past, and did not feel comfortable doing so. Not to mention, I was not too keen on working undercover with an unproven CI. To appease our neighboring sheriff's office and keep the political relationship going, we decided to go through with the deal.

About thirty to forty-five minutes earlier, we had deployed

surveillance units to the area, so they had eyes on the target house. We handed the CI $50.00 of department money to make the purchase. He got in his minivan, and our other surveillance units followed him out to the predetermined buy location. Thankfully, we had a substantial number of narcs in the area, more than a normal deal. We had all of our narcs and all of the narcs from the neighboring sheriff's office. The CI pulled up in front of the suspect's house. He parked in the roadway instead of pulling in the driveway. This was a busy road, and parking out front was the best place to be, in case he had to make a quick exit. So far, the CI had adhered to our directions with this act. He exited the vehicle and walked up on the front porch of the target house. All our surveillance units were in place; so far, so good.

He knocked on the door, and one of the two suspects answered and let him in. As he entered the front living room area, the other suspect got up and walked behind the CI while the other talked to him. We did not know this was happening because the guy standing behind our CI was blocking our view looking into the front door. He took a quick peek outside to see if anything suspicious was going on, turned, and closed the door and locked the two deadbolts on the old wood-framed door. The body wire reception was crystal clear, so we could hear the door being locked. This was one of those old shotgun, or mill-style homes, located in the center of the older section of the downtown district. Without any indication this was coming, the other suspect asked the CI if he had a body wire.

The CI, never trying to deny it or the target otherwise, lifted his shirt, and said, "Yeah, you got me. I have one."

Listening to the audio of the body wire, I could not believe what I had just heard.

The other narc and I looked at each other, and we both said, "Oh, Shit!!!"

We immediately came over the radio to all units, letting them know to move in and that our CI had been compromised. This was repeated three times to ensure they heard it.

We knew there was about to be trouble. Next, we heard what sounded like multiple thumps and scratches on the body wire. The body wire was clear up to that point; then, it sounded like someone playing with the microphone. That is when the suspects attacked the CI. They struck him several times with closed fists. Somehow he managed to break away from them and ran towards the rear of the house. I guess he did not have time to unlock the bolts to the door, so the next best thing was to run where the people beating him were not. You could hear the CI screaming on the body wire and the heavy breathing. Most of the time, these body wires often lacked reception; but it seemed like this time, we could hear every move as clear as if we were in the house ourselves.

The CI's voice went up several decibels and became really high-pitched. He tried to warn the guys, "They're outside," as he ran towards the back of the house. He was referring to the police being just outside. I guess he thought this would cause them to stop the assault. The CI ended up detouring into a bedroom, where he tried to slam the door behind him. Since the suspects were on his heels, he did not get the door closed in time, and they followed him into the room. That is when the CI made a split-second decision that he was going to dive headfirst out the second-story window. At that point, we pulled up in front of the house.

The CI jumped up on the bed, located directly in front of the double window. He used the bed as a springboard and closed his eyes while crunching his head, jumping towards the window. It all happened so fast, and he was so scared that he missed the center part of a single window, striking the center sash between the two windows instead. This knocked him backward onto the bed. He later told us that he hit his head so hard that it nearly knocked him unconscious. The next thing the CI knew, he was being pummeled by the suspects who pulled him off the bed deeper into the bedroom. He then made his second and final attempt at exiting through the second-story window. Thankfully, he was a skinny, wiry guy that was able to break loose from the suspects again. Working off of pure adrenaline, he jumped off the bed again and straight through the window headfirst. Over the body wire, I heard the sound of breaking glass, then a short delay while he fell before the CI made a loud gasping sound as he struck the ground. This was a second-story window just above the driveway. He landed on his shoulder and neck area, causing a neck injury. After that, he jumped up and ran towards us as we ran to the front of the house. He collapsed in my arms, shouting, "Get 'em! Get 'em! They tried to kill me!" At this point, he went limp; the adrenaline wore off, and the pain from his neck took over, so we stabilized him and started to render first aid to his lacerations.

Narcs breached the front and rear doors of the house at the same time. We were not thinking about tactics, other than getting in quickly. This went down almost simultaneously as the CI jumped through the window. Not knowing where the CI was, investigators searched the house. They found one of the suspects in the bedroom where the CI had jumped out the window. The other suspect was in the bathroom, attempting to flush the drugs, but he was unsuccessful due to the old house's lack of water pressure. Both suspects gave up without physically resisting us. We found a crack cookie floating in the top of the toilet water during a search of the house. A "cookie" is the street slang for a one-ounce cookie-shaped quantity of crack cocaine. This amount of crack can be sold wholesale for approximately $800 to $1,000. It can also be sold in a smaller quantity, one-tenth of a gram, for $20, commonly referred to on the streets as "twenties."

We also found several thousand dollars in cash and a semi-automatic pistol. This house was being rented by a third party, who did not live at the house. The house had a bed in one room, without any other furniture in the room. The only other furniture in the entire house was in the living room. The living room had two couches, a big-screen television, stereo system, and a play station with assorted video games. These guys stayed here all-day playing video games, waiting on customers to show up. It was clear that this house was set up with only one thing in mind; 'to make money selling drugs.'

During post-arrest interviews, the suspects knew they were busted and decided to talk to us. They told us that they knew immediately that the CI was working for the police when he called to tell them he was coming over, almost immediately after he was arrested. They said he never called them in the past because he just showed up. This was the opposite of what the CI told us: he always called them first and never talked drugs on the phone. Who knows what the truth is? But the fact is, the case did not go the way we would have liked. The CI injured his neck jumping from the window and left the scene in the back of an ambulance. Since he was working for us as a CI when this deal went down, we were sworn to protect him and take care of his well-being. We decided to have him go to the hospital and get checked out to ensure he did not have any serious injuries for which he could come back later and sue the county. The neighboring county dismissed the CI's charges due to the 'mental stress' that he endured during this case. We did not ask him to do any further work for us after this deal, and as far as I know, neither did the other sheriff's office.

The CI received about ten stitches for a laceration, had a mild neck strain, and a concussion. He was treated at the hospital and released that night. We took him home to his family to ensure he did not attempt to drive. Overall, he was extremely lucky not to have broken his neck from the jump or been killed by the suspects.

Case Conclusion: Both suspects were charged with Kidnapping, Trafficking Crack Cocaine, Interfering with an Investigation, and Unlawful Possession of a Pistol in the Commission of a Violent Crime. One of them pled guilty to the drug charges in return for his willingness to testify against his partner for the kidnapping. He said that the other suspect was the one who physically tried to harm the CI, once he found out he was wearing a wire and working for the police. He said he never intended to harm the suspect, immediately ran into the bathroom,

160

and started to try and destroy the evidence by unsuccessfully flushing the crack down the toilet. The second defendant ended up pleading guilty to an unrelated Armed Robbery charge, in a package deal that included dismissing all other charges in this case. He was sentenced to 12 years in state prison on the Armed Robbery charge. The case could be considered semi-successful because we ended up taking two violent drug dealers off the street, put them in prison, and nobody was seriously hurt or killed. Even though things did not go smoothly, it was a learning experience for me, to always listen to my gut to prevent a disaster before it happens next time.

This situation was kind of funny later after we realized the CI was not seriously hurt or paralyzed. We listened to that audio recording of the informant's body wire over and over. Other than the CI's heavy country accent and southern drawl, which were hilarious, we were just in shock that he did not try to convince them he was not an informant. It is hard to believe that anyone, within seconds of entering a drug house, when asked if they had on a body wire, would say, "Yeah, you got me; I have one." He may as well have just walked in with a shirt that said "Informant" across the front. The way this country boy said this so quickly, and lifted his shirt to show them the wire? It was beyond anything I had ever seen. Most people would fight you before they let you see their body wire since it could result in their death if revealed.

Mom Willing to Sell Her Child to a Pedophile

This case was one of the most memorable that I worked as an undercover, but not for any positive reasons. The case involved the sale and purchase of a child, which was nothing I had any experience with, nor did I know any other UC who had ever done a case like this. Back in the early 2000s, sex trafficking was not openly discussed, and many people in mainstream society had never heard of it. In this case, we had an informant who approached us about a woman who offered him sex with a nine-year-old child. The informant may have been a dirtbag, but one thing he was not was a pedophile. He was immediately offended that she would even ask, but as an informant, he knew how to handle this. He told the woman that he knew someone that would definitely be interested. That was when he called us, and we opened an investigation.

We debriefed the informant and then had him place a recorded phone call to the woman. Sure enough, everything he told us was true, and the woman was even ready to meet right then to sell the child for sex. We confirmed the age of the child to be nine, and that it was a little boy. The woman even had the audacity to tell us, as potential repeat customers, to call her any time because this was her son and that she would make house calls or allow us to come to her residence. I am normally pretty composed and do not let my emotions get the best of me, but this case bothered me deeply, as a man with children of my own. Also, being raised by two loving parents, I could not imagine not having them to go to when I was scared or needed comfort while growing up. I cannot fathom the nightmare to which this little boy was subjected. To cut the informant out of the picture, so that it just involved undercover law enforcement, we arranged for an undercover to call this lady.

A couple of hours later, I was the one that placed a recorded phone call to the mother. I will call her Sherry for the sake of this story. Sherry picked up the phone on the second ring, and I told her who I was, and named the informant as the one that gave me her number. Sherry wasted no time and told me she had just spoken to the informant and knew we wanted to have some fun with her nine-year-old son. There was no hesitation in her voice, and it was almost as if she was excited like she was doing a good deed or something. I explained to her that I was interested, and we wanted to know if she would meet us at a local hotel. I wanted to clarify that this verbal agreement was for her facilitating the abuse or sexual acts on a nine-year-old boy, so I asked her if she had any pictures she would send me of the boy. She said she would send me pictures after we hung up the call.

While discussing the deal, I stayed away from law enforcement lingo and was brutally vivid in what I was asking for her to allow me to do with her child. Despite sounding obscene, it was all business for me as I gathered additional evidence to make a solid case against this child abuser and neglectful poor excuse for a mother. My UC partner, Lyle, was instrumental in pointing things out along the way, to ensure that we hit every element of the crime to have a slam dunk case. Although he was not initially involved in this case as a UC, he was still working diligently behind the scenes to support the case. Lyle was like my brother, and a badass UC, so we always looked out for each other any way we could. We did not want her to be able to say that she misunderstood what my intentions were. Of course, I was never actually going to do any acts with the child or put him in a more vulnerable position. The conversation was so thorough that if she showed up with the child at the predetermined time, we had enough to make an immediate arrest. This woman sealed her fate when she spoke about her son as if he was an object to be sold, having no remorse or care for his well-being. Our goal was to make sure she was forced to plead guilty and nothing less. We never wanted the child to have to take the stand, so as UCs we were making sure we did everything in our power to make a solid case. Any good defense attorney that heard the recordings, in this case, would tell her it is in her best interest to plea with a sentence recommendation, versus taking her chance with a jury. We all know that a jury consists of regular citizens with true feelings and emotions, and nobody likes a child molester, and they would agree that a mother that forces this type of abuse upon her child is the lowest of low.

Any time you charge someone with Conspiracy to Commit Criminal Sexual Conduct, or a charge like Conspiracy to Commit Murder, the undercover officer cannot carry out the criminal act, of course, so the details must be discussed prior to an arrest being made. This is often very difficult because some people do not like to talk openly about these things with anyone. They often fear that we are the police, or an informant, recording them. So, to have Sherry openly talking about this made our case easier. The casual nature she had when we discussed this deal made me wonder just how many times her son had been victimized. I also wondered if she had any other children and why anyone would do such horrific things.

To get her to talk more and gather more evidence, I told Sherry that I had a fetish or fantasy with which I needed her to help. I told Sherry that I wanted her to bring different flavors of jelly when she came so that I could rub them all over my body and make the boy lick them off, and I could do the same to the boy. This was a sick proposition, but she only had one question when that was proposed. Sherry wanted to know if I would pay her back

166

for the jelly that she would purchase upfront. I assured her I would pay her extra for getting the jelly, and I told her my favorite flavors. We talked a little more, and I tried to inquire if she had access to other kids. It appeared that she did not, but she was willing to make any deals concerning her son.

After we hung up the phone, I questioned my informant more about Sherry. I wanted to know what would cause a woman to stoop to the level of selling her own child for sex. Also, she cared more about being reimbursed for the jelly than she did for her son's safety and well-being. She had been a hard-core drug addict for many years. The informant had known her most of his life. He said they used to drink and smoke weed together during their teenage years, but then she moved on to cocaine and then eventually to methamphetamines because the high lasted ten times as long for the same price as crack cocaine. After she tried meth, the rest was history.

Now she was a full-blown meth addict, willing to do anything to get the money to stay high. She prostituted herself many years for money, but as her looks faded, so did her clientele. That all changed one day when she was propositioned by a drug dealer to allow him to have sex with her son in exchange for drugs. The little boy was probably five or six years old at the time. Now, she did not have to do anything but take the child with her to the dealer, and she could get high. She took advantage of this arrangement for some time, which led to this undercover deal. This, yet again, was one of many reasons that I am so passionate about going after drug traffickers and trying to get help for addicts to stay clean. Hard-core drug addiction makes people lose their minds, and this case is a prime example of that fact.

Within an hour of placing the phone call to Sherry, she sent me a series of photos of the boy on my cellphone. I never specified what type of pictures that I wanted her to send, so whatever she decided to send only further showed her sinister intentions. Every move was calculated to build a solid case, and not allow her any defense to her actions. She decided to send me nude pictures of the boy in sexually explicit positions, rather than pictures of him in clothes or headshots. These pictures were sickening, and I found them extremely offensive, but they only made for a more solid case. Possession, receiving, and distribution of child pornography were separate offenses for which we could have arrested her. We held off because we wanted to get her on selling her child for sex so that she would get more time in prison, and we could rescue the boy that day. We wanted to end this young boy's living Hell forever, so we took calculated risks.

We arranged a meeting location at a local motel the next day. Before we met up, we had to brief the entire Vice and Narcotics Unit about the investigation, and plan the takedown operations. We wanted to start running surveillance on this suspect from then until we had her in handcuffs. Our goal was to have evidence of her leaving home with the child and driving to the motel. This allowed us to get a search warrant for her residence; in search of evidence of human trafficking, child porn, or other drug-related offenses. During the briefing for this operation, we could tell that the more details we gave, the more people were getting emotionally invested in this case. We made it very clear that we did not want anyone crossing the line, or using excessive force during the arrest because it would possibly jeopardize the prosecution of the case. It went without saying that if she or an accomplice were dumb enough to resist, they would regret it. We had a solid group of professionals in our unit, but it did not mean that images of what we would like to do with people like this had not crossed our minds. However, we channeled those thoughts into driving us to make the most thorough case as possible. Getting people to put in extra hours to take out scum like this was never anything that required any prodding.

After the briefing, the surveillance team set up in their posts early the next morning while others met at the office to discuss the case. I placed one phone call to Sherry that morning to make sure we were still set for everything and confirmed the time and location, and of course, that she would bring the jelly. She agreed and said it was all set. We did not bother getting an actual room at the hotel, because we were not going to give her time to get inside a room upon arrival. We had enough probable cause in the phone conversations and photos, that if she showed up with the child, which is considered the overt act, then we had enough to make the arrest and hopefully get a conviction, should the case go to trial. At the minimum, I had to present enough facts, no matter how emotional the case was so that a jury could find her guilty beyond a reasonable doubt.

The designated time set for the deal, 3:00 pm finally came

around, and my undercover partner and I were at the hotel parking lot waiting. Like clockwork, she pulled into the parking lot with her son and some unknown male subject. As she made cye contact with us because we were sitting in the parking lot inside the exact car we told her we would be in (i.e., red Nissan pick-up truck), she exited her car. The new issue was that she left the boy or victim in the car with this unknown male subject. Many things happen in undercover deals that you cannot plan for, but you better be prepared to adjust and overcome them as they happen. We were hoping she would be alone and approach us with the child or leave the child alone in the car so that we could take her down without the child in the mix. Of course, that did not happen. No matter what, that child's safety was our ultimate priority.

When she approached us, we did not immediately give the takedown signal. We told her we wanted to see what the boy looked like in person, after flashing her with the $300. We did not hand her the money, so she was still eager to be cooperative. She motioned for the child to come to her. Her son exited the car, and the unidentified male stayed inside the car.

That part worked out perfectly, so we could deal with the

unknown male alone. Originally, when she got out of the car, she had a single plastic grocery bag containing Welch's Grape and Strawberry Jelly, as requested. As small of a detail as some may think that the jelly is, it shows another overt act outside the presence of the undercovers, to further facilitate this illegal and immoral act.

This child looked emotionless, almost like a zombie, but still had hesitation as he walked towards us on his own. I could not imagine what was going through her son's head at that moment. Once the boy reached his mother, he hugged her. This blew my mind but showed me all he knew was this woman, and he thought this was what love was. There is no telling how she brainwashed this boy into believing what he was doing was good or right. My heart was ripping apart, seeing this unfold, but I had to stay focused. I took out the $300 and went to hand it to the lady in exchange for the child. Suddenly, I intentionally dropped all $300 in twenty-dollar bills on the ground, our takedown signal. Once the team saw it, and the surveillance leader gave the radio call to "move in," the arrest teams approached. We did this physical takedown signal, as well as a verbal one (i.e. code words),

172

for several reasons: It drew Sherry's attention to the money, and she immediately bent over to pick it up; at that moment my UC partner (Lyle) grabbed the child and took him out of the potential crossfire, in case the suspects resisted arrest; the takedown team could also concentrate on the male subject in the vehicle without the fear of the innocent child getting harmed; the arrest team could approach her and be up close and personal before she spotted them, which gave her little to no chance to resist arrest; and it gave some element of surprise and allowed us a tactical advantage.

As an undercover involved in a "buy-bust" scenario, never depend upon audio takedown signals alone, since the body wire may not be functioning properly. If the surveillance team missed one of the signals, then they usually saw or heard the other. Redundancy is important because of human error and equipment failures.

Sherry was taken down without incident, but the male in the vehicle failed to obey commands and started to resist arrest. This was not the situation where anyone wanted to resist a group of narcs who were all fathers themselves and had emotions high. This man was quickly slammed to the ground, and he accidentally landed on his head before being placed in handcuffs. It was over as quick as it began for this guy. During a search, we found a loaded 9mm semi-automatic pistol in his waistband. It was clear this guy was the 'muscle' if someone tried to rip them off or not pay. Thankfully, for his sake, he was not dumb enough to go for his gun. Therefore, he lived to see another day and to go to jail. We later determined that he was Sherry's longtime boyfriend, and they worked as a duo to sell the child many times in the past.

After we arrested his mother and the boyfriend, it took us some time to calm the child down, and let him know we were there to help him. His initial thought was that he was being kidnapped. Although some of our team had on raid vests that said "Sheriff," we did not look like typical police officers. Also, my undercover partner who grabbed the boy had on no police gear. This traumatized the child more but was worth the risk to prevent him from being harmed or victimized yet again. We had a child forensic investigator on standby to help us interview the boy. We were considerate enough to realize the sensitivity of interviewing a young traumatized victim like this, so we sought help from an expert. As expected, at first, he denied his mom wanting to hurt him, and was very protective of her. After a short period, he quickly changed his tune and broke down. The abuse had been going on for years, and it was hard to estimate, but he had likely been raped/ molested more than one hundred times over the last three to four years. This was beyond horrific in my mind. I could not imagine how this boy felt or the lifelong damages caused to him mentally. Since this type of case was not my field of expertise, we had the assistance of child sex crime investigators from our agency. They consulted with us often and took over any sexually related crimes and investigation.

During the execution of a search warrant at her residence, we found pornographic pictures of the child, that she had been sharing in private groups, via email. This was her marketing plan and how she found new customers. The male figure never admitted he knew what was going down at the scene, but the mother did cooperate and told us everything. It was not because she was suddenly upstanding, but because she was caught and knew we had her. I believe, deep down inside, she was ashamed and was grateful to be arrested because it was the only way her addiction would ever be stopped.

Case Conclusion: Both subjects pled guilty to charges that put them on the sex offender registry and sent them off to prison. Sherry received twenty years in prison, and the boyfriend received five, as part of a plea down to a lesser included offense, and a willingness to testify against Sherry had she not taken a plea agreement. He pled first, so this was a risk we took to get a conviction and ensure there was no trial. We did not want the little boy to take the stand and testify in this case, because it would only serve to re-traumatize and victimize him. This is why cases like this are pled so often, not to mention the court system being overwhelmed and backed up. A plea means an automatic conviction, and that is what counts here. I would have liked to have seen them both get life in prison, but the fact that the victim will grow up away from the evil he had known was the best possible outcome. I lost contact with the child over time, but I know he was taken into state custody or Emergency Protective Custody (EPC) as we call it. I pray he got all the psychiatric help he needed to deal with this unfathomable trauma, and that he was placed with a loving family or adopted. I know his mother lost her parental rights; I attended that hearing in family court.

In the name of full disclosure, I would have loved to have beaten this woman and guy to death on the scene, but I did not, of course. I know my fellow narcs, who are all parents, also felt the same way. We did not, because we knew that if we crossed the line doing anything wrong or illegal, we would lose our jobs, and they would both walk. Then more kids might become victims. I did not want that on my conscience, so we did it by the books like always.

It is like the Bible says in Ephesians 4:26, "Be angry and sin not," and Romans 12:19, "Vengeance is mine; I will repay, saith the Lord." We are not the suspect's jury, judge, nor God. As an undercover, you have to remember that there is no place to outwardly show emotions because you are only there to arrest and uphold the law, not convict and punish, because justice will be served one way or the other.

These types of cases stick in your mind forever, and may seem unconscionable to others. Many years after this incident, when I was running for Sheriff, I told this story, and even fellow police officers did not believe it happened. Thankfully, my undercover partner, Lyle, who was a Captain at that same sheriff's office, quickly set them straight. This case never made the news, like many of our cases. As a narc, most of our work is behind the scenes. We never seek out recognition and do many covert things. The fact that we saved this child gave us all peace of mind, and all the reward we needed. This case opened my eyes to the world of human trafficking, and how many other victims were likely all around us, of which we are oblivious.

CI Tortured and Murdered, and then My UC Deal that Led to the Suspect's Arrest

One confidential informant that had worked undercover for my old narc unit and also worked for the city police department was kidnapped, tortured, and murdered. His body was then wrapped in a carpet and later found dumped in one of the rougher areas of town. For several years, the police department had their suspicions of who did this but did not have the evidence to prove it. After about three years the case went cold, it was revived with one of my UC dope deals with the county.

I received information from one of my CIs at the time about a certain group of individuals working together, selling drugs in the county. After looking into the preliminary information we received, it was determined that these dealers had ties to the city's drug trade. So, I contacted the city police department's narcotics unit. This is when I found out that one of the drug suspects was also suspected of being responsible for the death of the city's confidential informant that was murdered years earlier.

The problem was that all the information the city had about this group of individuals was hearsay, because it was, "I heard that so and so told somebody something." Nothing they knew was anything more than 'he said-she said' about the informant's death. Knowing that all we had was second-hand information, I wanted to get something on members of this organization to perhaps help homicide investigators flip them into talking or at least ensure that they went to prison for a long time. Through my CI at the time, we arranged for a dope deal with one of the gang's higher-ranking individuals.

This dope deal was to take place in the parking lot of a business located at the bottom of the hill, behind the county law enforcement center. I thought this was a weird place, but it was also just on the outskirts of a rough area and a neighborhood where the gang sold drugs. What better way to stay off of the police radar than to do it right under their noses, undetected?

Somehow this trick worked for them for several years. The informant was driving his vehicle, and I was in his front passenger's seat. While sitting in the parking lot waiting on the suspect, the informant proceeded to tell me more about the suspect that he forgot to mention during our debriefing. For the sake of the story, I will refer to the main suspect by his street name, "Tax." According to the informant, Tax was ruthless and feared on the streets. He was known to be a violent person with a short temper. They called him the "Tax Man," but "Tax" for short, because he collected on drug and other debts by any means possible. He had allegedly killed several people over drug disputes. There was also an unsolved triple homicide in the neighborhood next to where we were doing the dope deal, and my CI and others on the street believed Tax and his guys were responsible for those deaths too. This triple homicide case has still not been solved to date. The alleged motive was that they suspected one of the guys in the house to be an informant. They decided to kill the other two guys in the house just because they were all together, and they did not want any witnesses.

This level of ruthlessness allowed Tax and his drug gang to remain on the streets terrorizing people. Most people would be afraid to testify against a crew like this, so they continued to rule their area's drug trade. While talking in the vehicle with the CI, our surveillance team spotted Tax in the area. We were almost surprised that Tax would come around for a dope deal in person since he was a higher-ranking individual that normally did not touch the drugs. Tax normally controlled things by sending in lower-level gang members to do the dirty work (i.e., deliver drugs), but we hoped he would show because of the informant's reputation, and the amount of crack we wanted to purchase.

Our surveillance team told us that they lost track of Tax's vehicle. I sat in the parking space facing the business, and the only place I could see behind me without looking around paranoid was through my passenger's side mirror. I did not even notice him walking up when a large black male suddenly appeared at my window. To be honest, it happened so fast that it startled me; I did not expect someone to appear before I spotted them coming. I was already on edge because I knew that this organization was allegedly responsible for killing multiple people, and they were greatly feared on the street. The guy leaned in the window and asked who I was. After the informant vouched for me, I was greeted with a handshake.

Thankfully, Tax was at my window, because I had the cash and wanted to do the hand-to-hand. I gave Tax the money, and the crack was dropped in my lap. He asked if the money was all there, and we both said it was. He quickly turned and walked away, disappearing into the darkness as abruptly as he appeared. We purchased an ounce of crack cocaine for $800 on this transaction. An ounce (28.35 grams) of crack cocaine put him at a certain sentencing threshold for Trafficking Crack Cocaine, which is why we selected that weight. We also hoped that a higher-ranking gang member, such as Tax, would show up since we were not purchasing a very small user amount. Our gamble paid off, and Tax showed up and did the hand-to-hand directly with me as the undercover, not the informant. This was about as good as we could have asked for it to go down.

Our surveillance team was able to watch and record the transaction. They watched Tax meet back up with an unknown man in a vehicle after the deal. We had enough to charge Tax in the dope deal, but nothing yet to charge him with the murder of the city informant. After doing some research, we were able to trace this vehicle to a female at an address in the area where the dope deal went down. The woman lived at a rental house in the name of an unknown male suspect, whose identity we confirmed via his driver's license photograph. My surveillance team positively identified him as the driver who drove Tax the day he sold me the ounce of crack cocaine.

We later retrieved a criminal history on this subject, which revealed a prior conviction for drugs and another prior felony conviction. This individual would be looking at a third strike, and a lengthy jail sentence if convicted of this current drug charge. With this knowledge, we decided to arrest the male subject without making a scene. We ran surveillance on him one day and conducted what appeared to be a normal traffic stop for a moving violation. Once pulled over, he was taken into custody and transported to our narcotics office. At the office, members of our team read him a warrant for the Distribution of Crack Cocaine. Of course, I was not in on the interview and did not allow the suspect to see me. Also, we did not want to burn the informant because he would prove beneficial for many more major cases in the future. After discussing what he was facing as far as a prison sentence, the suspect decided to cooperate. He ended up giving a statement on Tax and his involvement in the murder of the old informant. Initially, we did not have enough to charge Tax directly with the murder, but we did supply enough probable cause to have him arrested for Accessory After the Fact of Murder. We let the homicide investigators take it from there.

Case Conclusion: Tax was arrested. The cold murder case was suddenly revived, and homicide investigators revisited other avenues for building their case. Eventually, Tax's charges were upgraded, and he was convicted of murder. He was sentenced to thirty years in prison. He tried to use an insanity plea, stating he heard voices, but that did not work. A guy like him needed to be taken off the streets. If it were not for this drug transaction that happened several years after the murder, they might have never solved a murder mystery gone cold. We did not do this takedown to get credit for anything, but we did it because we had an opportunity to get a criminal off the streets. This case was great to show cooperation between narcotics units from other agencies, which was not always commonplace. The rivalry and ongoing friction between city and county narcotics units were alive and well, but somehow eased slightly after this case.

The saddest part about this case is what motivated this informant, who lost his life, to cooperate and assist police in a drug investigation in the first place. The informant's son, when he was a senior in high school, got caught up with the wrong crowd. He occasionally used marijuana and let someone persuade him to smoke marijuana laced with some crack cocaine. He was addicted almost instantly. He started using daily and escalated to using straight crack cocaine multiple times a day. His grades went from A's and B's to F's in all his classes. He started to miss school and got in trouble with the law. He was eventually arrested for Possession of Crack Cocaine and dropped out of school. The informant stepped in to help his son get clean and sober, but rescuing his son was not enough for this father as the dealers were still out there.

He decided to take to the streets and help police get rid of the dealers who got his son addicted to drugs. He did some controlled buys for law enforcement, and the cases came up for a trial. The investigators did not want him to have to testify and were willing to drop the charges, but he insisted on making sure they went to prison. The CI took the stand and bravely faced these dealers in open court. His testimony was damning and led to convictions. All of these individuals belonged to the same street gang as Tax and worked under him. Just days after the informant had testified in court, the CI was seen walking down a public street, which would be the last time anyone saw him alive. Some facts of his death remain uncertain, but they believe he was abducted by a group of individuals, and taken to an unknown location. He was tortured then killed, and his body was later dumped on a dead-end road of a rough and rundown apartment complex. His body was wrapped up in a carpet and had multiple gunshot wounds to his back. Besides being shot, he had been clearly brutalized. He was bound, had small burn marks in multiple places on his body, and his fingernails were removed. No human being deserved this type of treatment, and I cannot imagine the type of evil it would take to perpetrate this level of torture. I am thankful that I was involved in reviving a case that led to a conviction for this murder. We will never know if we got all those involved, but we did our best to hold someone accountable.

Tax admitted being the trigger man in the informant's death, and that is what led to his thirty-year prison sentence for murder. Criminals involved in violent crimes are often, almost always, involved in some form of drug activity because of the lucrative monetary potential. Due to this, sadly, if you take one drug dealer out, there is another one ready to step up and take over immediately. Since Tax had very high street cred and was greatly feared, I used this to my advantage for future cases. Later in the book series (Vol. 3), I discuss a murder-for-hire case, where Tax's street cred helped me. I had an informant introduce me to the suspect, who was paying us to kill someone else, as 'guys who had done previous hits,' or 'murders for Tax's drug trafficking organization.' Since he was somewhat of an urban legend, it automatically gave us street cred for a successful murder-for-hire deal while working undercover.

Professional Informant

Working with informants can be a stressful game. You must always remember that they can only be trusted to a degree, and they may be using you to further their agenda. For example, an informant works with the police to apprehend rival drug dealers to ensure they cannot encroach on his clientele. This is a win-win situation. The dealer wins because they get rid of a rival drug dealer(s), and the police win because they take another drug dealer(s) off the streets. The unintended consequences are that we may have just doubled someone else's drug clientele, or increased their potential for profit from drug sales. With that said, I still used informants with the notion in the back of my mind to always watch them closely and to try not to solely depend upon them to make any of my cases.

At this point in my career, I had worked with many different informants. Most of them worked until they got the assistance they wanted with the solicitor's office in a reduction or dismissal of pending criminal charges, and we never saw them again. Occasionally, one would come back to me with information in exchange for money, but nothing on a routine and continuous

188

basis for several years. That was until I was introduced to a man who was referred to as a "professional informant." A professional informant is someone who does this for many years and makes a living doing it. These individuals are rare, and many narcotics investigators never have the opportunity to work with a true professional informant.

This professional informant was like no other informant that I had ever met or like anyone I will ever meet again. He was what we called a 'once-in-a-lifetime' type of informant. This guy was a high-ranking member in the Crip street gang. When I found this out, I wondered how he stayed alive, being labeled as a snitch. I ended up asking him this same question. I found out that he was such a well-respected member of the Crip gang, that whenever someone from a rival gang called him a snitch, nobody believed him. He told me that he could be an informant for nearly forty years because he never snitched on a fellow Crip gang member. No matter what, he was loyal to his gang, and they were loyal to him. I am sure he put in work and did some really bad stuff for the gang in the past, but I had no direct knowledge of that, and he was not volunteering the information. Some gang members may prove their loyalty by killing rival gang members, but this guy did it by taking them out of the drug game and having them locked up in prison. Either way, you look at it, the threat is removed. It was a different approach than I had seen before, but it worked for him successfully for almost four decades.

Over the years, it was inevitable that, being a paid informant, he would have to testify. Sure enough, this guy testified on numerous occasions. He managed to do this without getting himself killed. I quickly learned that this guy had the gift of gab and could talk his way into and out of any situation. This made me more cautious of him, and I had to watch his every move and analyze what his intentions might be. An informant like this did not come to me without any baggage. Apparently, years before I got involved in law enforcement, he was an informant for the DEA, FBI, ATF, and several other local law enforcement agencies. He was well paid, and traveled the east coast, making cases for the federal government.

When I was introduced to him, he had just been released from prison on a child molestation charge. There is an unwritten rule in law enforcement, kind of like the criminal code against child molesters, which is *We do not work with child molesters*. They are considered the scum of the earth, preying upon innocent children. One of the persons that the informant had worked hundreds of cases with years earlier was now a sergeant with the sheriff's office for which I worked. The sergeant, Mike K., called me into his office one day to tell me about this informant. He told me that he used to work for him, and he was like no other, but you had to watch him close. After speaking with the sergeant, I contacted the informant to hear his story, since the sergeant told me his charges were not what I thought they were, and I should hear him out. I had a ton of respect for this sergeant, who used to run the county vice and narcotics unit for many years.

Initially, I was told that he had served a nine-year prison sentence for allegedly molesting his stepdaughter. Around year eight of his ten-year sentence, he received a letter from his stepdaughter, the alleged victim, about the false allegation that he raped her years earlier. In the letter, she confessed that her mother put her up to it, and now that she was eighteen and on her own, she wanted to apologize for making up the allegations against him.

Of course, the informant brought this to the attention of

the correctional staff while incarcerated in state prison. Once he got the ear of a concerned correctional officer, he was able to bring it to the state law enforcement division's attention. Law enforcement contacted the young woman who was the alleged victim, formally the stepdaughter of the informant. Over the course of months, she was interviewed and eventually put on a polygraph machine. She passed it, stating that she was not raped or inappropriately touched by the informant. Since the informant was about to complete his sentence at this point, he did not have much time to get out of prison early. Once he found an attorney that was willing to take the case pro bono, his sentence was overturned, and he was released from prison. Now he was out of prison and looking for work. However, he had been blackballed as an informant with federal agencies because of his false conviction of child molestation. The only thing he knew how to well do was work as an informant, so he was very eager to get back into the mix of things. Being with a local agency, I was his only hope to get him reinstated or off the blackball list. I knew it was going to take some work, but if this guy were half as good as the sergeant told me, it would be worth it. I did not mind working with him, as long as he was truly innocent of child molestation charges, which it appeared was the case.

I spoke with the CI and got some further details on what exactly happened to him. He told me that even though he was an informant for many different law enforcement agencies, he was illegally involved in kilogram-sized dope deals for most of his life. He facilitated dope deals on the side for larger dealers, by introducing a supplier to a purchaser. In return, he received a nice payment. This was how he got into working with law enforcement, when he was linked to some major players early in his drug-dealing career, and did it to avoid being charged in a drug conspiracy. He arranged deals and introduced new buyers to the dealer for a finder's fee. So he played both sides of the fence. Right before the allegations of molestation came out, something else significant happened to the CI. He had arranged a multi-kilogram cocaine deal with some Cubans. This was not a deal for the police, but one for his own profit. Unbeknownst to him, his wife had been having an affair with one of these Cubans. She wanted them to kill her husband, the CI, and rob him of several kilograms of cocaine he was supposed to sell for another dealer.

On the day of the dope deal, the informant showed up with the kilos of cocaine and met the Cubans. According to the CI, they tried to kill him. They pulled a gun on him, and somehow, he took the gun from the one guy and shot both of them. He fled the scene and hid the kilos, and disposed of the gun somewhere. Fearing for his life, he fled the United States and went to Jamaica. He was allegedly laid up in a safe house with some other Crip gang members, waiting to see what happened with the shooting investigation back in the States. When he did not come back immediately, the informant's wife talked her young daughter into saying that the informant had molested her. Now he had these child molestation charges pending on him. I do not know whatever happened with the two Cubans being shot, but as far as I know, they lived but they did not cooperate with law enforcement. The informant did not give me enough details on that encounter to follow up on it. I did track down a case that appeared to match the details. It involved two Cubans that were shot, but there was no mention of drugs, with which the informant said he fled the scene. Looking at the case as an investigator, if the Cubans did not cooperate, the police would have no clue about the drugs, and the suspect (the informant) would be unknown. The case was kept open for years but subsequently closed because the victims declined to cooperate.

Now the CI was in Jamaica and feared coming home because he had a warrant for his arrest for Criminal Sexual Conduct with a Minor. Allegedly the sergeant from the sheriff's office, who use to be the CI's handler and someone he built a strong bond of trust with, convinced the CI to come back and face the allegations. The CI listened, came back, and was placed under arrest for the child molestation charges. He sat in jail on a no bond pending his trial or a plea, since he was viewed as a clear flight risk. I cannot say he was not a flight risk since he had just come back from hiding out in Jamaica. Being very familiar with the criminal justice system from his work as an informant, he knew that he was facing an uphill battle with these new charges. He understood that it was his young stepdaughter's word against his, and she appeared to be an innocent child. He was a hardened street guy, and the jury would have surely convicted him. The solicitor's office offered him a plea agreement of ten years, rather than going to trial and possibly facing over twenty-five years if found guilty.

Something compelled the CI to take the deal. So, he went to prison.

While in prison, he faced some of the guys that he testified against years earlier while working as an informant. However, due to the fact that he was so well-respected in the Crip gang, and was a high-ranking member, he had protection from those other guys. The CI was also well-respected because he was born into this gang since his father was a member. He had Crip tattoos underneath his fingernails and had the letters "CRIP" across the fingers on both hands. The more than $100,000 worth of platinum, diamonds, and gold surgically implanted over his teeth alone was the craziest and most distinctively flashy looking thing I had ever seen in my career. I am not sure why he got this done, but allegedly he did it while hiding out in Jamaica. I could describe him further, as his look was quite distinctive, but to protect his identity and safety, I will not.

I had this informant that the Feds refused to work with because of something that he was wrongfully convicted of doing. Since I took a long shot at assisting him attempting to get the previous conviction dismissed off his record, I gained his respect.

Based upon all the facts (i.e. the stepdaughter's statement and the pending legal battle to have his record cleared of this conviction), he was allowed to work again as an informant. He was very grateful and told me that he would work a bunch of cases free of charge, just to prove that he was trustworthy. I gladly took him up on his offer. The difference was I did not want him purchasing drugs for me as he was used to doing. Instead, I used him to vouch for and introduce me to multiple high-level drug dealers in the area. I did it this way because I would much rather make purchases myself than use an informant with a criminal past. If he ever had to take the stand for me, then his criminal past could be brought up, and it would not look favorable towards our case. I could just imagine a juror thinking to himself, 'Why should I believe this child molester?' or 'Why do the police trust this child molester at his word for anything?' Despite him being innocent, as explained, it would distract the jury's attention away from the facts of the case, if we had to explain his innocence each time he testified. Thankfully, I prevented this from ever becoming a reality.

We ended up making more than thirty transactions where this informant introduced me to dealers. Just about all of them went so smoothly that I was becoming impressed with this CI. I do not know what he told them about me, but I apparently was known as a badass, because no one ever disrespected me. It was hilarious to look back at these cases because, on a few occasions, he would introduce me to guys who just got out of prison days earlier to sell me drugs. The people that he was incarcerated with respected him, and when released, he apparently hooked back up with them. On one occasion, one guy just got out of prison three days earlier, and I was his first deal. He was trying to make quick money to get back up on his feet. He was an old school drug dealer who had just served seven years from a prior drug conviction. Months after the deals, we arrested him, and he went right back to prison for a twenty-year sentence for multiple distributions of crack cocaine. We wanted to protect the informant, so most of the arrests were made six months to a year after the distributions. During those many months, they dealt with hundreds of other drug customers, making it almost impossible for them to pinpoint the snitch or undercover. Since I only used the CI for the introduction, not the actual hand-to-hand transaction, he did not have to testify in court as to the facts of the actual distribution of a controlled substance. This protected the CI further and allowed him to keep working within the same inner circle of people.

Now, this informant had proven his loyalty to me; he would made himself somewhat trustworthy again. I started to pay him $50.00 or a little more for each introduction he made for me, which led to a drug purchase. This was small-time money to him, but it was not about the money as much as it was about him being shown I appreciate his ongoing assistance, and that I was not going to take advantage of all he had already done for free.

If the target was worthy, a big drug dealer with a prior conviction, I could get authorized to pay him more for introductions. He was also appreciative that I was able to get him back into being a professional informant, and he started working with other agencies again.

During an unrelated investigation, some FBI agents came to our narcotics office, asking if we knew of a big drug dealer named "Big G." They advised us that 'Big G' was responsible for distributing over fifty kilograms of cocaine per month in the upstate area of SC. Once I heard the name Big G, I knew that my informant knew him, based upon prior conversations about this

199

guy. Months earlier, I had even been introduced to Big G and purchased powdered cocaine and crack cocaine off of him. At the time, I did not know how big a dealer he was; I had only purchased $200 worth of drugs from him. I did start to talk with him about trading a kilogram of cocaine for labor at his house. At the time, I was still posing as a person who owned and operated a painting and remodeling company. This work arrangement never panned out because we did not have the resources to paint his house, renovate, and then do the transaction for a kilogram of cocaine.

This is another example of several instances you will read about in this book, where I came up with an innovative and out of the box type of idea to trade drugs for something, when we did not have that much cash to allow to walk away (also called a buy-walk), and the idea was shot down. The problem was Big G had a large house, and it would have taken several teams a while to do the job; plus, he was not going to provide any drugs upfront. He said he would pay us in full after we did the work. This was not my first rodeo, and I was not going to have him potentially rip me off with no up-front product to show good faith that he was going to pay in full after the work.

Knowing that my CI knew Big G, I told the FBI about the above buy and drug conversation. I also showed them the active distribution warrants we had typed up on Big G but had not asked a judge to sign them yet. In full disclosure, I told them about the CI's situation of being blackballed by the FBI in the past. They were interested in speaking with the CI, so I arranged the meeting. After they met and interviewed the CI, we waited several weeks without hearing anything. Nothing happens fast for the federal government. Finally, they were able to get permission to remove his blackball status and use him as a federal informant, referred to as a Confidential Source (CS) by the feds. So we assisted the FBI on a long-term operation where the CI was going to personally work his way up to start making large (kilogram) quantity purchases of cocaine from Big G.

After several successful purchases from other members of the Big G drug trafficking organization, the CI was able to arrange a kilogram deal. For this buy, we had several FBI agents and our entire narcotics unit assisting in conducting surveillance of the transaction. The CI was given an amount of money from the FBI to make the purchase. They arranged the meeting location, and it was to take place at a night club that Big G owned. At the time of the transaction, the club was closed, and this was during non-business hours. The CI was equipped with an audio listening device (body wire) and briefed on the transaction rules, even if he thought he knew everything. He went in, and for some reason, the audio on the wire went to static or was so badly muffled it was inaudible at times so that we could not hear the entire conversation. We were able to make out small parts, but they talked in heavy street lingo and code words. It was apparent that the CI had been speaking with Big G, outside of the control of the FBI and my knowledge. This was a violation of their rules and a betrayal of my trust. They wanted and needed to control everything, as you should do when dealing with informants. They told the CI that he was to stay away from Big G on his own time, and if he did accidentally run into Big G, or received a phone call, he needed to contact the FBI immediately. After a confusing conversation, the CI exited the buy location and drove to our predetermined meeting place.

Once at the meeting location, the CI handed the FBI agents the kilogram of cocaine and answered any questions. Something just did not sound right about the deal. Upon further searching the informant's person, we found approximately $800 in one hundred dollar bills. The serial numbers on the bills revealed that this was part of the buy money given to the CI to purchase the kilogram. At that point, the CI had attempted to steal from the FBI, thereby proving himself as unreliable. He was getting paid pretty good money from the FBI (i.e., in the thousands), but he still got greedy and wanted this extra $800.

This made me look bad because I vouched for him as reliable based upon approximately thirty deals I did working with him undercover. I was very upset and pissed at the CI. I grabbed him by the shirt collar and slammed him against the wall and told him we were "fucking done." I was so close to beating his ass, but I stopped myself because he was not worth it. They did not arrest the CI for the attempted theft or interfering with a federal investigation. They allowed him to leave that day, but he was permanently blackballed from being a federal informant. From that point forward, I had to cut ties with this CI. I learned a valuable lesson from this 'professional informant'; no matter how good they are, they are still con artists or criminals at the end of the day, so always watch your back and search them closely before

and after deals. It is unfortunate that this occurred because I could

have made hundreds of cases with this informant over the years.

(BELOW) This is a screenshot of an undercover buy where my professional informant is introducing me to a guy that just got out of prison. I purchased crack off of him and he ended up in a shootout with police weeks later.

APR-14-8   3:28:59-P
COUNTY SO

Informant Turned Soldier

Individuals should not be defined by their past actions or

mistakes. Many people deeply regret their poor life choices and

strive to mend their ways and live the rest of their lives on the up and up. All of us make mistakes, and some learn and move on, which is what happened with this next informant. Just like my career in law enforcement could have ended before it started had the circumstances of the bonfire fight gone worse as described in Volume 1 of this series. The informant in this instance was faced with turning his life around so that he could build his life from that point forward. When dealing with informants, they are not all rough-looking thugs. When asked to describe an informant, I would say they can be anyone; a neighbor, coworker, friend, or family member. In other words, they can come from various backgrounds.

The next informant, whom I will refer to as 'Z,' got caught up in the glamour and perks (i.e., money and women) of the drug culture. He was in the U.S. Army Reserves when I first encountered him but was arrested for dealing drugs. I personally became acquainted with Z during an investigation into a location known for the distribution of cocaine, methamphetamine, marijuana, and other prescription drugs. What drew our attention was the fact that these drug dealers did not care who their customers were. They would sell to anyone at any age, even a child, as long as the buyer had the money to pay for the drugs. We received complaints from the local middle schools about people from this location, selling to some of their students. After a month-long investigation, we obtained enough probable cause to execute a search warrant on the primary drug sales location. During a search of one of the bedroom closets, we found U.S. Army uniforms. This surprised me because it was the first time I had seen U.S. military uniforms in a drug house. Although Z was not there at the time, we executed the search warrant I was able to catch up with him at a later date and time. He ended up being charged with Trafficking Cocaine and Possession with Intent to Distribute Marijuana. These charges stemmed from drugs being found in common areas of the house where Z lived. After Z was arrested, he immediately started to cooperate with us. When a suspect does not have a prior arrest record, it is just as motivating to cooperate with law enforcement as it is for someone who is facing a third strike. In either situation, the suspects have a lot more to lose; such as a good job or their freedom. I ended up being the primary case agent with Z, and I worked with him as an informant on more than twenty cases.

Z became very good at introducing me to different dealers and then pulling himself out of the picture. This allowed me to do my job as an undercover, and develop a trust relationship with the dealer(s), minus the informant. Z eventually did enough cases and was willing to testify against some major players in court, so I recommended to the Solicitor's Office that his charges (Trafficking Cocaine and Possession with Intent to Distribute Marijuana) be dismissed. They were eventually dismissed without prejudice, and he then paid to get his arrest record expunged. He then went on to serve more than ten years in the active duty with the U.S. Army and achieved the rank of Sergeant. Even as I write this book, he and I have stayed in touch via emails or phone calls. This is one of the few success stories of a person caught up in the dope game (high-level trafficking), who changed their life and managed to stay on track long term after his brushes with the law. He has served several tours in Iraq and Afghanistan, and I am very proud of his all of his successes since long ago when we first met.

This type of conclusion makes me satisfied with my decision to recommend that his charges be dismissed. Since he is no longer involved in drug sales, and a citizen who positively contributes to society in United States, he falls within the class of people, I call a good American. I tell this story to show that even addicts can change for the better. Each time we talk on the phone, he thanks me for giving him a second chance. He is forever grateful, but to be honest, I only did what was right, and he did the hard part by staying sober and staying away from drugs and criminals. His life could have easily gone in a totally negative direction, but thankfully it did not. One time I got to speak to his wife and daughter on a video chat. That was really special. His wife knew all about me, and she was very appreciative of my support. Seeing what a good father he is, and how he was happily married, made it all worth it to me. I wished more stories ended up like this one.

Deputy Shoots My Informant

When working with informants, you must ensure that they are not doing anything illegal in your presence or while under your control (i.e. while making a buy). You take steps to make sure they act right outside your presence, by having them sign an agreement that outlines their code of conduct and potential consequences for any violations. You hope they can stay away from getting involved in criminal behavior, but it comes with the territory of a criminal informant to be around other criminals. The reality is that we have no control over what an informant does outside of our presence. We know the inherent risk in dealing with the criminal element, but you never truly know what type of things they are up to outside of working with you.

In this case, I had a newer informant that I just started using for some local drug buys. So far, we had only used him to buy user amounts of cocaine and heroin. Things were going smoothly as far as we knew. He was working towards getting a Possession of Cocaine charge dismissed, which was made by a uniformed patrol deputy. The deputy handed the suspect and case over to me to work him. The deputy was a community-oriented guy, and all he wanted out of this was for his beat area to be cleaned up. The deputy knew that there was no way for him to get the mid-level dealers while in uniform, so he trusted that we would use the informant to do buys, and gain probable cause for search warrants.

Our goal was to raid these drug houses and arrest the dealers, thus helping the deputy clean up the community. The deputy said that if that occurred, he did not care what happened with the drug charges he put on the informant. Whenever a deputy collaborated with me like this, I always made the extra effort to continually build a positive working relationship.

We made about five buys in the area and were starting to gain more trust in this informant. The next thing I know, my phone is ringing, and I am being told this same informant was in a shootout and shot by fellow deputies who caught him burglarizing a residence. Apparently, he was out committing home invasions/burglaries in the very same area we were using him to clean up.

(BELOW) This is a copy of a newspaper article about the above informant being shot while committing a burglary.

Gunfire exchanged during break-in

Two charged after deputies called to ████ Street home

By E. Richard Walton
STAFF WRITER
rwalton@████ews.com

A ████ man and a ████ man were charged with burglarizing a home on ████ Street after an exchange of gunfire with sheriff's deputies early Saturday, authorities said.

████, 22, of 600 ████ ████

████ and ████, 29, of 300 ████ Road, No. ████ ████, were charged with first-degree burglary, Master Deputy ████ said.

He said deputies responded to a burglary-in-progress call after two men broke into 11 ████ St. at 4:35 a.m. He said there was an

exchange of gunfire between one of the men and unidentified deputies after the men were spotted exiting the home, which is near ████ Road.

No deputies were injured, ████ said, but he referred other questions about the incident to ████ which is investigating.

████ is called in to do an independent investigation if a deputy fires a weapon.

See SHOTS on page 2B

SHOTS
FROM PAGE 1B

████ said.

████ spokeswoman ████ said the Sheriff's Office requested that her agency investi-

gate a shooting in ████ ████ early Saturday. She declined further comment.

The suspects came to ████ Street in a car, but fled on foot, ████ said. Deputies called in extra units, including its K-9 team, to find the suspects, he said.

They were captured in a

wooded area near a set of railroad tracks shortly before 8 a.m.

Deputies took a third man into custody who was with the suspects, but he was released later when it was determined he was not involved.

████ said a gun was seized, but he wasn't certain

what type or what caliber it was.

Both suspects were being held at the ████ County Detention Center; neither was eligible for bond, a jail spokeswoman said Saturday.

Chapter Four

Police Corruption

When working undercover for an extended period of time, one is bound to run into other law enforcement officers who are not on the up-and-up. Not that police corruption is a major phenomenon, but allegations of the actual act of corruption have plagued the badge since the beginning of law enforcement and continues to do so today. Social media has only made this worse, with everyone having a platform to tell partial truths against anyone. Law enforcement, specifically undercover work, has evolved in a positive light over the years, but corruption remains as a constant black-eye to any department. No matter how many good deeds are committed by an individual officer or a department, what everyone remembers is the one bad deed. In part, this is enhanced by the media, which rarely reports positive stories, and saturates the news with negativity. *If it bleeds, it leads.* The same goes true with most scandalous or salacious news. The old saying of *One bad apple spoils the whole bunch,* holds true in this case. One corrupt cop tarnishes the image of law enforcement officers everywhere, it seems.

As an investigator, I was able to assist in apprehending corrupt police officers on several occasions. This was some of the most rewarding work that I did during my years working undercover. When someone takes advantage of the public's trust in a position to which they have been sworn to serve and protect, it should not be taken lightly. As a police officer, I am sure that most other officers would agree that we are harder on punishing one of our own who is clearly in the wrong than the courts could ever be. Once your name is mud in the close-knit law enforcement community, then it stays that way forever. Police corruption can have many different aspects and come in many different forms. It can range anywhere from using excessive force continuously to stealing drug proceeds seized during an investigation. Throughout this chapter, you will read about some of my most memorable operations that dealt with police corruption.

Surprise in the Closet

This investigation started with a tip as to what we were told was a methamphetamine house operating in our jurisdiction. The tip came from an informant involved with an undercover operation with myself and Lyle, my UC partner. This informant had provided trustworthy information in the past, so we had no reason to believe that what he provided this time was inaccurate. The information we received told us about a drug house that was also involved in prostitution. This was not the informant's direct firsthand knowledge so that we could not get minute details of the level of drug sales or prostitution involved. Although the informant did not have direct knowledge, he/she stated the information came from a reliable source. These allegations did not seem out of the ordinary, because vice crimes, such as prostitution and gambling, commonly go hand in hand with drug distribution and use. Not having any *inside* information on the inner workings of this operation was one of our initial setbacks. We still wanted to deal quickly with this case and decided to use a 'knock-n-talk' investigative technique. We wanted to look into it quickly since we had lots of tips coming in daily, and when you procrastinate, the work piles up.

A knock-n-talk is where law enforcement officers go to a house and do just as indicated. You knock on the door and talk to the occupants. The gift of gab comes in handy here. Also, this intelligence gathering technique is perfect for undercover officers because they do not look threatening. Not looking like a cop usually lowers the person's guard and makes them more open to talking and inviting you inside. The officers' objective is to legally be invited into the residence and receive a voluntary consent to search. Gaining the suspect's trust is a true art form, and your success depends upon your actions and how you interact how with the person you are talking to or the owner of the residence.

A slight modification to the knock-n-talk that we used was to downplay what we were actually looking for or act like we were looking for something else. Yes, police can lie during an investigation, and it is perfectly legal. We did this so that the individual felt almost compelled to grant consent because they knew beyond a doubt that we would not find what we said we were looking for. This also gave the perception that we were going to be in and out of the residence as quickly as possible. This less intrusive or quick search of the premises is more appealing to the person giving consent than an all-out search of the residence (i.e. executing a search warrant). The end goal was to try and find evidence of something illegal as quickly as possible. If we found evidence of a crime quickly, then it granted us probable cause to get a search warrant for the premises, even if they withdrew voluntary consent after initially giving it. Once consent is withdrawn, you need a search warrant to continue searching. Anything you find during the voluntary consent search would grant you probable cause, which is the minimum standard for a search warrant. When this happens, it allows the search to continue after voluntary consent is withdrawn, and the judge issues a search warrant.

We used the ruse of searching for something other than what we said we were looking for successfully on many occasions. The key is to claim you are looking for a small item, which allows you to look almost anywhere. This is called the "scope of the search" in legal terms. For example, if I said I was looking for a stolen car, I could not open cabinets and drawers because a car could not fit inside those areas, and that type of search would be deemed illegal. If I said, I am looking for a stolen golden ring, and I can look anywhere that the ring can fit or be hidden.

During this incident, members of the sheriff's office vice & narcotics unit went out to the house to do a knock-n-talk. We told the occupant of the house, who also claimed to live there, that we were looking for large quantities of marijuana (i.e. 100 pounds or more). In actuality, we were looking for evidence of methamphetamine and running a prostitution house, but where there is marijuana, there is the likelihood of other drugs. Since we stated that we were looking for something we knew they more than likely did not have ("large quantities of marijuana") in their house, they granted us voluntary consent to search. Once we started the consent search, the clock was ticking, and we had to work quickly before they got annoyed and withdrew consent. We always left one investigator to chat with the homeowner while the others searched. This was done for several reasons. First off, the investigator had to be present to immediately notify all officers on the scene to stop searching, if the person in control of the residence withdrew voluntary consent. The investigator who stayed with the homeowner had to have a calming and friendly personality to keep the person happy and answer their questions. Sometimes this investigator was someone they already knew and trusted. In other investigations, where nothing is found in a knock-n-talk or consent to search is denied, the police presence alone may cause the illegal operation to shut down temporarily or permanently out of paranoia. In this specific case, we quickly found some drug paraphernalia in the residence, which gave us probable cause for a search warrant if we needed it.

A further search revealed small quantities of methamphetamine and evidence of the distribution of methamphetamine (i.e., scales and numerous clear plastic bags, 1 in. x 1 in. with logos on them, commonly used to store drugs). Now we knew that the tip was based upon good information, and we needed to search the residence more thoroughly. In the past, some of the tips that we received ended up being only linked to personal vendettas against someone who pissed another person off, so we would not find anything. When this was the case, we wanted to be in and out of the occupant's hair as quickly and painlessly as possible.

At this point in the consent search, we decided to stop what we were doing and send one of the investigators to meet with a judge to sign a search warrant. Why risk the chance of the homeowner being able to say they felt they could not withdraw consent after drugs were found and lose the case when we had probable cause for a search warrant.

About one hour later, the investigator returned with the signed search warrant in hand, and we continued the search. We quickly noticed that each bedroom closet had locks on the doors, which was very unusual. While searching the closet area of one of the first bedrooms, we found a hidden closed-caption television/video recording station. Tracing the wires, we found that there was a pinhole-sized hidden camera built into the drywall, which was not visible to the naked eye from more than a foot away. Even if you knew it was there, it was still hard to locate where it was. We noticed this camera because we used the same type of equipment for covert undercover investigations. This pinhole camera was linked into tech equipment that could record whatever went on in the bedroom, specifically on the bed. It was common to find residences where individuals recorded personal sex videos, especially in a drug house, but they usually did not need hidden covert style cameras; they just used handheld video cameras or a cell phone. In this situation, we found this same hidden camera and recording set up in two other bedrooms. It was now clear why they had locks on the closets where they kept the recording equipment. Each bedroom was sparsely furnished. They each had only had a bed, nightstand, and clock radio. Inside the nightstands were assorted sex toys (i.e., handcuffs, whips, paddles, lingerie, dildos, etc.). Reusing the same dildo with multiple people is disgusting, but at least they had a bunch of condoms in the same drawer. This all supported the suspicion that this was a house of prostitution yet apparently; also additional crime was being conducted here. Having this many hidden cameras inside of the private rooms indicated that these videos were used for more than personal viewing pleasure.

On the outside of the residence, there was an elaborate video surveillance system. The residents use this video feed to see if the police or anyone else may be coming to the house. This was quite common with operations involving drug traffickers, or other serious criminal violations. So, this alone did not alarm us.

220

After further investigation, we learned that this operation was set up to record various people having sex and using drugs. Later they would blackmail, extort, or take valuables or money from the clients for keeping silent about their involvement in these vices. Since some of these clients may be known as upstanding or prominent citizens, they had a lot to lose if it was revealed that they slept with prostitutes for money or used drugs. The individuals running this operation knew this and demanded money to not release these videos to wives, co-workers, or even the media (i.e. blackmail or extortion). This extortion operation could be pretty lucrative for your common criminal since they recorded their vehicles, vehicle license plate, the person approaching the residence, the person paying money, and that same person having sex or using drugs. This amount of footage made for irrefutable evidence of prostitution or drug use. It was an elaborate set up from criminals to take advantage of other criminals.

What made this incident stand out, even more, was that during a search of one of the closets holding the video recording equipment, a live grenade booby trap was found. Another narc and I started to search through the clothing in the closets. We both started on opposite ends and worked towards each other. It was not uncommon for money or drugs to be found hidden in the pockets of clothes hanging in the closets. As we got closer to the center of the closet, we both began to search through a jacket. I felt something hard and round in what appeared to be one of the jacket sleeves. I could not make out what it was immediately. I just knew it was not normal, so I manipulated it with my hand. As I did this, the other investigator pushed up against the same item from the opposite side, where it hung inside the same leather jacket. The other investigator, who is a former U.S. Marine, instantly knew that it was a grenade.

He said, "Oh shit! Don't move! It's a grenade!"

Stopping, I did exactly what he said.

He reached underneath it to prevent it from falling. He grasped it from the outside of the sock it was in to prevent it from detonating, in case the pin had already been removed. I backed away and walked out of the room to get our sergeant, a former U.S. Army Special Forces Operator. The grenade had the pin pulled, and it was dropped down into a long tube sock.

They put three layers of socks around this grenade. The elastic of the socks held the grenade tightly along with a tape around the top portion of the sock in contact with the grenade, not allowing it to release the handle and start the countdown to detonation. The bottom of the socks had been cut off, and the grenade was packed tightly between multiple items of clothing. The pressure from the socks, the tape, and clothing hanging in the closet did not allow the grenade to slip out and fall to the floor, which would have caused it to detonate. I had no idea if this would have been successful or not. I think the tape was too tight, but I was not going to take any chances. Thank God that we never took the pressure off of the grenade once we felt it. We never found out if this grenade was there to destroy the video recording devices or do harm to whoever went into the closet without permission; perhaps it was both.

The bomb squad came out to the scene and detonated the grenade, which was live. Due to the fact that an explosive device was found in the closet, we had to evacuate the house. A bomb team came in and searched the remainder of the house with a bomb-sniffing dog. We waited outside to go back inside and finish a more thorough search after the bomb squad left. Hours went by, and they never let us go back inside.

The investigation revealed that an investigator from the sheriff's office was somehow involved in this illegal operation. Rumor had it that a local politician was also involved, but I never got any more details and was prohibited from viewing the video recordings seized in my investigation. I never found out the complete truth because our Office of Professional Standards (same thing as Internal Affairs) came in and took over the investigation. As a result, the investigator resigned from the sheriff's office within a day or so of the search. To this day, I do not know if he was ever charged with anything criminally from the above incident. What was ironic about this was that this investigator used to be one of the best sources for providing us with information about methamphetamine labs within the county.

In hindsight, no wonder he had so much intel; he was personally involved in the drug and prostitution business. At the time, we just thought he was an excellent investigator with many informants. Looking back, the only thing shady about his actions was that he never told us who gave him the intel, other than saying "one of his trustworthy informants." This did not draw any particular red flags because once you developed a good informant, you had to be careful that another officer or agency did not steal him/her from you to make cases. So, as I have indicated, protecting an informant was not really that suspicious.

Something else though that struck me as odd, and gave me the feeling that we must have hit on something very sensitive was the fact the Sheriff came out to the scene in the middle of the night during the execution of the search warrant. As I mentioned above, we were not allowed back in to finish the search once the grenade was rendered safe. Considering we had found drugs, and this was a drug house with prostitution and prostitution fall under our jurisdiction as vice and narcotics investigators we should have handled the investigation. The fact that it involved a deputy, or possibly more than one politician, did not mean anything to us. We should have finished the criminal investigation by calling in the state law enforcement division to assist so that it would not look like a conflict of interest investigating one of our own. This never happened. I do not know what they were trying to hide, but something did not smell right about this case just besides the dirty cop. Why did the Sheriff come to the scene when he never did on the hundreds of other similar incidents? I have my thoughts on who else may have been caught on some of these videos having sex with prostitutes, but we will never know the whole truth. I wonder if the evidence ever made its way into the evidence vault, or if it mysteriously disappeared. Again, we will never know, because once the Sheriff arrived, we were kicked off our own investigation and crime scene.

I asked my supervisor later on about this matter. I was quickly shut down and told to focus on my other cases. The fact that that grenade could have killed my partner and me, and there was no real resolution, upset me. Thankfully, when this occurred, I had already started the application process to become a Special Agent with the DEA. I secretly made a vow to myself that day that if I were ever Chief of Police or Sheriff, I would never try to cover up the bad deeds of anyone, especially not a cop or politician. Fifteen years later, this promise would come back to me when I was Chief of Police. My mayor and head of investigations were criminally indicted for crimes ranging from misconduct in office to extortion to destroying evidence in a murder investigation.

About a year after this prostitution and drug case, I had a similar situation occur on a gambling operation we busted. We got a tip from an informant about a gambling operation that ran out of a commercial business. I reported it up the chain of command, and we followed up on it and went inside, undercover. We immediately discovered a large-scale gambling operation, so we shut it down. We seized about $5,000 in cash, and the manager of the business was very cooperative. About a week later, I noticed cars at this same location, so I called a few of my fellow narcs and we hit it again. We did not notify our supervisors what we were doing, because it happened so fast. This time we got about $30,000 in cash and the manager was not at all cooperative. He asked why we were back so soon, and acted like we were only supposed to hit them every once in a while, (i.e. quarterly). We seized nearly six times the amount of cash when we hit it unexpectedly, and did not let our supervisors know. Not to mention, we busted them in the middle of the week; these were not even peak gambling days.

After this happened, I almost immediately got called into the office with the upper brass. I was told point-blank to concentrate on my drug cases. They never outright said it, but it was clear that they wanted me to leave the gambling operations alone. Being that we were a vice and narcotics unit, I considered gambling one of the primary 'vice' crimes, and it was my duty to do this type of enforcement. They saw it much differently than me. At the time, I had no clue why they treated me like this, but my gut instinct said someone was in on the take or accepting bribes. Almost ten years after this incident and long after I left the sheriff's office, the front page of our local newspaper indicated that yet another person in charge at the sheriff's office was being criminally indicted. This time it was for misconduct in office and extortion (giving an illegal gambling operation information in exchange for money).

This gambling operation was the same one that we had busted years before. It did not take a rocket scientist to realize that I was encroaching on some of the upper brass's illegal activities all those years ago and wanted it to stop. What I just did not know was, who else, if anyone, in the upper brass knew of this. Being a low-level narc at the time, I did not have any opportunity to affect change on corruption cases like this, but I sure as Hell would have if I were given full support. I was grateful to see how the FBI and

State Law Enforcement Division were the agencies that made this bust many years later. In the name of full transparency, the Sheriff was the one that was said to have turned the intel over to these agencies to have one of their own officers investigated. With that said, I will always wonder how much money in kickbacks or hush money was paid to certain law enforcement officers over that ten-plus year period. If there is one thing I hate, it is a dirty cop or government official.

Sold Out by One of Our Own ("Dirty Cop")

In the peak of my undercover experience, I was asked to go into one of the local strip clubs to assist with an investigation. This strip club was suspected of being linked to a larger national chain and believed to have ties to an organized crime family in another state. The initial goal was to gather intelligence, not to publish any written reports on the matters which could be obtained outside of our unit, since police reports are public information. This meant that we were going to go into the strip clubs and gather intelligence regarding any criminal activity, but not divulge what we found out. We were given government funds to carry out this operation. As you could imagine, even the officers who normally did not work undercover, gladly signed up for this detail. I knew that strip clubs were a huge hangout place for drug traffickers, so I looked at it as an opportunity to develop further drug targets.

About a month into this operation, we had gathered indisputable evidence of ongoing prostitution and drug sales inside the club. The problem was that we could not prove that anyone beyond the dancers or bouncers, such as the owners/operators, were involved. The ultimate goal was to prove a case against the owners, which could result in shutting down the club and seizing any assets associated with the business (i.e. property). Major seizures have a long-lasting negative impact on the criminal organization, versus just arresting a few dancers for prostitution; or patrons for drug sales in the club. This specific strip club was considered a nuisance property for the area in which we lived (part of the Bible Belt), so I believe this operation was political in nature. This was most likely why they wanted to keep the paper trail to a minimum and provided more funds than usual to gather intelligence.

One night, another investigator, Brad, and I worked undercover in the strip club. We went into the club just as we had many times in the past. We got a drink and mingled in with the crowd and dancers. Since we had become almost like regulars and were known to spend a little bit of money, we were very popular in the clubs. This was what it took to get an inside track on things at the club. We had been in the club for an hour or two and had been propositioned for sex several times. We pretended to arrange a weekend of sex with several of the girls to go down in the near future. Of course, we could not do the act, so we had to plan the sex for a later date, to buy us some time. Our cover story allowed us to pretend that we owned our own business and had important clients coming into town, for which we needed the hottest girls to ensure they were entertained and had a good time. The dancers bought this story hook, line, and sinker. Apparently, this was a fairly common practice in the business world, when one company is trying to close a deal. As they say, "sex sells," or was it, "sex seals the deal?" Maybe it was both in this case.

Both of us had just received lap dances from two dancers, which is when things got weird. After they finished dancing, we asked for another dance because we were in the middle of a conversation about the prostitution deal, when the song ended. All of a sudden, the girl giving me the dance was called up to the Disc-Jockey (DJ) Booth. This was not uncommon, so I did not think much of it. I watched her walk into the booth and come back out and down to us after a short duration. She whispered something in the other dancer's ear while she danced for my partner. She then walked back over to me to finish our dance. Her open-demeanor and dancing style immediately changed. It was like a switch had been turned off. The girls were no longer grinding on us like they had been just moments before the DJ Booth conversation. When I started to talk to her about hooking up with us for the prostitution deal, which we were negotiating earlier, she blew me off in a playful way by laughing and saying how silly I was for wanting her to be a bad girl.

We had already discussed her and a friend doing anything we wanted for the entire weekend for $500 each, including all the alcohol and whatever our entertainment was for our guests (i.e.

renting a yacht or party bus/limousine). We knew something was wrong, but at that moment we had no idea what happened. Once the girls walked away, Brad and I talked it over for a minute. This place was huge and had almost one hundred dancers, so another group of dancers soon approached us. We started all over again with the weekend proposition deal. As they were dancing, another girl walked by and whispered something in their ears. Next thing we knew, they were also following all the legal rules of dancing for the state (no grinding or allowing us to put our hands on them).

After the dances, they immediately got dressed, and we watched as one of them walked up to the DJ Booth. The DJ Booth had a one-way mirror on the outside, we could not see in, but anyone inside could see the night club dancers and patrons. When the girl opened the door and entered the booth, she turned on a light, illuminating the inside and could see in slightly. At least we could make out a person from a distance, and my partner immediately recognized one of the guys in the booth as a deputy with the sheriff's office. We knew we were burned at that point, but the worst part was by one of our colleagues.

Knowing we were burned, but not wanting to run out quickly and tip them off to anything we saw, we sat there for a few minutes. We finished our drinks and then made our exit. We notified our surveillance teams of what had occurred and drove out of the area. The surveillance team maintained a constant visual on the club until the officer left the establishment. Several hours later, the plain-clothes off-duty officer left the club and got into a van. The van was marked with vinyl decals indicating that it belonged to a carpet cleaning business. He was followed back to his residence, where surveillance ended for that evening.

Over the next week, we did some investigating and learned that the deputy owned a small carpet cleaning business as his secondary employment. He had been cleaning the carpets for the strip club for several months. The deputy began by legitimately cleaning the carpets in exchange for a monetary payment. As time went on, and he started to hang out at the strip clubs more often, he somehow got to the point where he started to trade their services for his (dances, drinks, and sex in exchange for carpet cleaning). The deputy eventually began receiving large sums of money for classified police intelligence regarding strip clubs. The deputy had been seen driving around in a very nice new car, plus had many other items which he could not have afforded on a police officer's salary, even if he had a side business. This alone was suspicious, but not illegal if the proceeds came from the legitimate side of his carpet cleaning business. It is not against policy to have secondary employment, so we checked if he had permission from the Sheriff. Sure enough, he did turn in his form, and it was approved since carpet cleaning in and of itself is not a conflict of interest to working as a deputy.

With all of this preliminary information about the deputy's questionable behavior, the sheriff's office opened an internal affairs investigation. Since there is no reasonable expectation of privacy in a patrol car, being government property, we put an audio recording device inside his vehicle. To do it without drawing suspicion, we waited until he put his patrol car in the shop for routine maintenance. After normal shop hours, we hardwired a covert audio listening device to the car battery. We did this so it would not run out of battery life quickly. Our unit started to run undercover surveillance on this deputy every day that he worked. Since he worked twelve-hour night shifts, we were on duty at the same time. Each evening we followed him from his house to the sheriff's office for his briefings. We ended each shift following him home. We got proof that he was frequenting the club, even on duty, in a marked patrol car. We now needed proof that he was supplying them with classified information to have him criminally indicted. To accomplish this, we set up a ruse.

On the day of the ruse, we called all narcotics investigators and we gathered on the bottom floor of the law enforcement center. Meanwhile, the deputy was to report for roll call, in order to go out on patrol with his platoon. All narcs came dressed in raid gear, thus appearing ready to be conducting a major drug raid, We made sure the deputies saw us and started rumors about conducting raids of strip clubs on the east side of town, where this strip club was located.

After his platoon conducted their routine briefing before the shift started, they exited the law enforcement center and went on patrol. Just as we suspected, the deputy was seen quickly exiting the building and getting into his patrol car. He did not even wait until he got out of the parking lot before he got on the phone with someone from the strip club. We later found out that it was the management at the strip club. We could only hear one side of the conversation since our audio listening device was in the patrol car, not on his phone, and he did not put it on a hands-free talk/speakerphone for this call. We heard him warn whoever he called that the vice and narcotics unit was coming to their area to raid some clubs, and it could be their club. He warned them how many of us were coming, and about what time. This was all that we needed, so we continued surveillance on him while others went back to write the reports of our findings.

After several hours went by without a raid, the strip club manager called the deputy. This call was put on speakerphone, so we heard both sides of the call. The deputy was thanked for the information and told that nobody came to their club that evening. This call corroborated the one-sided conversation we had heard hours earlier. This deputy was now interfering with an investigation, which was a clear Misconduct in Office charge.

The next day, we drafted a search warrant for the strip club, and the deputy was called into work early. He was stripped of his gun and badge and placed on non-paid administrative leave, pending the investigation results. The club was raided before the deputy was released from questioning by the Office of Professional Standards (i.e. the same thing as Internal Affairs), to ensure that he did not have time to call and warn them of this situation. During the execution of the search warrant, we found something that shocked us a bit and really opened our eyes. A yellow sticky-note was found on the strip club manager's desk. Written on it was my and Brad's full name. They did not have my undercover name, but my real name, which is very distinctive. This was what we needed to close the case on the deputy. It scared me because the strip club manager was known to have links to major organized crime nationwide. We did not know exactly how deep the corruption went. This made me fear for my wife and our son more than anything.

While searching the strip club, we found a video link recording all our actions in the club, going directly to an internet hook up. We later found out that this link sent the video, via the internet, to a server in Atlanta, Georgia, where some other related strip clubs were located. This was where the organized crime group controlled all of the organization's assets and sister companies.

Case Conclusion: The officer was indicted for Conduct Unbecoming of a Police Officer, which is a felony that can carry up to ten years in prison. Since he was a police officer with an unblemished record, no record of criminal activity, he took a plea. He did not go to prison and was only sentenced to probation for five years, which was a slap in the face and an insult to us. He risked our lives and careers as undercover officers. As I have mentioned before, there is not much "justice" in the criminal justice system unless you are a "criminal." It should be revised and renamed the victim's justice system, which would include a total re-evaluation of the system's goals as a whole. Providing justice to victims and their families while ensuring the rights of the accused should both be the priority of any modern system.

We were betrayed by one of our own, and more than a little pissed off. I always feared getting burned during a major operation, but I never thought it would be because of one of our own; a fellow brother in blue. If I was burned because I made a mistake, I could live with that and use it as a learning experience. However, getting burned by a fellow officer stings to the core.

During the many visits to the strip clubs during this operation, we had another close call that never burned us but easily could have. During this incident, I was wearing a covert audio and video recording device. This was the first time that I tried to wear such a large piece of equipment in an environment where the people are so touchy-feely. During a lap dance, one of the dancers kept repeatedly bumping my recording device.

At one point, she asked me, "What's that?"

I quickly replied, "An insulin pump."

She never blinked an eye or mentioned it again. One bit of satisfaction I could still walk away with after this investigation was knowing that it was not our actions or mistakes that caused us to get burned. I take personal pride in my undercover work and would be much harder on myself than anyone else if I had caused myself to have my undercover status compromised.

Corrupt Corrections Officer

Corrupt cops were something that I rarely had to deal with, but I really enjoyed putting a stop to them. I would honestly rather take down a dirty cop than a major drug dealer, merely out of pride for my profession. For this undercover deal, I was approached by the State Department of Corrections to assist them and work undercover with an investigation involving a corrupt corrections officer. Being sought out for your undercover skills by local, state, and federal agencies was the ultimate compliment for me, and I never minded helping anyone.

This case got started when state investigators had an inmate's wife call them. Her motivation for becoming an informant and giving up a corrupt corrections officer was to try and get her husband's sentence reduced. As previously discussed, with confidential informants, there is always a motivation to make people snitch; and it almost certainly is not out of the goodness of their heart to do the right thing. The department of corrections was not about to reduce his prison sentence, because the courts had ordered that, and they had no control over it.

One thing they could do was give the inmate back "good time," for the number of days served, or more privileges inside the prison. 'Good time' is when an inmate serves a preset number of days without having any disciplinary matters or write-ups. If they do this, they get a reduction in the overall days they are required to stay in prison. For example, a person who constantly gets in trouble will be required to serve the entire length of their sentence. A person who gets credit for 'good time' may get thirty days of 'good time' credit for every year served. This would mean that every 'good year' equals thirty fewer days off the original sentence. 'Good time' also makes them eligible for parole, and grants them a better chance of parole being granted. This inmate's wife was a single mom, supporting three small children because her husband was in prison. Therefore, she was motivated to do anything to help her husband get out sooner.

I met with the department of corrections investigator, who worked for the state. We discussed my posing as this lady's nephew and supplier of drugs. She was going to introduce me to a corrections officer, and I would give him drugs to be smuggled into the prison. In a situation like this, officers are normally paid well for taking these major risks, but not in this situation. This officer was not being paid by myself or the female, so I did not know who was paying him. He was doing this as a favor to an inmate that he owed for some prior favor. I do not know if this inmate beat down another inmate who was harassing the correctional officer or what, but it must have been something very worthwhile, considering the risk he was taking and the value of drugs in prison.

On the day of the deal, we got wired up with covert audio recording and listening devices underneath our clothes. Then we got into my undercover vehicle and rode out to the Home Depot parking lot, where we pre-arranged to meet up. As we pulled in the parking lot, the large SUV that the correctional officer was supposed to be in was already on the scene. This was totally a cop thing because dope dealers are never on time, but cops are known for being a little early. I found this kind of funny since I was posing as the drug dealer and running late like they usually are. I pulled up right next to him, and we all exited our vehicles. He wore his department of corrections uniform, but it was hard to tell because he had a non-uniform issued jacket over the uniform shirt. We stood between both his SUV and my undercover vehicle. The female introduced us, and we talked for a short bit. I handed him the one ounce of marijuana and twenty-five Xanax pills, which we had previously arranged.

Just as I gave him the drugs, he pointed in his car at a small child and said he had to run him home before going to work, so he was in a rush. This shocked me because I scanned the car up to that point but did not see anyone inside. I guess I was initially looking for a grown-up; not a small child slouched low in the seat, playing a handheld video-gaming system. The child could not have been more than twelve years old. After the deal, the target jumped in his car, and we got in our car. He rolled down his window and told us, "I'll take care of this tonight," Then, he started to drive off.

After we gave him the drugs, I gave our pre-arranged takedown signal to the arrest team that was covertly spread out in the parking lot. They were not right on top of us, to prevent us from getting burned, so they took a while to approach. Instead of rolling up on the car covertly and blocking him from the front and rear to prevent a chase, the department of corrections unmarked

SUV approached with blue lights on. This only gave the corrections officer a chance to see us coming, and he got spooked. He quickly accelerated just as one of the vehicles moved in to block the front of his car.

Since he was in a full-sized Ford Excursion, he managed to push one of our smaller trucks out of the way and make a hole to escape apprehension. We also had another large truck with us, and they tried to block the corrections officer's SUV from leaving through the entrance of a restaurant adjacent to the Home Depot parking lot. This did not work, and the larger SUV was easily rammed out of the way. Another one of our vehicles tried to block him again, at the last exit before getting onto the main road, but was also easily moved out of the way by the much heavier and more powerful SUV. Once he got to the main road, the chase was on, and the speeds kept climbing.

While all of this occurred, I tried to alert everyone on the Nextel that there was a small child in the car. Amongst all the chaos on the radios and Nextel's, nobody heard my first few transmissions. Finally, I was able to get through to the sergeant, who called all of our guys off the chase. This was a great call because we already had this guy identified, and they could pick him up at a later date and time, which should have been our original plan.

The problem was the Department of Corrections Investigator did not have the same radio frequency as us, and we could not communicate with him other than by cell phone. We tried to call his cell phone, but he was so neck-deep in the pursuit of the SUV that he never heard it, or at least, he did not answer it.

The chase went on for more than twenty minutes, and Highway Patrol eventually got involved. The corrections investigator ended up wrecking the corrupt officer's SUV, causing it to overturn and roll over sideways several times. When he did, he also overturned his state vehicle. Fortunately, and miraculously, the child was not injured. Thank God he had on his seatbelt, or he would have likely been ejected and killed.

As for the corrupt corrections officer, he received minor injuries and was taken to the hospital, treated, and released that same night. The Department of Corrections Investigator received the worst injuries of them all. His injuries were so severe that he was forced to retire on permanent medical disability. The inmate was charged with Assault and Battery with Intent to Kill multiple times for ramming police along the way, as well as a series of other charges. Unknown to a lot of people not involved in the drug game, drugs in prison are valued around ten times what they cost out on the streets. This is in part due to the high demand and extreme risk taken to get them into prison. He was subsequently convicted and sentenced to more than 10 years in prison on a plea deal.

(RIGHT) Photo of what I looked like on the night of this deal.

(BELOW) This is a copy of the newspaper article/press release after the above incident. As you can see, the corrupt corrections officer was charged with Child Endangerment for fleeing with the minor child in the vehicle and Assault and Battery with Intent to Kill for almost killing the corrections investigator during the pursuit, as well as ramming other law enforcement vehicles to get away. As far as the charges in the article about the second corrections officer arrested, we were not involved in that matter. It is also interesting how they referred to me as an "Informant" working with the State Law Enforcement Division. For some reason, when a police officer from an outside agency works undercover for the state, they sign them up as an informant, which makes no sense to me. I went with it because it did not really bother me if they were stuck on old policies from decades ago and not keeping up with the evolving world of working undercover.

Corrections officers arrested on drug charges

By Jason ▮▮▮
STAFF WRITER
▮▮▮ news.com

Two state corrections officers, one from ▮▮▮ were arrested and charged with trying to smuggle drugs into prisons, state officials said late Saturday.

Lorenzo ▮▮▮, 42, of 1104 ▮▮▮ Drive in ▮▮▮, was charged with possession with intent to distribute marijuana, possession with intent to distribute a controlled substance, violation of the state contraband law, misconduct in office, child endangerment and assault and battery with intent to kill, according to warrants.

▮▮▮, an employee at ▮▮▮ Correctional Institution, took marijuana and the anti-anxiety drug Xanax from an informant working for the State Law Enforcement Division, according to the arrest warrant. The warrant also states ▮▮▮ planned to distribute the drugs inside the prison.

The other charges stem from a chase that ensued when police tried to pull him over, the warrant said.

▮▮▮ had his 12-year-old son in his car when police attempted to pull him over, the warrant said.

SLED officials said ▮▮▮ arrest was a joint operation involving SLED, the state Department of Corrections and the ▮▮▮ County Sheriff's Office. The Highway Patrol also assisted in the case.

The other officer arrested was Earl ▮▮▮, 25, of ▮▮▮. According to warrants, he took crack cocaine from an undercover agent and planned to distribute it to an inmate in the ▮▮▮ Correctional Institution, where he worked.

Cop or Crook?

You see a lot of crazy things working undercover, but on this occasion, I can say I was absolutely stunned with what I saw. One memorable case was not even during an undercover deal or operation. A couple of years earlier, I had purchased some ecstasy in a local night club while working undercover for the city. I made two purchases from a Hispanic drug dealer in the night club, whom I will refer to as *Jose* for the sake of this story. After making two purchases off Jose, I intentionally stayed away from him to start working on other drug targets in the night club. I never tried to stack more than two distribution charges on a person, unless they were a huge target, or one of my previous UC cases was not as solid as I wanted it to be. Jose was eventually arrested in the drug round-up of dealers from *Operation Lights Out* from A Narc's Tale Volume 1. Nothing extraordinary happened during those transactions with Jose, which is why I had not mentioned them up to this point in the series.

Due to the high number of cases I worked, I do not always find out what happens with the cases unless they go to a trial. Many cases are plea-bargained between the prosecutors and defense attorneys, without the knowledge of the case agents or undercovers. I do not agree with this, but it is the nature of the beast; with a backed-up court docket, not everything can go to trial. Unbeknownst to me, Jose put in for and was accepted into the Pre-Trial Intervention Program, or PTI, for first-time offenders. He was accepted into the program and successfully completed it one year later. After completing the program, he went to the Clerk of Court's Office and paid to have his criminal record expunged of these charges. This wiped his record clear of this drug arrest and conviction.

A few years later, Jose applied for a position with a local law enforcement agency. One day when I was going to that agency to pick up some paperwork, I noticed a guy sitting at the front desk in uniform. This was not unusual, because there were always officers working the front desk detail. The thing that got me was I recognized this guy, but could not remember where I had seen him before. I went into the building and went on about my business when it finally hit me that this new officer was Jose, the drug dealer.

I quickly went to the photo section of the criminal processing unit at the local law enforcement center. I attempted to see if I could pull an old mug shot from several years earlier when he was arrested for Distribution of MDMA (Ecstasy). He had gotten his record expunged, but thankfully the city records personnel failed to go into the booking computer and remove his photograph. I did not even know if they were required to remove an old booking photograph. I was not able to find a copy of the old police report since that had been removed as part of the expungement process. I remembered that as part of the investigator's files, which were kept in the vice and narcotics office, we kept a copy of every undercover report. These reports were much different than an incident report but did have all the same information and many more details.

I got a copy of this report the same day and drove back to the law enforcement center. I brought the undercover report and mugshot to the on-duty supervisor, and he immediately contacted some of his higher-ups at the department. It was not more than thirty minutes before Jose was removed from his assignment and terminated for falsifying his application package. I never heard if he was prosecuted for this, but it was unheard of for an ex-drug dealer to blatantly apply to work in law enforcement in the same area that he was originally arrested.

Jose had selectively failed to mention that he had been arrested for a felony, times two, in the last seven years and this somehow slipped through the cracks of the background checks. At the time, he was pulling desk duty while waiting to go to the police academy. I often wonder if anyone would have ever caught this major oversight if I had not recognized him and put two and two together.

Chapter Five

Operation Straight Shooter

Operation Straight Shooter was only an aspiration in my mind to do a major long-term undercover operation when I came over to the sheriff's office. I wanted to impress the sheriff and make the largest undercover case in the history of the county and perhaps state history, so I took on this challenge. I could not do an investigation of this caliber alone, so I chose one of the best UCs I have ever worked with, my close friend, Lyle K. We sat down and came up with a game plan to do an undercover operation using little to no dope transactions using confidential informants. We noticed a trend in the courts, where informants were making most of the buys, not the undercover agents. This resulted in them disappearing, failing to testify, or doing a terrible job in court when it came to prosecution time. After an initial arrest, most cases were lost or forcibly dismissed, because the informant was not available to testify, or discredited on the stand. Our goal was to make every deal involve an undercover, one of us actually making the drug transaction, not a potentially untrustworthy informant. This was what we wanted, so we talked to our sergeant and lieutenant, and they agreed to it.

Our supervisors were great because they gave us free rein to implement our plans and mission. Throughout this chapter, you will read about some of the more memorable cases made during *Operation Straight Shooter*, which ended up accomplishing our goal of being the largest undercover operation in our county's history.

Twenty Dollars of Cocaine Equals Twenty Years in Prison

As discussed in Volume 1 of this series, working undercover in homosexual night clubs was somewhat uncomfortable for a heterosexual male like me. Then as I began *Operation Straight Shooter*, I found myself training other undercover police officers on how to overcome some of the obstacles that I went through infiltrating clubs of this sort. Not that I am homophobic or anything, but I found these clubs to be unsettling, and an unusual environment and lifestyle of which to be a part. This made for a rather uncomfortable assignment, but I was willing to pour myself into it because it was my job and a mission in which I believed.

Based on many complaints about flagrant drug use and sales in the homosexual night clubs, plus my previous knowledge and work experience in these specific night clubs I teamed up with two other less experienced undercover investigators to infiltrate the club and to look for possible targets. The club that we decided to go to was known for its flamboyant crowd, where many people were cross-dressers or transsexuals. I knew this could be an uncomfortable environment, because this type of crowd talked with their hands as much as they did with their mouths. This could be a serious problem when wearing a body wire. For that reason, we decided to pose as a group of young men who were lovers in a ménage à trois, a three-way relationship. This would help us fend off unwanted sexual advances while we searched for potential drug dealers in the night club. This type of cover story helped prevent others from touching any of us sexually, possibly finding our body wires, so we thought this was our best approach. My two narc partners were fresh faces in the club scene and therefore had never been burned or labeled a narc or snitch, always a positive. However, the guys also had done very little undercover work, and this lack of experience made them vulnerable to mistakes. So, I took them under my wing and guided them through uncharted waters for both of them.

We dressed in semi-preppy clothes that allowed us to fit in with the night club crowd and dressed somewhat comfortable matching undercover 'personalities.' We drove out to the club but did not have a membership to get into this private club. We hung out in the parking lot and "flirted" with the first group of guys who pulled up into the parking lot. This idea worked perfectly, and a group decided to sign us into the club as their guests. If this did not work, we could have gotten a membership but would have had to wait the twenty-four-hour grace period before we were allowed inside. This company policy was to prevent problems (or undercover cops) from just showing up and making entry.

We bought those guys drinks for getting us in and then ditched them in the club since they did not appear to be into drugs when we probed them. We mingled among the crowd and spotted a few potential targets we wanted to get close to and attempted to make a purchase. Before we could get a purchase, one of us had to use the restroom. We decided to go together because of the type of environment we were in, and I did not want to leave my new undercovers alone. These bathrooms had a single toilet and a urinal on the wall, but the walls and ceiling were covered with mirrors. We noticed that men walked in and out on each other all the time, and we did not want this happening to us. All three of us walked in and started to close the door behind us. Just as the door was about to shut, a hand reached in and stopped it. They pulled the door open and stepped inside. It appeared to be a rather large female.

She said, "Go Ahead. Don't mind me." We all just kind of stood there, and she just pulled up her dress, dropped her pantyhose, and sat down on the toilet. The *she* ended up being a full-blown male. She struck up a conversation with us while she pissed, sitting down.

She said, "I bet you thought I was a woman."

We all answered at the same time, "Yes," even if we could tell immediately it was a man. We did this to be polite and complimentary on her look. We then started to play on her ego about how pretty she looked. After she finished her business, she got up, fixed her clothes, and washed her hands and walked out of the bathroom. That is when we locked the door, and each of us took turns, relieving ourselves, and got out of there. Everyone knows that the restroom is not the place to hang out in a homosexual night club.

We walked back out into the club, and I immediately noticed a guy I will refer to as Michael, who I had purchased drugs from years earlier when I worked undercover for the city police. At the time, I had platinum blond hair, but now my hair was long and black. I noticed him standing alone, and we walked over and struck up a conversation with him. To break the ice, we bought him a drink. This served the purpose well, but it also caused him to believe that we were flirting with him, which was not our intention. For some reason, he grew fond of me quickly, and when I went to get another drink, he told one of my undercover partners his sexual thoughts about me. When I got back, one of my partners could not help but start laughing at me. He pulled me aside and told me that Michael had the hots for me. I knew that this was my 'in' with him, and I was so relieved that he did not recognize me from dealing with him years earlier.

We stood around dancing to the music for a while, as I appeared to be zoned out, but I was really looking around for a drug target. At this point, Michael asked me if I was ok. I took advantage of this opportunity since he opened the door, and I told him that I was bummed because I wanted something to make me feel better and help me party longer. Michael asked me if I wanted some of that "white lady," which is the street name for cocaine. I put my arm around him and whispered in his ear, "I would love some. How much?" I asked how much because I wanted it to be clear I wanted to pay and was not accepting his gift, so he did not expect anything from me in return. I knew he was a drug dealer from past experiences with him, and I wanted to keep it all business with nothing sexual being implied.

Michael told me he only had a little left and gave me a price of twenty-dollars. I pulled out a single twenty-dollar bill and handed it to him. He reached in his pocket and pulled out a 1-inch by 1-inch, blue-tinted, mini plastic-style bag containing cocaine, and handed it to me. This was a very small user amount of cocaine, but it did not matter on the weight.

The weight is irrelevant for small purchases because no matter how it is viewed, a distribution of a controlled substance is a felony under the law. After the transaction, I dismissed myself and acted like I was going to the bathroom to get high. I went into the bathroom alone, waiting until it was empty, and locked the door. I went alone because the quantity of drugs was only enough for one person, and I needed to act accordingly like I was using what I purchased. I waited for about five minutes and then went back outside to my undercover partners. I told them we were good, and we mingled with the crowd and made a few more contacts. I believe one of my partners made an unrelated ecstasy (MDMA) purchase and got a contact number for a future deal. After about an hour, we slipped out of the club to process the evidence and write reports.

Case Conclusion: At the end of this operation, during a large-scale round-up/arrest operation, Michael was arrested. He was currently out on probation for my previous dealings with him when he had his day in court. He walked into court, confident that he would get his probation extended because he only sold a small quantity of cocaine or less than a half a gram.

He had a public defender assigned to him, and when his name was called, he entered a plea of guilty on the charges. Due to our past dealings, I wanted to be present in court that day. After the prosecutor told the facts of the case to the judge so that he could determine an appropriate sentence, Michael's probation officer spoke. The judge then asked if anyone else would like to speak on behalf of the state. I asked the judge if I could say a word and was granted permission. Michael looked over and immediately recognized me from our most recent drug transaction at the club. He started to get dizzy. He had to be held up by his defense attorney with the bailiff's assistance because he almost passed out before I even started speaking.

I explained to the judge that this was not the first time this defendant had sold me drugs. I explained that he was convicted of two prior distributions, for which he sold me ecstasy (MDMA) in a similar situation; while I worked undercover for the city. I reminded the judge that he had pled guilty to one distribution in exchange for the other one being dismissed as part of a plea deal. I then asked that the court consider this a third distribution or strike, and sentence him accordingly. I looked over at Michael as the judge looked down to write something, and he looked like he had just seen a ghost. I think realization finally hit him that I was not only the undercover that he sold drugs to recently but also the guy with platinum blond hair that he had sold ecstasy to years earlier.

The judge took a few minutes to deliberate and then sentenced Michael to twenty years in prison. I must admit, even I was shocked how hard he hammered him. I was expecting the probation violation, and maybe five or a maximum of ten years for this distribution but not twenty. Michael busted out in tears and literally had to be carried out of the courtroom while sobbing like a baby. Never before had I seen a man sell $20 of cocaine to an undercover cop, and get twenty years in prison. As you can see, there was much more to the story, but '$20 Equals Twenty Years' was Michael's fate.

On a side note, in our interview and interrogation room in our vice and narcotics office we had a wall that we put up mug shots of suspects and the number of years they were sentenced to on their pictures. We put these pictures all over the wall as a reminder to the person(s) being interviewed that we did not play games in that office. Michael's mug shot and the caption of "$20 of cocaine = 20 years in prison" became the subject of many discussions over the years. This wall served as a reminder for people to cooperate with us or face the prison sentences that will would most certainly become their new reality.

(BELOW) Photo of the three undercover officers that went into the night club for this deal.

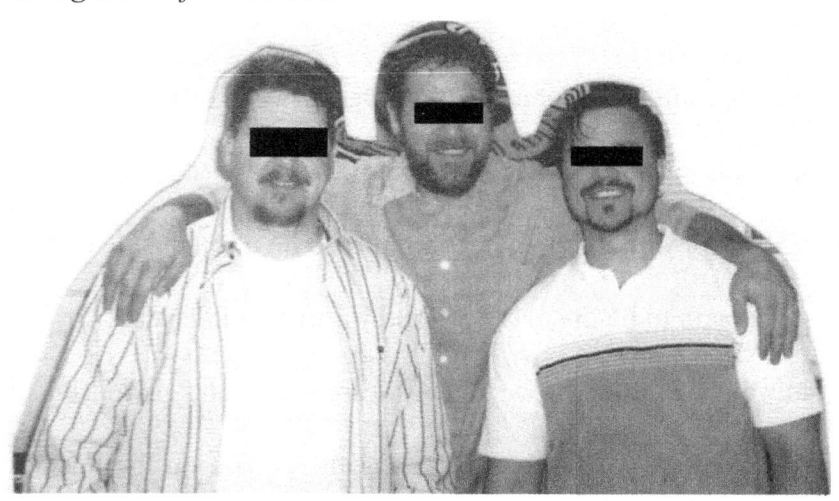

(BELOW) Printout from the State Department of Corrections website, showing the Defendant in the above case and his prison sentence.

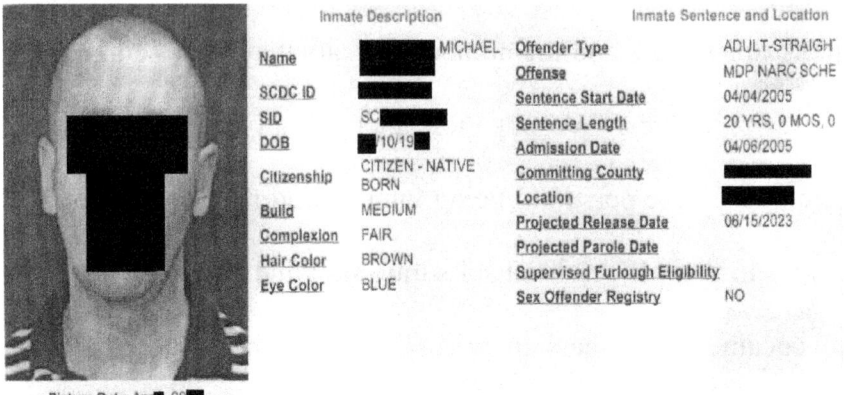

Inmate Description			Inmate Sentence and Location	
Name	███	MICHAEL	Offender Type	ADULT-STRAIGH
			Offense	MDP NARC SCHE
SCDC ID	███		Sentence Start Date	04/04/2005
SID	SC███		Sentence Length	20 YRS, 0 MOS, 0
DOB	██/10/19██		Admission Date	04/06/2005
Citizenship	CITIZEN - NATIVE BORN		Committing County	███
			Location	███
Build	MEDIUM		Projected Release Date	06/15/2023
Complexion	FAIR		Projected Parole Date	
Hair Color	BROWN		Supervised Furlough Eligibility	
Eye Color	BLUE		Sex Offender Registry	NO

Picture Date Apr██, 20██

Kicked Out for Smoking Weed

During this operation, we did an array of different types of drug deals, from street level to night clubs. In this memorable moment, we went out to a new night club on a rough side of town that was said to be the new hot spot for drugs and dealers. Prior to going out to the club, we did some research and pulled up the registered agent of the business, and the person on the business license. The owner had a checkered past, but many years prior. This information alone was nothing more than something good to know, just in case we had to use it. In this case, it turned out quite beneficial.

One evening, my undercover partner Lyle and I drove out to the club. Before we went out, we went through our usual ritual of getting dressed and going over our cover story that evening. We usually kept the cover story similar, so that we did not make mistakes or get confused. Simplifying things was key when you worked an array of undercover operations.

The last thing an undercover needs was to be worried that they would say the wrong thing because that could distract them and become very dangerous.

While getting ready, I decided to roll a couple of joints using a fake marijuana product we had called "Wacky Weed." It smelled and tasted like marijuana, but had no "THC." Tetrahydrocannabinol or THC is the active ingredient in marijuana that makes someone get high and makes the product an illegal controlled substance. This was in the days before any state legalizing marijuana for recreational use, and it was barely being discussed as a legitimate medicinal substance.

We had used this fake marijuana as a prop on deals in our vehicle and in hotel rooms in the past, but not at a busy night club. We had it with us but were not sure we would get to use it. Once ready, we headed to the club with our two-person surveillance team ready to be inside with us, and another two-person team out in the parking lot.

When we got there, we noticed they had security with metal detectors searching people before they were admitted. This meant we had to have specific weapons on us, which could be concealed, to make it past the security. I had a North American Arms .22 magnum pistol; tiny enough to be hidden in my palm with a closed fist, and a plastic knife. The knife was made before 9/11, and all plastic knives now must have a metal rod in them to help them be discovered by metal detectors at airports. This knife was 100% plastic, but could easily do as much damage as regular metal knives. It was uncomfortable, but I took the cylinder with the bullets out of the revolver and put it in one shoe, and the other part of the gun in the other. I knew that if the metal detecting wand was actually used properly, from the ground to above my head, and it alerted, I would blame it on my steel-toe boots. The plastic

266

knife was in my groin. Thankfully, that day the security guard stopped at my calf muscle, and it never went off.

Once inside the club, my partner and I got a drink and found a spot to watch the crowd for a few minutes. We did this to figure out who might be a possible target. After about an hour and some small talk, but no success with a few people, we went to the bathroom. Waiting outside the bathroom in a line, we met a guy, who I will call Jimmy, that said he had some cocaine. He did not agree to sell us any at the time, and we were just *'talked shit'* with him. Once inside the bathroom, I saw him snort a line off the top of the urinal. I wanted to take advantage of this moment, so I decided to pull out my joint while in the doorway of a toilet stall, still *'shoot the shit'* with this guy. I lit it up and started smoking it. My UC partner took a hit, and within minutes the whole bathroom smelled like weed. Jimmy then asked for a hit, and of course, we obliged him. This was the perfect opportunity to test our Wacky Weed product. We knew that when a person is already high and around friends, they can mentally make themselves act or feel a certain way that has nothing to do with the drugs or substance consumed. It is kind of like a lightweight drinker that acts more inebriated and sillier than they should be, based upon the amount of alcohol consumed. The guy took his hits and talked about how strong it was. My partner and I just looked at each other and smirked. After he was done, he walked out of the bathroom. We stayed to finish the joint. We even shared it with another drunk guy that asked for a hit, and he went as far as to cough uncontrollably and he had gagging reflexes as if it was strong weed. It was so funny, but we maintained our composure.

After Jimmy was out of sight, security came barging in and caught us red-handed with the joint in hand. We were not about to say it was fake, so we let them do their thing. They took us to the office, just off to the front entrance to speak to us. The owner of the club just so happened to see the commotion and he approached. The owner looked like he was straight from the '70s, with a shirt unbuttoned by two to three buttons, with a wide expanse of his hairy chest showing. Security told him what happened, and he looked at us and told us that he could not allow this type of thing in his clubs or else the police would shut him down. He said we had to leave but could come back another time. We apologized to the owner and started telling him how we had never been to this club before, but we loved the environment, the music, and the crowd. We told him that we had a lot of money to spend and wanted to have a good time. As I said this, I pulled out a pocket full of cash. I made sure he saw all the hundred dollar bills I had on me, since money talks to a business owner. I pulled a one-hundred-dollar bill from the wad of cash and handed it to him. As I did this, I promised no more problems and asked if we could stay that night and have a good time. We shook hands, and he told security to let us stay.

We walked back into the main floor and open area of the club. My partner spotted Jimmy off in the corner, with a few guys and girls. We got another drink and slowly made our way over there to Jimmy and his crew. Jimmy spotted us and introduced us to his crew like we were old friends. I guess the Wacky Weed did its job. A few minutes later, we asked if he had any more of that "white," another street slang word for cocaine, that we could get off of him. He sold us an 8-ball (one-eighth of an ounce) without hesitation. The funny part was he asked if we would sell him some weed. We had that other joint but decided to tell him that we were out, and that was our only joint we shared with him earlier. We made small talk for a bit, and we decided to make our exit. We exchanged phone numbers and left the area, to act like we were going to the bathroom to get high. Instead, we made it through the crowd and exited the club.

We sat in the parking lot for the next two and one-half hours waiting on Jimmy to leave the club, which is the part of undercover work that sucks. Once he exited the club, we notified our surveillance units and described him and his vehicle. We followed him out of the parking lot, but only until we confirmed our surveillance team had him. We then backed off and let them pursue the suspects. We did not want to be spotted or to burn our undercover vehicle. Deputies followed him for about fifteen miles. They ran the vehicle license plate, then pulled up a driver's license photo of the registered owner and sent it to my cell phone. Both my partner and I positively identified Jimmy as the same guy that sold us the cocaine.

For this reason, we did not have to conduct a traffic stop on him. Surveillance units pulled away and let him go. Many months later, he was arrested as part of the much larger roundup to close out this operation.

Working Undercover in the Raves Again

The MDMA (Ecstasy) business became lucrative in the late 1990s into the early 2000s because of the all-night dance parties referred to as 'raves.' Anyone who hosted a rave could charge $10 to $25 a head and potentially have thousands of kids show up. All they really needed was a safe location, a DJ with a decent sound and lights system, and the kids were ecstatic. An old barn on farmland was perfect for this since police cracked down on locations where they rented public buildings (i.e. civic centers) to throw large raves. Besides a cover charge, they could charge for bottled water, other drinks, snacks, and even select who sold drugs at their raves; of course, for a kickback at the end of the night. Some of the more elaborate set-ups sold glow sticks, drug paraphernalia, clothing, and other items.

We started to receive tips about underground or field rave parties that were taking place on farms out in the middle of the countryside in the neighboring county. We reached out to the narcotics unit in the corresponding county that was having these raves. They did some research, and through informants, they confirmed this information. We asked them if they would like to work a joint investigation to see if we could infiltrate this close-knit group of young adults and teenagers, who traveled from rave to rave. They were interested but stated that they only had one female undercover narc that they felt could fit in this environment, but it was too risky to send her in alone when the backup was nowhere in sight. For these types of deals, you needed a team, preferably two separate two-person undercover teams. They could operate as two separate teams to scout out potential targets, or come together if needed. We selected four undercovers for this operation; three from my agency, and the lady from the other.

I must admit that I was excited about this opportunity, mainly because I was not the lone undercover. I had previous experience working in raves from my time with the city. I felt a little more polished and experienced with raves since I had made forty-seven successful undercover buys during my last operation.

Since this was not my first rave, and I knew what to expect, I came to the table with lots of ideas for undercover props. We had fun with this one and got each of us a pacifier, blow pops, glow sticks, and clothes that glowed in the black lights. Kids in raves commonly used the pacifiers because being under the influence of ecstasy gave them something referred to as 'the clinchers,' where they grind their teeth and bite down uncontrollably. Many rave kids often had something in their mouths to alleviate this aggravation and pain.

Our two narcotics units met, and as the undercovers, we reviewed our cover stories. We had been researching a couple of raves we wanted to hit in the area over the course of the next week. We got dressed up and headed out to the rave in two separate vehicles. Upon arrival at the first location, it looked like a very small rave party of under one-hundred people, or else, we were there early. The crowd was very young, and we were likely the oldest ones there. It was hard to blend in when the crowd was so small, but we did our best. We went inside this old abandoned farmhouse that had no furniture in it. It was clear that they had put in some work to get this place ready. They painted graffiti art throughout all the rooms, and set up DJ lighting, with a sound system. It was clear this crew had never thrown a rave before, but they were trying, and aesthetically, it looked and sounded decent. The reality was that the people there were enjoying themselves because they were high, so the things we saw as dirty or in bad condition, they most likely never noticed.

We purchased bottled water and began to scout out the area. One of the other undercovers and I decided to blend in by cracking some glow sticks and dancing as if we were already rolling on ecstasy. This got others to come around us and start dancing as well. I guess you can say we kind of got the party started. After about twenty minutes of dancing and sweating profusely, we asked one of the guys dancing next to us if he had any "rolls," which is another street name for ecstasy. It was clear he was high at the time, and you do not know unless you ask. Without hesitation, he asked us to go outside to his vehicle to do the deal. As we were outside, it was clear that more people were starting to arrive. The crowd was not your typical rave crowd. Many of these guys looked more like the wannabe crowd. Wannabes are people that dress like they want to be gangsters in hip-hop attire. They tried to look tough and hard but clearly were neither. What made the first buy at this location memorable was not the purchase, but what happened during the purchase. As we stood outside the dealer's vehicle, waiting for him to count out pills for us, we noticed a guy get into a vehicle next to us, and it looked like he was jimmying the ignition. Upon closer inspection, that is exactly what he was doing. He was actually stealing the vehicle. He got the car started and drove off as we were making our hand-to-hand transaction. I put the ecstasy pills in my pocket, and we started to walk back towards the farmhouse.

As we walked back inside the main house, a couple of guys came running up on us in a confrontational manner. They had seen us standing next to their car, which was just stolen, and thought we were working with whoever stole their car. We tried to play dumb, but they were getting aggressive. A shoving match ensued, but thankfully no punches were thrown. Just before it got out of hand, the guy who just sold us ecstasy stepped in between us and vouched for us being over there buying, having nothing to do with that situation. Apparently, this guy had some street credibility with them, so they backed off.

The interesting thing about this was, as we went back inside the rave to find our partners, who also did a deal at the same time. It was ironic how victim of the car theft handled this situation. Since he was an illegal rave party with lots of drugs, he could not immediately call the police. I am sure they reported it stolen later, because one of them mentioned doing that. It just shows you never know what you will come across or see in these raves.

As I said, a rougher looking crowd than a normal rave was starting to flow in, so we decided to exit the area while we had two successful undercover buys completed. We had written down the license plate number of the dealer's vehicle. We ran it in the DMV's database, but it came back registered to an older male in his 60's. We did a skip trace on that address, and it had four adult males and one adult female living there. The driver's license, state identification card, or mugshot photographs of each person were retrieved. Some had criminal histories with a mug shot, and others had only a driver's license. Out of the four males that we reviewed their pictures, one was the guy from which we purchased drugs. Warrants were issued for his arrest, but he was not arrested until the end of the operation and the large drug roundup many months later.

The next evening, we went to another rave nearby. This rave was similar to the first but had twice the number of people in attendance. It was still a rough-looking crowd. We quickly made a buy of cocaine in the barn area where they held the rave. Almost immediately after the transaction, a fight broke out, and thankfully we managed to avoid it. We quickly went to our vehicle before things got out of hand. As we pulled out of the field, the SUV we all rode in drove a little sluggish in the muddy field. When I stopped to see what the problem was, I noticed we had two flat tires. We were not sure if the tires were slashed, or someone let the air out of them because it was very dark. Since it was more than one tire, this was not the result of mere chance. We drove out of the area and to the roadway, where we called our surveillance team to bring by two large cans of Fix-a-Flat to help us get enough air to get out of the area, hopefully.

About twenty minutes later, they brought us the Fix-a-Flat, which contains a gel to clog the holes in a tire. We filled both tires and got the vehicle drivable. We managed to get to a safe location and parked the vehicle. We jacked it up, took off both tires, and took them to a local garage/tire repair shop. Thankfully, the owner came outside after hours and helped us out since he was a strong supporter of the local sheriff's office.

Neither one of these buys were anything substantial, but the events around them were quite memorable, from the stolen car to having two flat tires. You truly never know what you will encounter working undercover, but you must always be ready to quickly adapt and overcome any obstacles.

*(**BELOW**) These is an image of my fellow undercover narcs (Lyle, Charlie, & Neysa) and I before going to two separate raves in a neighboring county while working undercover.*

(BELOW) These is and image of one of my UC partners (Neysa) and I at a rave on a different night.

Trade You A TV For Drugs

During this deal, Lyle and I were introduced to a target by a new Confidential Informant (CI). We were told that this guy was a multi-ounce level methamphetamine and cocaine dealer in an older section of town. His name was John, but for the sake of this story, I will refer to him by his nickname, "JJ." JJ was your typical meth dealer. He was a white male in his early twenties, with nothing more than a high school education, a history of drug abuse in his past, never married, had a child out of wedlock, and lived with his baby's momma in a trailer.

On the day of the introduction, all three of us, my UC partner, the CI, and myself, drove to JJ's residence. When we arrived, JJ had a few guys over there, carrying out a large projector-style flat-screen television. This was one of the old large ones that required at least two people to carry and took up a lot of space. JJ was distracted by this, and pissed off because the night before, his trailer house was struck by lightning and it destroyed his television and other electronics. Knowing that we barely had enough money to buy an ounce of meth from him, I told him that I could maybe find a new TV for him. This got us talking about what I wanted in return, and led straight into the negotiations on drug prices. He wanted $1,500 for an ounce of crystal methamphetamine. This was a high price, to be honest, so I asked him about the quality. He did not respond and walked over to a small desktop safe that sat on his kitchen counter at the time. He opened it up, pulled out an eight-ball (one-eighth of an ounce) size bag of crystal meth, and threw it to me across the room. I looked at it, and the quality seemed ok, but it was not crystal clear and had a slight yellow tint, which normally indicated a less pure product. The shards were also small and not large chunks, which meant it was likely stepped on and cut up at least one time or more. I commented to him about this, and he admitted this batch was not the quality he normally gets and that he was going to be "re-upping" or getting a new supply that day. This was music to my ears because now we knew a timetable of when he would have his source of supply get him more drugs. Instead of having to run surveillance for prolonged periods and never see who they had as a supplier, we now had a more specific window of time. We also knew that 'today' could mean in the middle of the night or even tomorrow, but the fact was he needed to re-up, and it would be sooner than later.

In order to ensure his re-supply happened quicker, I went back to the conversation about the television and asked if he was interested in a partial trade of cash and the TV for an ounce of crystal meth. I emphasized a higher grade and quality than the stuff he just showed me, as I told him my buyers would not take this "shit." I also let him know that this was a small sample or test buy, to see the quality of his product, and if it worked out, I needed much more than this in the near future. Putting the vision of dollar signs in his head, I played on his greed for money. This also caused partial blindness of sorts and made him an easier target for an experienced group of undercovers to bust. While this took place, I remembered we had a similar-sized TV; even newer than the one he had and maybe slightly larger, in our evidence room. This TV was seized in an illegal gambling operation and had just been adjudicated in court.

Part of the plea agreement involved signing over all the property seized in the case to the sheriff's office. Normally, this TV would be sold in a public auction, but nothing prevented me from using it to further a drug investigation first. Also, the Property & Evidence (P&E) Custodian at the sheriff's office needed that TV out of her P&E room, because it was too large and took up valuable limited space. Since it was unusually large, they kept it in the hallway, and it was a nuisance trying to squeeze by it each time they walked down the hallway. If we did not get rid of the TV, they would be forced to pay a monthly fee and rent storage space to hold this item until it was sold at a public auction. Lots of money each year is spent storing evidence, especially older evidence that was already used to get a conviction. However, it must be maintained for the period of time while the appeals process is valid. This can be five years or up to life, with a piece of evidence related to a murder conviction, per state law. As you can see, maintaining and storing evidence can be costly and takes up more and more real estate each year. Removing any items is a welcome sight to the P&E supervisor.

Eventually, we agreed on a price of $400 cash and the big-screen television, for an ounce of higher quality crystal meth. The deal was set to take place the next day, and we left the area. I normally would not have left the eight-ball of meth like that, but it had to be done to get him to order up a higher grade and larger quantity for our next deal. This also helped our probable cause and the likelihood of proving there were drugs inside the target location.

We immediately drove to the P&E room and spoke with the supervisor about getting the television out the next day for the deal. This was a great opportunity to bring in two more undercovers to help carry this large television. When I saw it, I was pleasantly surprised, because it was much larger than the TV he had before, and I knew he would be happy.

The next day, we prepared our buy money, got two other narcs that normally did not work undercover to volunteer to help carry the television inside the target location, and got wired up. Since the CI did the introduction, and I was now in direct contact with JJ, we decided to cut the CI out of the loop without telling the target. The less the CI knew, the better. It was to protect the CI and create a stronger case involving only undercover officers. This worked perfectly because, during the deal, JJ never asked where the CI was ever again.

The day before, after our initial meeting, we continued running surveillance on JJ's residence to identify his dealer. Nobody showed up that evening, but my surveillance team called about 8:00 am the next day, and let me know that they believe the source of supply showed up.

They recorded video of this guy carrying a small bag into JJ's residence and coming back out empty-handed less than five minutes later, which is an action consistent with a drug deal. Part of the surveillance team followed the source of supply, and the others stayed behind to watch JJ's house. The surveillance team discovered that the driver of the vehicle matched the picture and physical appearance of the registered owner's prior mug shots. This guy had two prior strikes for Distribution and Trafficking Cocaine and Methamphetamines. He had already served more than ten years in prison and was not new to the game. Our team got him identified, then pulled off and went back to JJ's to help with our deal. We took it one step at a time, but the source of supply was ultimately the bigger and better target in this situation.

Meanwhile, we went to the P&E room and loaded the undercover pickup truck with the big-screen television. I signed it out as part of an investigation and left details on the chain of custody of the TV's value. About 9:30 am, I placed another call to JJ to confirm he was ready. JJ said he just re-upped and was ready whenever we were. This just corroborated that it was his dealer that our surveillance team spotted. We set it up and immediately drove over to his house.

Once inside, I introduced my other two new undercover partners to JJ. We made conversation and then took him outside to see the TV. He was very happy to see how big it was and told us how he would be able to watch all the games on it with his boys. JJ also boasted and commented on how he would win lots of money on the games, all while sitting in his living room watching them on his new big screen. We chuckled, but saw the inner irony, considering the gambling operation used this TV to watch and bet on games; but now it was being used to take down a drug dealer that was going to watch sports games on it and gamble with others involved in the drug game. If TV's could talk, I bet this one could tell some stories.

We carried the TV inside his residence and helped him hook it up. He was happy, and his girlfriend and their son got even more excited when the first picture on the screen was a cartoon. We handed JJ the $400, and he went to the same safe, which sat open on the kitchen table, and retrieved a one-ounce bag of crystal meth. Sitting next to the safe was a Glock pistol. This batch was clearly different from the last one and looked like clear shards of ice. This was normally indicative of some high-grade crystal methamphetamine. After the deal, I acted like my helpers needed to be somewhere, and we left soon after.

We went back and got a search warrant for this dealer's residence, and arrest warrants for distribution. Normally, in long term operations, we did not like to bust someone so quickly, because it may jeopardize the UC or operation. This time, we were in a catch-22 because of the small child that we knew was crawling around the house, where drugs and guns were openly sitting out on the kitchen table, and God only knows what other areas. Once we got a search warrant, there was a period of up to ten days by which it had to be served, or else it was considered null and void. We did not want to do it immediately, because it would have burned us and the CI, so we waited a few days and ran more surveillance on the suspect. We decided to put a GPS tracker on JJ's supplier's vehicle, via court order, to track all of his movements. We wanted to identify his supplier's drug source, and to know when he was going to re-supply JJ again. We set up what they call a "fence" around the area, within a mile of JJ's residence, using the computer program for the GPS tracker. This alerted us anytime his vehicle moved inside that area and gave us his exact location in real-time. Within three days, he was already at JJ's, re-supplying him. We got the alert, and it was confirmed through our surveillance team that the source of supply walked in with a bag and came out of JJ's residence three to five minutes later without the bag. This was consistent with the last transaction.

We knew that JJ now had more drugs, and we had not dealt with him in three days, so our deal was not fresh on his mind. Not to mention, he had people coming and going from his residence a lot over those three days, and likely did dozens of deals each day. This was the perfect time to execute the search warrant on JJ's residence since he would not immediately suspect it was us or the CI who snitched on him.

Our high-risk narcotics entry team hit the residence and discovered four one-ounce packages of crystal meth, $5,500, three pistols, 1 AK-47 rifle, and other paraphernalia to use, make, or sell meth (i.e. scales, bags, cutting agents, pipes, etc.). We called in the Department of Social Services because the girlfriend and child lived there and were present during the buys and search. Under the

Drug Endangered Child Program, the child was immediately taken to the hospital for testing. The child tested positive for both methamphetamine and cocaine in his system. Albeit, they were trace amounts of the drugs, likely because of crawling in the residue and putting hands in the mouth or rubbing eyes, but it was still a positive test. Therefore, Child Endangerment charges were added to Felon in Possession of a Firearm, Trafficking Methamphetamine, Possession with Intent to Distribute Cocaine, and several other charges. Due to the weight of drugs found, we seized the cash and took back our television. We made it look like we were seizing anything of value in the house that he could not prove were not proceeds of drug trafficking, which we knew the TV was, so he was not suspicious of us taking it. We also seized a good quantity of gold chains found inside the residence, many of which were probably stolen and traded for drugs. The mother was also charged with Child Endangerment and Possession of Drugs.

Case Conclusion: Subsequently, JJ pled guilty and took all the drug charges in return for us, dismissing the drug charges on his girlfriend. It was a win-win for us, because we got another dealer off the street, hopefully saved a child from a lifetime of abuse, and cleaned up an area.

We continued the investigation into JJ's source of supply and eventually got him after extensive surveillance, phone toll records, and executing a search warrant on his residence. He was in possession of over a pound of meth and more than $20,000, as well as a money counting machine when we busted him. The Drug Enforcement Administration (DEA) got involved and took over the case. It ended up turning into a wiretap investigation that spanned across multiple states and ties into Mexico. Never underestimate where a case will take you if you follow the money and drugs. Many people would have just stopped at JJ, but that would be a rookie narc mistake. Always take the case to the next level until you hit a dead-end, and do not be afraid to think outside the box as an undercover (i.e. trading a piece of evidence for drugs like this TV that cost us nothing then seizing it back later).

Not that I need a disclaimer to this fact, but let me start by saying that I am no rapper, and do not even claim to be able to sing at all. With that said, this case goes to show you, if an undercover is willing to step outside his/her comfort zone, swallow their pride, while doing whatever is necessary within the law and then any deal can be made and great work can happen. You will also see how lowering your inhibitions can lead to a little extra fun during undercover operations.

For these undercover deals, I worked to infiltrate a group of gangster wannabes that were terrorizing a certain side of town. They were known for selling weed to the young crowd (teenagers of middle and high school age), and auto break-ins. We had many complaints in this area from parents and homeowners about this group, and the Sheriff wanted something done quickly. It did not take long to identify the key players, which meant this group was not very good at either of their chosen paths to make money.

For this undercover situation, I visited hangouts and developed contacts with the younger crowd so that unwitting parties could introduce me to a guy that we thought was their unofficial leader. Just like with anything, if you cut off the head, the body dies with it. This was the approach we took for this investigation. We chose to use a young guy named Bobby as the primary unwitting informant to get an introduction. We chose Bobby because he was very outgoing, and appeared friendly with everyone; at least that is what one of our sources of information told us. Being an unwitting informant means Bobby had no clue we were police, and we were using him to get to someone much more important to us. He was also never criminally charged with anything in this matter. Bobby was merely a pawn we used to get to the bigger target.

On this particular day, I went to pick up Bobby, and we drove out to the area where the target (referred to here as Tyler) hung out. When we arrived, I could see that this was clearly a young crowd of people, range age from fourteen to twenty-three. They were drinking, smoking weed, playing music, and some of them were skateboarding. This hang out was behind an old, abandoned building that seemed *'out of sight and out of mind'* from anyone passing by the area. At this gathering, they were doing their own backyard brawls, which they recorded on their cell phones. The main fight was pre-arranged, but secondary fights occurred as individuals called each other out. Surprisingly, they had rules and kept it somewhat civil. It was funny to watch since some of them could not fight very well. One of my secondary objectives was not to get on any of the cell phone recordings. For this reason, I tried to stand off to the side and away from the circle of people around the fight. That was where I was able to spot Tyler with his buddies, sitting off to the side, listening to rap music, and dancing.

Bobby introduced me to Tyler, and we hit it off pretty quickly. He kept commenting on how I was a big guy, meaning muscular, and he wanted to see me fight next. I told him that I do not fight for fun, so if someone fucked with me, they would get shot. I was harsh like that for several reasons. First off, I did not need to be fighting anyone, because no matter how much pressure they put on me to fight, it was not something I would have needed to do as an undercover. Second, I wanted to intimidate them and let them know I was crazy since I was the lone undercover on this deal. Third, I wanted them to assume I was armed, by saying I would shoot someone. Usually, guys of this type will not mess with a guy they think is armed and crazy enough to use it.

As a new face, I knew the mob mindset could backfire on me, and I might get jumped or robbed if I did not put a certain image out there. Back yard brawls give crowds a mob mentality, so I needed to be extra cautious if things went south in a hurry. This only added to the many other dangerous factors of working undercover and came with the territory.

I hung out for a little while and spoke to Tyler about anything from fighting to drugs. When drugs came up, I let him know I used to move some weight in marijuana (i.e. 10 pounds a week), but my supplier got busted, and I would not mess with him anymore. We talked about snitches, and I made him feel comfortable in assuming I was not police or a snitch. This made Tyler more prone to talk with me about dealing drugs. Before the end of the meeting, I exchanged cellphone numbers with Tyler, and I left the area.

I called Tyler the next day, but before I did, I made sure I looked up a few of the newest rap artists and songs that were up and coming on the charts. I used that as part of my small talk in our conversations. We agreed to meet up the next day for Tyler to give me a sample of the weed that he sold. We set up the deal for the next day, and it went down quickly. I made one short phone call, drove up to his house, he came out to my car, and handed me the drugs. I handed him the money and drove away. It took under two minutes for the actual transaction. This initial deal, with him walking away without an arrest, was important to gain his trust. He merely gave me a 'dime bag of weed.' A dime bag is $10 worth, just enough to roll a joint and sample his product, so it was not a big deal. However, as I have said before, it does not matter the weight when you sell drugs. A distribution is a felony, no matter what type of drug or the quantity.

I called Tyler back that night to brag about the quality of his weed. I told him I was interested in buying more weight from him but that I wanted to be careful not to move too fast because I really did not know him well yet. I held off making a big purchase right up front, so he would not suspect me of being a cop. I told him I wanted three ounces of the same quality weed as last time. This time he said that he was down on his supply, but made me an offer. He asked me to come pick him up and take him to 'his guy' to make the buy. I could not believe what he was offering, but apparently, he was desperate, and his car was broken down. We arranged for me to pick him up the next day and do the deal.

Tyler lived right on the county line, and we had no clue where his supplier lived, either in our county or a neighboring county. If it was in the other county, I had no jurisdiction, and making the deal would be illegal. To err on the side of caution, we contacted the neighboring sheriff's office vice and narcotics unit to assist. We had about eight surveillance vehicles to follow me if we had to drive a little distance. This was more than enough, considering I only had one to three on a normal undercover deal, and four if I was lucky. Any undercover deal where you have to "trip," meaning travel with the target, increases the danger factor. It is multiplied even more when you do not know where you are going. If the target is driving the undercover around, that increases the danger factor further. Thankfully, in this deal, I drove my undercover car so that I could control some aspects of the deal.

Before I went out to pick up the target, both narc units met up, and we discussed the game plan. We got along well with this other county narcotics unit and were cutting up as we prepared everything. Recently, a comedy cop movie, *Super Troopers*, had been released. There was one scene in the movie where two cops bet each other that one could not say 'meow' ten times during a traffic stop. The officer in charge of the stop easily and hilariously won the bet.

As my narc colleagues helped get my undercover car wired with a listening device, one of the guys in the unit was laughing about a video he had seen. It was a video of someone making fun of rapper Snoop Dog, and how he spoke saying *for shizzle, or for shizzle my nizzle* repeatedly. *For shizzle my nizzle'* was Snoop's catchphrase, meaning *for sure, my friend.* One of the narcs, in good fun, bet I could not say "for shizzle" thirty times during my undercover deal that day. Being competitive, I asked, "What we were betting on?" We agreed on lunch. I took them up on the bet and decided to have fun with it. My thought process was, *Hell. Nobody will ever know about it, so why not?*

When I picked up Tyler, he jumped in the car with me. The goal was to make sure he was not looking behind us and that he stayed relaxed. Before him getting in the car, I had preset his passenger-side mirror to make sure it did not allow him to see right behind him without an adjustment, just in case he decided to take a glance. I did not want him to spot my surveillance team, following us. I noticed that he had a small backpack with him.

I greeted him with, "What's up, my nizzle?"

One time down and twenty-nine to go.

He shook my hand and did not blink an eye with what I said. It was at that moment that I knew this bet was going to be a little less nerve-racking for me to execute, and maybe one I could even win; but this was certainly not going to be as easy as saying the word 'meow,' which rhymed with the word 'now' among several other common words. On the drive, we listened to music and only spoke when he asked me if I wanted to hear something.

I said, "Hell, yes!"

He reached into his backpack and pulled out a CD of music that he made, and said, "This is my fresh new mix."

Apparently, Tyler was an aspiring DJ and rap artist. He put in the CD and began to rap for me. He was not too bad, so I got down to the beat as I drove. After the song was over, I told him that this could be on the radio one day, and I asked for a copy of his mix or the CD. I was playing up his ego a little bit. Little did I know, but he had a burned copy of that song in his backpack. I offered to pay him, and he said, "No," and that it was on him, but I could buy his next one at the stores. He was optimistically implying he would be famous one day, with his music sold in the stores or online.

His supplier's location was about twenty minutes away out in the country which was into the neighboring jurisdiction. So it was a good thing that I deconflicted or let my counterparts from the neighboring county know ahead of time, as previously discussed. When we arrived at the target location, he told me to wait in the car because he was going to run inside and meet with his guy. I truly did not expect to get out of the car on the first time he was bringing me to his supplier's residence to re-up. It was already odd that he asked me to drive him, and showed me his suppliers' residence, so I just took what I could get at that point. After about ten minutes, Tyler came back out with his backpack full. He sat down in my vehicle and pulled out one of the three large one-gallon sized Zip-lock bags containing a pound of marijuana each. He handed me the bag and said, "I got him down to $3,000." I was taken aback by this because he had three pounds, and I plainly told him I wanted three ounces. When I told him I only wanted three ounces, he looked deflated and shocked.

He said, "What?"

I said, "Yes. I told you that on the phone, and you confirmed."

Tyler said he thought I said pounds, and that he would not have needed to leave his house for this deal because he had three ounces at home. I only had enough money for three ounces, so there was no way to buy it all, and he was not about to front me that much on our first big deal after only buying a small sample. I gave him the money for three ounces, and he ran back inside his supplier's house. I wish I could have heard that conversation and how he explained it.

While waiting in the car, I decided to have some fun talking to my fellow narcs over the body wire.

I made sure I said "For shizzle" thirty-plus times.

They messaged my phone that it did not count unless I said it in the presence of the target and that I was only up to twelve. I knew I needed eighteen more for the win. After about ten more minutes, Tyler came out with the same backpack, looking much lighter, and got in the car. He handed me the three ounces and we pulled out of the driveway to head back to his place. For his troubles, I offered to grab him lunch at Burger King. He took me up on it, and we hit up the drive-thru. While eating and driving, he put back in his mix CD of beats he created. He was rapping, and we were cutting up. I said "For shizzle" as much as possible, but his rapping dominated the small cabin space in the car. I knew I needed at least a dozen or more "for shizzles" to win, but was not sure I would get them in before we finished. After he rapped, he pointed at me mid-beat to take over. I was in the moment, despite not being a rapper, so I went for it. To this day, I do not remember precisely what I rapped about, but it seemed like I rapped for five minutes. However, it was only a couple of minutes. I do remember that I said "for shizzle" nineteen more times, though, which put me over the thirty. I know this because we replayed the recording with members of my unit afterward to get an accurate count. We were not listening to it for sound quality, or to review the details of the undercover deal, but merely for the purpose of counting "for shizzles." It was hilarious. I still cannot believe I did that, but it was all in good fun. I won the bet hands-down, and I got a free lunch out of the deal.

When we arrived back at Tyler's house, I dropped him off and let him know I would be in touch. I had already made two buys on the guy, and to be honest, he was not a big target, so I disappeared and never contacted him again. About a year later, he was arrested as part of the much larger round-up involving over one hundred different drug dealers. He did not plead guilty like most other people and decided he wanted to go to trial since he was classified as an adult, but would be sentenced as a first time/youthful offender. This meant he would get leniency during sentencing if convicted. His attorney gave him good advice, and he had little to lose going to trial, versus taking a plea, because either way, he was not likely to go to prison.

During trial prep with the solicitor, we went over the details of the deal. Everything was fine and professional until we listened to the audio recording of my undercover deal. YES!!! The "For Shizzle Challenge" was going to be played in open court during a trial in front of the jury, judge, prosecutor, defense attorney, and many of my peers. I was so embarrassed, but there was literally nothing I could do to stop it. We all got a good laugh out of it while preparing for the trial, so I prayed that the jury would too.

The day of the trial came, and I arrived decked out in a very nice suit and as clean-cut and professional as I could look, considering I was working undercover. The time came for the audio recording to be played while I was on the stand testifying. I had just gotten sworn in as an expert witness. They had to play up my professionalism and extensive prior experiences working undercover, as well as other expert witness testimony I had provided in the recently. So the jury was looking at me as a complete professional. At least they did until the recording began. I managed to contain my laughter and held it together on the stand, but I could see that several jurors wanted to laugh, but they too held it in. When a courtroom is in session, the atmosphere is similar to that of a funeral. It is not the place to laugh or joke around. After my testimony and the judge went into recess, several people approached me in the hallway to talk about the recording. It just so happened that there were about a half a dozen law students in the courtroom that day, who were getting in their mandatory hours of watching trials. They thought it was funny as Hell, and we had a good time laughing about it in the hallway outside the courtroom.

Later, the jury came back with a guilty verdict on the two counts of Distribution of Marijuana. During sentencing, the judge sentenced him under the first-time offender and youthful-offenders act and sent him off to a shock boot camp to scare him straight. I honestly did not care what he got and felt the sentence was fair. After sentencing, the court adjourned. We are not allowed to approach a juror after the trial, but if they approach us, we can speak to them. Two of the jurors approached me afterward. One of them greeted me with a "for shizzle" and a handshake while laughing. Then we started to talk about the rap I did. It was at that time that I told them about the bet. We all thought it was a hoot. The jurors and I got a good laugh out of it, as well as many others, and they said it was the highlight of the trial.

It is important to have fun on the job, but never think what you do will not come to light for all to see someday.

Thankfully, we were able to get a conviction on the distribution charges, and it became something we can laugh about years later. If this bet had cost us the trial because a juror felt we were unprofessional and not trustworthy, it could have ended with a not guilty or hung jury. If that happened, I certainly would not be laughing about this today.

Outlaw Motorcycle Gang (OMG) Member OR Not

During this deal, I worked as a lone undercover agent to purchase a couple of ounces of crystal meth. A confidential informant who was busted on an unrelated drug charge put me in contact with this dealer. The CI called the target by phone and told him that I was cool and potentially a pound quantity dealer of methamphetamine. This meant that they had a chance to pick up a new customer who might purchase thousands of dollars' worth of crystal methamphetamine each week. I later called the target dealer using the phone number that the CI gave me. I talked to him about getting a sample buy of crystal methamphetamine. I told him that I did not want to talk anymore about it over the phone until we got to know each other. This was typically a smart move to do when working undercover; I wanted to appear to be very cautious. Most drug dealers are cautious and hypervigilant, and when they think you are just as cautious, if not more, then they feel more comfortable dealing with you.

We arranged to meet across town. I was alone in my undercover truck and I had the truck wired up. My surveillance team followed me out to the buy location. I called the target from a nearby payphone. He questioned why I did not call him from the same number, and I explained that I was at a payphone close by to the meeting location, and that I liked to mix it up all the time to make sure nobody was tracking me. This was just another attempt to take his mind further away from thinking I was an undercover police officer. He said "they" had to make a quick stop, and would be on their way to me.

Now, I knew that he was likely coming with at least one other person since he said, "they." I relayed this information to my surveillance teams. About thirty to forty-five minutes went by, and I did not hear anything from the suspect(s). We had a surveillance team covering all entry points into the parking lot, but nobody spotted our potential targets. I did not want to sit at the meeting location for too long, in case this was a setup for a robbery. The dealer could have told me to meet at a certain location of their choice to intentionally be kept waiting. While sitting there in my truck, they could rob me or pay someone else to do the deed. It is common for dealers to rob one another because if it is over drugs, they cannot call the police for help. This was the survival of the fittest or meanest on the streets.

Being cautious, I drove out of the parking lot and cruised the area so as not to be sitting in the same spot the whole time. If he had counter-surveillance, I wanted to keep them guessing as much as they kept me in the dark with their whereabouts. After about another hour, when I was ready to give up and call the deal, I received a phone call from the suspect(s). I told them I was a little upset and felt like they were jerking me around. They assured me that they were close by, and had the drugs with them. I maneuvered my vehicle in the parking lot to be in the best position for my team to cover me and get to me the quickest if things went bad. The suspects finally showed up a short while after their call. Now, we had pulled our vehicles to the top of the parking lot side by side, where the driver's side windows were facing one another. Located inside of his newer model Acura Legend was another unknown male subject in the passenger seat. There were two of them, and I was alone.

They told me that they were sorry it took them so long, but they were working another deal that did not go well. They picked up a grocery bag, and showed me a kilo-sized block of marijuana; they said that the other guy was supposed to buy it, but he never showed up. They asked me if I wanted any weed. I told them I just brought enough money for the two ounces of crystal methamphetamine but would be interested in a future deal. This deal was arranged to be a buy-bust operation, where they would be immediately arrested after the deal went down. The reason for the buy-bust option was because we could not identify these suspects before the deal. We knew very little about them, which drastically increased the danger factor. If the police make an undercover dope deal with you, they already know who you are most of the time, especially if they are spending thousands of dollars.

The government is not going to let that much money go for an unidentified suspect. But they do not mind letting it walk, if the suspect is a mid to upper-level dealer, they are positively identified, and it could lead to other cases. After the transaction went down for the two ounces, I gave both the verbal and visual 'takedown' signal to my team. As they pulled in to block our vehicles from fleeing the scene (eliminating a chase), the suspect vehicle started to pull off. The first surveillance vehicle came in and touched his front bumper to the suspect vehicle's front bumper, with the target vehicle and the rear vehicle doing the same. The suspects had no way out and by the time they figured out what was going on, our takedown team had already opened their doors and extracted them from the vehicle. Another team also did the same thing to me while I was sitting inside of my undercover vehicle. The UC should always be arrested, just in case counter-surveillance teams for the dealers were watching us. This temporarily protected me, the undercover, from being discovered or burned. Of course, my identity would be revealed in court documents down the road, but we were worried about the initial impact and rumor mill to protect the UC and ongoing operations.

They handcuffed each of us and put all three of us in different patrol cars. The guys in my Narc unit decided to have a little fun with the suspects at my expense. They pointed at me and asked the suspects if they knew who they were dealing with. They were talkative and stated that they had just met me for the first time. They denied giving me the meth that was found in my vehicle when the arrest team came in. The guys told the suspects that I was a member of a national Outlaw Motorcycle Gang (OMG) who was on the run from the law for several murders. They told the suspects that they had been following me and tracking me through multiple states. It just so happened they decided it was safe to do the arrest on me when they saw me meeting and conducting what looked like a dope deal. These guys both looked over at me while I was sitting in the back of a patrol car. I head-butted the window of the patrol car and started yelling obscenities at them. Like two scared little boys, they both looked away without making any further eye contact. From that point on, they were scared to even look at me. The guys in the unit told the suspects that they were lucky that I did not rob them or kill both of them. They laid the story down thick and told them that I was notorious for robbing and killing drug dealers across multiple states. When they told these dealers all this stuff, I had no idea what they were saying until they told me later. To add fuel to the fire, before they put me in the back of the patrol car, they searched me while I was face down on the pavement in handcuffs. When they found the three guns that I was carrying, they made sure to call it out so the suspects could hear them when they said, "I got a gun. I got another gun and another gun."

Now, these guys thought I was a gun-toting outlaw, and the police busting them was a blessing in disguise and even may have prevented their deaths. This thought though was short-lived. After their arrests, they both got attorneys and filed for discovery to receive all paperwork in the case. The paperwork divulged the fact that I was an undercover narcotics investigator, which is something we are forced to reveal since every suspect has a constitutional right to *face their accuser.*

Case Conclusion: Both suspects pled guilty to Possession with Intent to Distribute Marijuana, the only drug found in their vehicles at the time of arrest (sure conviction). In exchange for the guilty plea, the Distribution of Methamphetamine and

Distribution of Methamphetamine within ½ mile of a school, as well as the Possession with Intent to Distribute Marijuana charge within ½ mile of a school were all dismissed. One of the suspects received an eight-year prison sentence because he had a prior non-drug felony conviction on his record. The suspect without any prior felony convictions was given a sentence of three years in prison. In addition to the prison sentence, I hope they both learned a valuable lesson about who they deal with and how to be more cautious or better yet do not deal drugs at all.

Job Application Ruse to Identify Suspect

During my first purchase of cocaine from a new target, I purchased an 'eight ball' or one-eighth of an ounce. I made this purchase without having the suspect fully identified, which is not the best practice. The guy was so nervous during the first buy that we opted not to pull him over to identify him as we had originally planned. Sometimes you have to change plans when you feel it may jeopardize the undercover operations. When we got a subpoena for his cell phone subscriber information, it was registered in the name of a white female, and he was a black male, so we thought it was most likely not one of his immediate family members. I had to develop an idea of how to identify this suspect without burning our cover story and blowing the deal. For this very reason, I always carried around blank job applications in my vehicle. I had these available if someone told me they were looking for a job, so I could have them fill it out to get a positive identification on them. I had this paperwork sitting in my UC truck but had never used it up until this point.

On the day of the deal, I drove out to meet with the suspect in the parking lot of one of the local Red Lobster Seafood restaurants. He pulled into the parking lot right on time. We both got out of our vehicles and started talking while standing outside of my truck, near the back of the truck bed. I was dressed like a painter and posed as working for a painting company, making pretty decent money. The small-time dealer told me that he needed to find a real job to be able to have legitimate income, so he could buy a newer car and get his probation officer off his back.

It is a common problem for drug dealers to have plenty of cash, but no means by which to purchase high end or costly items like vehicles or houses. You cannot just walk in and pay cash for these items and think it will go unnoticed, because the IRS has reporting requirements for any transaction over $10,000, as well as other lower threshold amounts of money. If a drug dealer wanted to purchase a $30,000 vehicle, they needed to finance it even if they had the money to pay for it up front. They would need to prove they had legitimate legal income coming in, and that they could pay back the loan. Therefore, drug dealers may have normal jobs to cover their true means of money - and to be able to purchase nice things.

Just as I suspected, the target brought up the topic of finding a job again. I told him that I could maybe talk to my' boss man' and see if he would hire him. I told him that we had a big paint job we were starting next week, and we needed more guys. Once he found out he could make $600-$800 per week, before taxes, he was very interested. I told him I had a job application in my truck. I went back into my truck and pulled out a blank job application. He started to fill it out right there on the hood of my

UC truck. He even told me that the address on his license was old, and this was his correct address on the application. He gave me his girlfriend's phone number because he sometimes stayed with her. He had no idea I was a cop, and that he just gave us more than enough information to positively identify him, to have warrants ready to arrest him at a later date.

The key to being successful with this job application ruse was to have a very short and easy-to-fill-out application, so applicants would not want to take it and bring it back later. This form was less than a half of a sheet of paper long. To make a more solid identification of the suspect, I took it a step further, getting a picture of him. Since he appeared physically fit and athletic, I told him about the guy my boss fired because he was slow, fat and lazy. I told him the other guy broke a ladder being over the maximum weight, and my boss said anyone I bring on the job site better be fit and high energy. I asked him if I could take a quick picture of him with my cellphone to show my boss that he was perfect for the job. The guy even smiled for the picture. I got a kick out of doing the extra things like this in my cases, and always tried to challenge myself to take it to the next level with each new deal.

Not only was it fun, but it also made a very solid case with soundproof and indisputable evidence from whom I was buying drugs.

(BELOW) Photo of the actual job application I had people fill out working undercover. Short and simple enough not to draw suspicion, but enough to help positively identify the target.

Case Conclusion: We arrested this suspect during a buy-bust about two weeks after this deal. He ended up working as an informant and did over twenty introductions of UC agents to drug targets. These introductions led to multiple purchases and arrest of different suspects, as well as the seizure of two nice vehicles. In return for his cooperation, I made a recommendation to the state to dismiss his charges. The prosecutors took my suggestion, and he was free to go without a criminal conviction for any drug charges, although he did three separate distributions hand-to-hand with me. This is a prime example of where it pays off to become a confidential informant, and cooperate with law enforcement. Almost everyone says I will never become a "snitch" or assist the police with any investigation. The truth is though most people have their breaking point and offer to assist the police in return for some type of lenience on their pending charges. This lures criminals into becoming informants. We have so many people wanting to cooperate with us that have to turn many people away, and we only work with a select few. Some people think they can outsmart us and play us to take out their competition, but we quickly see through these people. They will give up small dealers most of the time, but not the big guy. This is the type of informant that we do not want to use because he is untrustworthy and withholding information from us.

Informants who agree to work with the government must be fully committed, and cannot play both sides of the fence - or else it will come back to bite them. Once, I had a guy we arrested on drug charges. He decided to cooperate, and worked for us for over a month, completing six good cases for us (i.e., purchasing drugs undercover and introducing an undercover to dealers). During this active investigation, our surveillance team spotted him purchasing drugs from our target on his own time. Part of the agreement that he signed stated he would not do this, and if he did, any agreement we had was off the table. This guy did these dangerous deals and was on the verge of being done with what we needed him for until he was caught again and arrested on a new drug charge. Now he had two felony drug charges pending and a charge for interfering with an investigation, possibly times six. Of course, he was no longer reliable, and all the work we had done with him up to that point could not be used to prosecute anyone (and was a waste of many hours). I decided not to charge him with Interfering with an Investigation on the six cases, but we did get him to plead guilty to one serious drug charge in agreement to dismiss the other. This guy received ten years in prison, all because he tried to play us. This is yet another reason that I prefer to use CIs only to make introductions and then cut them out of the picture as soon as possible.

(BELOW) This is a screen shot of a video recording from the UC deal where the suspect filled out the job application, which gave up his identity

Dope Deal at the County Court House

After many years of undercover work, my undercover partner, Lyle, and I developed a knack to be able to detect dope dealers wherever we were. We could convince anyone willing to sell drugs to trust us. The courthouse steps were one of the last places someone would think of doing a dope deal. Lyle and I were at the courthouse discussing a case with the local solicitors/prosecutors. After the meeting, we went outside and observed the suspect, who I will refer to as Brad for the sake of the story.

Brad was standing around smoking, waiting on his ride to pick him up. When working undercover, we never passed up an opportunity and decided to strike up a conversation with Brad. Considering this was a courthouse, there was a high probability that we may run into law enforcement officers that we knew. For that reason, we often did training for young officers. We told them never to initiate a conversation or say hello to an undercover that they see on the street unless spoken to first. This simple rule saved me many times from being compromised over the years. Brad, looked a little rough, and appeared to be the 'doper-type.' We found out that Brad was there to complete the Pre-Trial Intervention Program (PTI).

As explained previously, PTI was a program set up for first-time offenders. They could sign up for this program and pay an entry fee of a few hundred dollars and complete some community service. After one year of no new arrests or charges being filed, the initial charge for which they signed up for PTI was dismissed. Then they could go to the courthouse and pay to have their record expunged, and their arrest will be gone. It is a great program for the person who makes a mistake and does not ever do it again. However, the problem is you may have some repeat offenders who happen to get caught for the first time enrolling in the program. They have no intention of changing their ways, but they get the charges dismissed after completing the program and they continue with their same lifestyle as before.

Brad was reporting for his weekly meeting, and we just so happened to run into him. We told him that we were there to talk to our public defender and the prosecutor about a plea for a gun charge, a charge they hit both of us with (allegedly) after we shot at some guys with whom we got into a fight. We claimed it was self-defense, but that we possessed the firearms illegally. Like I have always said, my partner Lyle and I were on the same page with everything, and we knew each other so well that we did not even have to set up this story beforehand. We both had the gift of gab, and once either one of us got started, the story just flowed like it was the truth being recollected from memory. This ability made us more convincing and great partners.

During the conversation, we eventually got on the topic of 'getting high.' Brad offered us his services in this area. We arranged to have him sell us some cocaine and marijuana. About a week later, we met him in the back of the courthouse parking lot when he was there for another meeting. We were allegedly going to be there for another meeting with the prosecutor and public defender's office. Brad sold us an "8-Ball" or one-eighth of an ounce of cocaine without any hesitation. We let him walk away after the buy, and he became part of the roundup in the larger operation.

Case Conclusion: By the time we got around to arresting Brad, he had successfully completed PTI on his other unrelated charges. So, he had a clean record. Despite that fact, once he found out that we were both undercover narcotics investigators, he knew he had to take a plea deal. He pled guilty to one count of Distribution of Marijuana in exchange for an agreed-upon sentencing recommendation of probation. When he was sentenced by the Judge, the Judge was almost reluctant to give him probation. The Judge stated that he felt this individual made a mockery of his court by selling drugs on the courthouse steps while court was in session, and the only reason he was not going to prison with a maximum sentence was because of the state's recommendation. Subsequently, he received three years of probation. Never underestimate the gall of a drug dealer to even sell drugs at the courthouse.

Go with Your Gut OR Risk Being Killed

A great undercover must learn to understand the feelings they have about different scenarios and act upon their instincts. Distinguishing the difference between natural nervousness and an uneasy feeling about a situation was sometimes hard to do, but vital for safety as an undercover. If you have natural street smarts, it is a tool that will keep you safe and alive in many scenarios. I was blessed with great instincts, but I also believe I have a guardian angel that looked out for me on numerous occasions over the years. One case, I remember like it was yesterday, involved a meth target known to everyone on the south side of town as "Meth

Man." The southern end of the county was also a more rural area that had been oversaturated with meth labs.

This target was a known meth cook, with a very violent past, and history of paranoia beyond the norm even for a meth head. Meth Man was said to have shot a guy one time over supposing the guy was going to rob him, but later finding out the guy had no intentions to do such a thing. He was a loose cannon, and a guy we desperately wanted to get off the streets because of the sheer fear he put in the community and the drug world.

I first met Meth Man on an unrelated dope deal, when he showed up to purchase from the same target, at the same time as I did. That day, he showed up wearing blue jean overalls, with no t-shirt underneath, and old boots. He had long scraggly hair and beard. He was in his early forties but looked to be in his sixties, because of meth use. At the time, I looked kind of rough myself, and we talked for a minute, but never exchanged numbers.

About five months later, we had a new informant who said he could introduce me to a guy named Meth Man. We set up a small meth deal with this CI, since he could not buy any large quantities and was only a user. I went with the CI on the deal and rode in the front passenger seat. My whole goal was to get him to remember me and get his number so that I could set up a deal later without the CI. For this deal, we met at a trailer park on the southern end of the county, which was known for meth activity. Within seconds of pulling up, Meth Man came out of the trailer. He approached my passenger's side window and leaned in, looking at me before talking to the CI.

He just stared at me for a second, and then said, "Deuce, What's up, man?"

He remembered me, and even my street name.

I was pleasantly surprised and started to small talk with him. He asked where I had been, so I told him I just got out of detention in a neighboring county for a Failure to Pay Child Support. He laughed and gave me five.

My CI butted in the conversation and asked for the gram of meth. As he leaned over to hand him the money, I snatched it out of his hand and handed it to Meth Man. The opportunity to do the hand-to-hand presented itself, so I jumped on it. Meth Man handed me the dope, and I acted like I gave it to the CI, but kept it clenched in my fist. I asked, Meth Man for his phone number to get something from him in the future and he gave it to me. After the deal, we drove away to process the evidence and do paperwork.

Over the course of the next few weeks, I had a series of text messages and phone conversations with Meth Man. I planted the idea that I was expecting to come into some insurance money from an accident that I got in a while back and was interested in purchasing a bunch of meth to flip for even more money. Meth Man saw dollar signs, and we eventually negotiated a one-pound crystal meth deal, which was contingent upon me getting my settlement check.

We knew how dangerous and unpredictable this guy was, so we waited until later the next week when we had all our manpower in the narc unit to assist with a buy-bust. I contacted Meth Man the night before to let him know I had the money. We negotiated $12,000 for one pound of crystal meth. We agreed to meet the next evening at a preset location.

The next day came around, and I contacted Meth Man.

So far, he had answered every call, and it seemed to be going as planned. We arranged for a meeting at a gas station off the main exit of the interstate nearby his last known address. This guy apparently moved all over the place. So we never really pinpointed exactly where he was living at the time, so we could not run surveillance on him. I got wired up, and my surveillance team went out about an hour before the buy to get in place. We planned on doing a buy-bust after I confirmed or saw the drugs. I set up a flash roll to look like $12,000, but it was actually only about $4,000 with a majority of one-dollar bills and several one-hundred-dollar bills on the outside of each roll. We had no intention of letting him count the money before seeing the dope. My intentions were to give the arrest signal immediately after seeing the dope and I was fine with that plan.

I drove out to the meeting location, and the time for us to meet came and went. I texted him and there was no reply. I gave it another fifteen minutes and called, but still there was no answer. This was not exactly unusual with drug dealers but was inconsistent with him and *all* activity prior to this point. After about four calls, he finally answered, but it was over an hour after the scheduled deal already. I asked him if he was good, and he said *yes* he was on his way. We hung up the phone, and I waited.

Another fifteen minutes went by, and I called again, but no answer. I texted him, and he replied, 'on the way.' I asked him what he was driving in since I had not met him in a car before, and he said a 'white Cadi.' I relayed this over the wire to my surveillance team.

Another thirty minutes went by and nothing. At this point, I had a bad feeling about this guy. I got to thinking about how I was just with a CI, and we had purchased one gram, and now I am purchasing one pound from the same guy. Could he be setting me up to rob me? I had never seen this guy with a pound but heard he had manufactured this much in the past. I decided to call him one last time. He did not answer, so I left a voice message. I told him I was not feeling good about this, and pulling out of the deal. I told my team I was pulling the plug on the deal, and they were not really that happy. As I told this to my team, my phone rang, and it was Meth Man. He apologized, and his tone was nice like he was trying to convince me to stay now. He said he was right down the road and told me where. I put it on speakerphone. My surveillance team listened to my body wire and relayed updates to the others on the team. I told him, ok, but I let him know I was not happy with him jerking me around. As I sat there waiting on him, I started to have the hair on the back of my neck stand up and got a bad stomachache. This was like no other feeling I have had before, and I also got dizzy. One-minute passed; five minutes passed, and then ten minutes passed, but Meth Man was not there yet. I thought back to undercover school, and the lesson I learned was never to get caught up in the "lust for the bust." At that moment, I decided to pull out and call the deal. As I told my team that I was pulling out in my vehicle, one of the surveillance units spotted a white Cadillac with a white male driving by himself approaching the meeting location.

Instead of stopping and waiting for Meth Man to pull in and do the deal, I decided to leave. I pulled out of the gas station as Meth Man pulled in. We drove right past each other. He looked at me; I looked at him and I pulled away. My phone started to get lit up by Meth Man, but I kept driving. I relayed to my team all my phone calls I had recorded. We decided that we had probable cause to arrest him on the previous Distribution, and enough for the Conspiracy to Distribute the one pound of crystal meth.

The team pulled up and blocked in Meth Man in his Cadillac as he was about to leave the gas station. They drew down on him and ordered him out of his car at gunpoint. They were not taking any chances with this guy, who had a history of violence and meth use. After his arrest, they located a package in the front seat area, under the center console, which was consistent with a pound or more of drugs, packaged and wrapped in duct tape. Also located under the driver's side seat was a sawed-off double-barreled shotgun, which was loaded. The Narcs could tell that Meth Man was cranked up on meth. He was talking crazy, but talking so they asked him questions. He told them that the package was not drugs, but a mini-phone book wrapped in duct tape. He told them he was going to meet a big drug dealer and rob him. He was talking about me. He said he had planned to hand me the bundle of drugs, which was actually a phone book, in exchange for $12,000. Once I noticed the weight of the phone book, and that it was not meth, he said he would shoot me in the face with the sawed-off shotgun and drive away. He made it clear that I was the target and he was robbing drug dealers who were the scum of the earth. He said it almost so convincingly, you would have thought he was a modern-day Robin Hood if you did not know any better.

After he was transported away and placed in the detention center on the Distribution of Meth and Conspiracy to Traffic Meth charges, he was given a $50,000 bond. He could not make bond and sat in jail for about one year. He filed for discovery and found out that I was actually an undercover narcotics investigator. As a result of this information, he took a plea deal and went to state prison for ten years on one count of Distribution. The Conspiracy to Traffic charge was dropped as part of the deal. About six months later, the feds adopted the gun charge (i.e., sawed-off double-barrel shotgun). He took a plea deal with the feds also. After he serves his ten years in state court, he is to report to federal prison and serve another five years.

This case could have ended tragically for me if I had not gone with my gut and pulled away at the last minute. I still remember how pissed off a few of the guys were on my surveillance team because they had been sitting out there all day waiting on this deal to go down, and I pulled out as it was finally about to go. As an undercover, you must never let anyone else tell you to do or not to do a deal. Going with gut instinct could be the very thing that keeps you alive.

The Undercover Deal that Turned into an Internal Affairs Investigation

In 2004, I decided I needed to tell my current supervisor about my application process with the Drug Enforcement Administration (DEA). It had been thirteen months since I applied with the DEA, and I was in the final phase of my hiring process. In the last phase, I had to complete my background investigation. I figured I was better off telling my supervisor, before he found out about me possibly leaving the sheriff's office from a complete stranger, calling him to conduct my background investigation. Coincidentally, I was called into our Office of Professional Standards (OPS) the following week after I told them I was seeking out other employment. For the purpose of this story, I will refer to OPS as "Internal Affairs."

When I walked into the office, the Lieutenant told me to have a seat, and he was not very friendly in his demeanor. I later learned that after twenty-two years of law enforcement and being a Chief of Police, this was not how you should approach any officer if you work Internal Affairs (IA). The best IA Investigators I have ever had the privilege to work with always took a respectful approach, tried to prove you innocent, never compromised their integrity, or took any part of the investigation personally. If they took this approach and you were still found guilty of a violation, you likely did something wrong and deserved to be punished. With that said, the punishment always seemed fair and to fit the offense. They were not out to get you or destroy your career for what could be perceived as a lapse in judgment or mistake with good intentions. How could you not have respect for that approach?

The Lt. threw down a sheet of paper in front of me, with which I was all too familiar. Although, this time, I was on the receiving end of the form that I normally read to suspects. It was my Miranda Rights waiver sheet (*i.e. You have the right to remain silent, anything you say can and will be used against you in a court of law. You have the right to an attorney...etc.*). The first words out of the Lieutenant's mouth were that this was a "criminal investigation." Now he had my attention, and I immediately asked what case this pertained to. He told me it was an undercover deal where myself, another undercover, and a Confidential Informant (CI) picked up a suspect and sent her into a house to buy some pills. I knew what case he was talking about once he mentioned the name of the suspect, whom I will refer to as Betty for the sake of this story. The problem was that I could not recall the intricate details of the case because I had done over one hundred buys over the past few months. For some reason, this made the Lt. look at me as if I was lying, but I did not care what he thought; I knew I always did what was right and necessary to stay alive under the circumstances. Most hard-nosed cops or narcs that are constantly in very dangerous situations cannot stand paper-pushing admin guys that never did anything tactical a day in their life (i.e. 'Monday-morning quarterbacking' the ones doing real police work). It is easy to scrutinize a person's decisions from the comfort of an office, but actually being there and living it was very different.

During this specific drug deal, one of my so-called friends worked undercover with me (no names mentioned, but it was not my trusted undercover partner Lyle), along with one of my long-time confidential informants. This was my best informant at the time, but one you had to watch the most. He had been an informant since 1976, and he had done over five hundred deals for the government, so he knew the system better than most cops/narcs. This guy had more experience than our whole narcotics unit combined. He was what we referred to as a professional informant in law enforcement. A professional informant is someone who does it full time for a living and has no other job but to work for the government. Informants like this are very valuable and are almost always motivated by money. They are also very rare and come with some inherent risk.

This type of CI knows that the more cases they make, the more valuable they are, and the more money they make for each drug deal or introduction of a UC. An informant at the low levels only makes about $25 to a few hundred dollars per buy. Contrary to popular belief, they are not paid thousands for every deal. Now, I am not saying that some of the federal informants do not make thousands per transaction. In the federal system, some informants work for a percentage of the total assets seized instead of an upfront payment. This was an incentive for them to work harder, and direct us to higher-level drug traffickers with many assets, which also came at a greater risk to the informant. Look at it this way; you had an informant who received ten percent of the total seized assets in a case if the investigation lasted one year and over fifteen million dollars' worth of assets (houses, cars, property, jewelry, etc.) were seized. This would land the CI an annual paycheck of 1.5 million dollars. Although this is very rare, I do know of more than one case where a DEA informant made millions of dollars working as a confidential informant for the government.

In this case, my professional informant told me that he knew of a guy, aka 'Pops,' who sold thousands of prescription drugs out of his house. The catch was that the informant could not purchase drugs from Pops directly, but had to pick up Betty, who would go over there with him. Being a *somewhat* trustworthy informant, we decided to go over to Betty's house and take her to Pops' house to purchase some illegal drugs. Intelligence revealed that the sheriff's office had received numerous complaints about Pops, but nobody wanted to mess with him because he was an older man. When I say old, I mean he was in his late seventies, making it almost pointless to some officers to mess with him because they knew the courts would not do anything to him. In my opinion, this was no excuse to just ignore him and do nothing. I wanted to rid the streets of any drugs, so I jumped on the opportunity.

Many people do not realize that the most abused drugs in America today are prescription drugs. This is such a huge problem that the DEA has devoted a whole division to controlling this problem, referred to as DEA Diversion. These DEA Diversion Investigators, not Special Agents, concentrate on the illegal diversion of legally prescribed drugs/medication. Pharmaceutical drug abuse is probably one of the only forms of drug abuse that affects every household type, regardless of socioeconomic status. The prescription drug abuse problem may draw anyone in, which was Betty's situation. Before getting involved with drugs, Betty was your average working mother of two. It all started to go downhill after Betty had a car accident several years earlier. She injured her back and neck, which required the doctor to prescribe her a mild narcotic to alleviate the pain. She took these narcotics for months, and eventually upped her dose to deal with her increased pain and medicine tolerance. She had two surgeries and was still in constant pain. She reached what the doctors referred to as maximum medical improvement, and healed as much as the doctors could help her heal, so they immediately stopped prescribing her high dosage narcotics pain meds.

They gave her a small settlement through the insurance company and washed their hands of her. She still had chronic pain and still needed something to alleviate it. She started out going to multiple doctors in neighboring counties, to get multiple prescriptions of different narcotics used to control her pain. This little technique is known on the street as "doctor shopping." She now had a daily habit of a specific number of pills that she needed every day in order to function. As one can understand, with increased tolerance to the drugs, her only recourse was to increase the dosage. This meant that her addiction was costing her quite a bit of money and would never have a resolution unless she either overdosed or got help. It is part of the never-ending downward spiral of addiction.

Eventually, doctor shopping did not produce the necessary number of pills to support her habit, so she resorted to purchasing them illegally on the streets, from different dealers, or selling their legitimate prescriptions to supplement their income. Now she was a full-blown addict who started out taking Lortabs or Hydrocodone and then she moved to a more potent time-release pain pill known as OxyContin. She started out taking the pill orally, then snorting it. Next, she took it intravenously with a needle. She was now a full-blown addict, taking only prescription drugs. The lack of availability of the large quantity of prescription drugs, along with the high cost, caused her to occasionally resort to heroin use (i.e. street drugs with no medicinal value). OxyContin is very expensive on the streets (i.e. $1 per milligram, on average). So, if you have a 10 mg pill, it costs $10, but if you have an 80mg pill, it costs $80 per pill/tablet).

Betty developed a habit of taking over 200mg of OxyContin each day. The $200 per day was outrageous, and she had to do something to get the money. This caused an addict like her to resort to theft or shoplifting, where she might sell or trade the stolen items to the dealers for drugs. Sometimes women resort to prostitution to get that quick fix, trading sex for drugs. Oftentimes, they set up drug deals and do occasional sales to finance their own addiction. One needs to know details like all the ones I provided about Betty's case, to understand why we took on cases like hers and her level of desperation or addiction.

This deal was supposed to be a quick one-deal case, where the unit would execute a search warrant on Pops' house several days later. On this day, another UC, my professional CI, and I drove out to Betty's residence. She lived on a rundown side of town, well-known for high crime and drugs. We all got out and went into her house. She was there with her two children, who appeared disheveled and not very well taken care of. She agreed to take us to one of the locations to buy some prescription pills off Pops. She described Pops as an old-time pill man, who had been selling thousands of pills to hundreds of different people over the last decade. When dealing with an elderly dealer, it is a little sensitive because he probably legally has many different prescriptions that he can carry. This prevented us from immediately arresting him for unlawful possession of a controlled substance if he was stopped by a deputy and in possession of a specific narcotic in a prescription bottle with his name on it. This was the perfect cover for an older guy and made him more of a challenge to bust. The only way to get him was with an undercover purchase, by an undercover narcotics investigator or informant, which is exactly what we did.

Betty told us she would ride with us over to Pops' house to buy some pills (specifically Oxycontin, Lortabs, and Xanax, which are all narcotics pain killers). The dilemma we had next was that she was going to leave her kids alone while she left. One of her kids was early elementary age, and the other was more than ten years old. The older one appeared to be mature enough to handle the situation, so we decided to follow through with it. I do not think Betty was worried about this at all, but we were. I am sure these children were more independent than most, since they practically raised themselves, having a drug addict as a mother. Drug addicts prioritize their desire to get high over taking care of their kids and other responsibilities. In order to make sure nothing happened to the kids while we lured their mother away, we sat a surveillance unit on the house to watch and make sure nobody came or went from the location. We were fortunate that nothing happened, and the kids were good during the deal. This is one of the many things we must do behind the scenes as a narc, who, first and foremost, are sworn law enforcement officers with a duty to serve and protect. If we had taken off and ignored the issue with the children, and heaven forbid - something happened to them; it would have been on us. We should have known better, and we had a duty to protect them, no matter how bad we wanted to make a drug bust. This is where character and integrity come into play, with a narc who works mostly behind the scenes. You must always be willing to do what is right, even though many others may put on their blinders and not bother to get the drug sale done. As you can see, we are not just worried about buying drugs during what may be perceived to an outsider as a simple pull up, buy drugs, and then leave transaction.

For this deal, we drove Betty over to Pops' house. When we were almost there, Betty told us we could not go in because Pops was crazy, and he would pull a gun on anyone new. She specifically told us he always had a sawed-off shotgun next to him, and she had seen him put it up to a guy's chest that entered his house that he did not know despite him being with a regular customer. He was paranoid about new faces and set in his ways, so he hated change. We wanted to make the deal ourselves and cut Betty out of the deal, so I did not like this, but I felt like I had no choice since we were almost there, and it sounded too dangerous to try. By this point, Betty was going to be more than an unwitting informant, being used to get to a drug target for us without her knowledge. Now she had become a distributor and one of our investigation targets for facilitating and doing the actual drug deal. We tried to cut her out of the picture, which would have resulted in her being used as an unwitting informant and not being charged criminally; but, she told us she had to do the deal or else it was a no go for her. Little did she know, she was writing her destiny with that decision. In hindsight, it is clear that she was only thinking about how she would get some drugs out of this, and she did not care.

As we pulled up to the house, we could see a group of teenagers, and guys in their late twenties, playing basketball in the backyard. The house had an eight-foot-tall chain-link fence surrounding it, with barbed wire around the top, with a rolling gate to enter the inner perimeter. This was a stereotypical drug house, fortified to keep out rival drug dealers and cops. This was not something you would see in a nice neighborhood. It also had surveillance cameras, showing the dealer everything going on around him/her, so they could have time to take appropriate actions (i.e., dispose of drugs or prepare for a fight, among other options). Two things drug dealers fear; being busted by the cops or being robbed by a rival drug dealer in a home invasion. As we pulled up, they recognized Betty, and they opened the gate and motioned for us to pull around to the back of the house. The gate closed immediately behind us, and the fence was locked with a chain and padlock. We were trapped on Pops' property, with no way out other than to ram or jump the fence in an emergency exit. Working undercover, you must always be thinking, "What will I do if...?" You need to plan for the unexpected, or else you may be caught off guard (i.e., getting robbed or killed). In this instance, I made sure the vehicle was strategically positioned facing the gate at the weakest part of the fence, so all we had to do was hit the gas and take off if things' went south.'

As I already indicated, Betty warned us that Pops would not allow strangers to come into the house. We agreed not to go in and agreed to give Betty the money to get the pills. Initially, I gave her enough money to purchase twelve Lortabs and twelve Xanax pills. Betty went inside and came back out shortly after that. We observed her enter and exit the residence. It was important for our probable cause to make sure she left our car, did not have contact with anyone else outside, entered the target residence, came back out, walked back up to us, and handed me the drugs. This helped show she got the drugs inside the residence and nowhere else, so we could get a search warrant.

After she exited Pops' house, she got back in the car with us. Betty sat in the front passenger seat, and I sat in the rear passenger seat behind her. The second undercover sat in the rear seat on the driver's side, and the professional CI sat in the driver's seat. Betty turned around, with her knees in the seat, and spoke to me. At the time, the CI and the other UC had their windows down (on the driver's side) and spoke to three unknown guys, setting up a five-pound marijuana deal. These were the young guys who more than likely pulled security for Pops or at least, they ran the gate for him. While they were setting up the future deal, Betty and I did the dope deal with the prescription medication. Betty had the pills in her hand, and she slowly dropped them into my hand. Just as almost all the pills were given to me, she pulled back the last two pills. She immediately took the pills orally and said that was for the trouble. It was obvious she was a pill head; she did not even have anything to drink with the pills; no water needed. It happened quickly and did surprise me, but there was nothing I could do about it without blowing our cover or jeopardizing the investigation or the safety of myself, my undercover partner, and the CI. So, I went with it and documented it later on in my report.

I put the pills she gave me in my pocket and did not panic after what she did. I knew that I did not give her the pills, and it would have been impossible to anticipate this happening or stopping her. Since the first deal went well for the Lortabs and Xanax, I asked her if she could go back in and purchase some OxyContin (Oxy's). Before going in on the first deal, I asked Betty to look around or ask what other types of pills Pops had for sale because I might be interested in something stronger than what I got. I told her that I had people (buyers) who wanted me to get them some Oxys. I sent her back into the house, and she purchased a quantity of OxyContin, which helped add to our probable cause for the search warrant. She did not attempt to take any of these pills, most likely because their value was a lot more. They were ten-milligram pills, which cost a dollar per milligram per pill ($10 each, so 10 for $100). The Xanax and Lortabs were $3-$5 each pill, depending on the number of milligrams.

After the second deal, Betty came back out of the rear door of Pops' house and immediately got into the vehicle. She handed me the pills, and we drove away. We drove Betty back to her house and went back to the office to do paperwork and process the evidence. This was just another of many cases in a larger operation, so we did not arrest Betty or Pops immediately. About one week after the purchase, we executed a search warrant on Pops' house in the early morning hours. We caught him off guard so he could not get to his sawed-off shotgun, which he had leaned against the wall right next to him. This proved that Betty was not lying about the shotgun, and Pops always had it close by him. We found an unbelievable variety of prescription medications. The people who sold these drugs to Pops were stupid enough to sell

347

them in the existing prescription bottles, with their names on them. This only left a trail of evidence behind to charge someone in the conspiracy at a later date. We seized over $15,000 stashed in different locations throughout the residence. Pops was taken to jail and bonded out not long after, within twenty-four hours. His bond was set at $80,000.

Approximately three or four months after the deal with Betty and Pops, we conducted the roundup and arrested all the dealers involved in the operation. All the arrests were made, and nothing new came up from Betty's arrest. About a month later, after Betty asked for a discovery of all paperwork dealing with her case, she filed a complaint against me. She made up allegations that I personally gave her drugs during this undercover operation. The immediate question I had was *how a pill-head remembers the specifics of a deal that she did while high*, which was probably one of hundreds she had done in the last few months. I also questioned her credibility and motive to make this up. Remember, she had a huge appetite and addiction for a daily dosage of pills. This meant that she probably did at least one dope deal every day for years, and she was like a zombie pill-head walking around. On many occasions, she may have done many more deals. The reality is we only did one deal with her, but yet she seemed to remember every intricate detail. I call "Bullshit."

I was a little shocked when my actions started to be seriously questioned based upon a complaint from a pill-head because I documented everything in my report, just as it happened. I even documented that she took two pills for herself, and I did not attempt to hide any facts. The one issue that came up was when the second UC wrote his statement. He said to me later that he did not actually see the dope deal, but documented facts in a summary as he thought I said they went down. He mentioned that I 'allowed' her to take the pills, which was inaccurate. If I had taken the pills and then pulled two out and gave them to her as a payment, that would have been illegal; but she took the pills and swallowed them before receiving all the pills from her. I had no choice but to allow this to happen because of the way it went down and the dangerous situation of me coming out of my role to stop it would have created. Even if I had come out of my role, she had already swallowed the pills, so there was no reason for me to have done anything differently. This discrepancy in two statements from officers that were both on the scene, and the fact that Betty said I gave her drugs, caused Internal Affairs to open up an investigation.

Initially, this was not a big deal because drug dealers commonly make up lies about cops to create a defense for their distribution case, of which they were almost always guilty. If a defendant cannot defend their actions, attacking the accuser's character and creating enough for reasonable doubt in the mind of the jury is their only hope. It comes at the expense of the honest cop that truly did nothing wrong, but criminals do not care about unintended casualties from their actions as long as they do not go to prison.

Without warning, I was told to immediately report to the Internal Affairs (IA) office at the law enforcement center downtown. Unbeknownst to me, my UC partner had been questioned about this incident three days earlier, and he did not even give me a heads up about any type of investigation. Yes, he was probably told not to mention this to anyone; but since I did not do anything wrong and knew it, my undercover partner should have given me a heads up about which case was being investigated. If I had known which case, but no other details in advance, I would have reviewed the case file to be able to answer questions immediately, with great detail. Instead, I walked in blind-sided and was told I was being investigated like a common criminal. This instantly put my guard up and made me defensive, since I had so much to lose and did nothing wrong.

I believe that the investigation went south a week before they opened it up. I knew that they did not have anything on me, and they were already upset that I was about to leave the sheriff's office. I had spearheaded the undercover unit, which gave us national recognition in the law enforcement community, so they knew their undercover success would lessen with my departure. In addition, their only other full-time undercovers were two people I trained, and they had never worked full-time undercover until I was in the unit with them. To make a long story short, Internal Affairs backed off once I let them know that I knew my rights, and knew I had done nothing wrong. Internal Affairs went from initially acting as they wanted me in jail for Distribution of a Controlled Substance, to wanting me terminated, to wanting me suspended, to wanting me written up, to finally settling for a verbal reprimand, which is the lowest form of discipline that can be administered. It was a clear fishing expedition. In the end, I was given oral counseling, with no punishment. The sheriff's office said, although I technically did not violate any policy with the sheriff's office, there should have been a policy in place, and I should have handled the situation differently. Next time, they said I need to pay the unwitting informant in advance for the transaction she/he was about to do, so they do not feel that they can take a portion of the illegal drugs purchased. I agreed with this statement, and I was asked to help train other undercovers on how to prevent this from happening to them in the future.

In hindsight, I realize that I was not clear in my wording in my incident report. I said that I allowed her to take the pills, which was partly true. I did not try to stop her because it happened so fast, but I definitely did not receive the pills and then turn around and distribute them back to her. I knew that would be an unlawful distribution, and then I would be no better than a drug dealer.

Initially, when I told my story to Internal Affairs (IA), they said it conflicted with the CI, Betty (suspect), and the other UC's stories. Of course, it conflicted with the suspect's statement, but the CI *and* UCs? I did not know why, and I was surprised to hear this. Well, I found out later that Internal Affairs lied to me, and only my fellow UC had a conflicting story. The problem they had was that they said that I took the pills from Betty first, and then gave Betty some of the pills for doing the deal for me. That would be a distribution if it happened that way, but it did not. They said that I could have told her no, and given her money instead of the pills in advance. Whatever she did with the money would not be my problem, but at least it would not be a distribution. At first, the Internal Affairs Investigators did not believe that she took the pills on her own before handing me all of the pills that she purchased for me. The CI advised Internal Affairs in an interview that I would never do something like what they were claiming. This was a relief to hear that the CI told the truth and knew me well. This was a CI that pushed the envelope with me, but he knew I always follow the laws. Of course, IA did not believe the CI, which is understandable, so he had to prove himself by taking a polygraph.

The CI passed the polygraph, which only further proved I would never have done what the suspect alleged. I was very disappointed to hear that my fellow UC said I got the pills and then gave them to Betty, but I also knew he did not see the transaction take place. The UC said this, but he was leaning out the window during the deal and not looking at our hand-to-hand motion, *or* the transaction, which all happened in seconds. Being a 'company' man like he was, this UC did not want to say he was not sure what happened, thinking he would lose credibility. All he had to do was say, 'I did not see the actual deal,' and document only what he saw happened with the surrounding *known* circumstances - but he did not. When I confronted him, he said I must stick with my first story. He stuck to this story and caused me a long Internal Affairs investigation. He knew that if he changed his story now, it would have gotten him put under investigation. So, he was now looking out for himself, but at my detriment.

Something else that made this case memorable was how badly I was treated and disrespected by IA and the sheriff's office during the investigation. It hurt me to know how badly I was treated, considering I had sacrificed my wellbeing to clean up the streets, and that was how they repaid my good hard work. During their investigation, I had to give four different written statements. I invoked my Miranda and Garrity rights in all but the last two statements, and this infuriated Internal Affairs. I was threatened with possible termination and told I could not put my rights on paper before I wrote my statement. I was basically told I had no rights, which in and of itself was unlawful. Even as a cop, I had the same rights as anyone being accused of an offense in our criminal justice system. I continued and wrote a third statement. In this statement, I was told by my Vice and Narcotics Lt. to explain why I put my rights in all the previous statements. When I turned it in, IA guys flipped out on me. They thought I was trying to be slick and mention my rights in a nonchalant way.

Little did they know, I was only obeying a direct order from my Lieutenant. I was only doing what I needed to protect myself from being done wrong by these guys. I later found out that the Lieutenant over IA was really mad because I was one of the original founding members of the first-ever Police Union in the sheriff's office, which had started to grow a decent following. They knew that employees having rights protected would make their job more difficult for them. Unfortunately, that union dream died not too long afterward, because SC has no collective bargaining rights in a right to work state, and many people saw what happened to anyone that tried to be part of a positive movement towards employee rights; they got unfairly targeted or treated. Well, they ordered me to give a fourth statement and remove that part. For my fourth statement, I just wrote the facts pertaining to the incident without invoking my rights since I was ordered to do so. I consulted with an attorney beforehand, and he told me not to be insubordinate and to do as they asked. I did, and they left me alone after the fourth and final statement. Although they left me alone, they did not clear my investigation for three more months. The moral of the story is that I realized that I could not trust anyone, not even my fellow undercover, in this case.

Only you have your own back. Thank God I did not let this affect my ability to work. The DEA eventually hired me after completing a polygraph examination and getting a Top-Secret clearance. I disclosed this with the DEA, and they asked me lots of questions, even on the polygraph, but I passed it with flying colors. Here is the most ironic thing about this case: I ended up receiving a Distinguished Service Award/Medal for this operation, including this case, and all of my undercover work, which resulted in the arrest of over one hundred fifteen drug dealers on over two hundred fifty felony warrants.

IA Investigation Still Haunting Me Several Years Later

It did not take long to learn that the lead Internal Affairs (IA) investigator for the sheriff's office held a grudge against me for the 'Betty' case discussed above. One of the things he did not like was the fact that I knew and invoked my constitutional rights to remain silent while the case was considered criminal in nature. Once the case turned internal, non-criminal, and only administrative, I invoked my Garrity Rights, meaning that any statement I gave could not be used against me in a future criminal proceeding. I did this to protect myself, which is what any officer should do when IA comes at them and accuses them of a crime right from the start, which they know they did not do. What really pissed them off the most was when I invoked my rights, and they tried to intimidate me into cooperating without using or documenting my rights. Still, I refused and told them I was a

357

member of the Police Union and wanted representation present. They did not like this at all, because it was something they were not used to, and SC was a state without collective bargaining rights. So, this meant that the Police Union was not powerful unless it had numbers or the majority of officers on the force.

At the time, the Union was a new thing for the sheriff's office, but the city police department already had over half of their officers as members. I knew that once we got over 50% of the staff on board, we would finally have a voice. As a leader that is not known to follow the same path as everyone else, I was one of the original ten Union members at the Sheriff's office, pushing this to look out for employee rights. The sheriff's office was notorious as a 'good ole boy' system, and the Sheriff, an elected official, ruled with an iron fist. Our county had the same Sheriffs for long periods of time, and before they left office, they would announce their predecessor, who would then get elected. It was the deep-rooted 'good ole boy' system, and I was not a 'good ole boy.' In other words, it was the Sheriff's way or the highway, and legally he could get away with it. Thankfully, I got along fine with the Sheriff himself, and we did not have any personal issues. It was just this one guy who was over IA that had a bone to pick with me because he got butthurt that I knew my rights, and used them to protect myself.

By invoking my constitutional rights and following legal guidelines to protect myself, I forced IA to work outside their comfort zone for the information that a rookie cop would just give without question, and potentially incriminate themselves for something they did not do. I had seen officers fired based on information they provided when cooperating with investigators, so I was cautious. The Fifth Amendment protections against "self-incrimination" still applies to police; we are people, too, and have the same rights according to our constitution. I do not know why it was so hard to understand that I have rights and will protect myself. The fact that I was not the least bit intimidated by a twenty-plus year veteran probably also got to him. Egos were a negative thing in this circumstance. I know you can always tell the size of a real man by the size of the problem it takes to get a rise out of them. This guy was a small man, although large in physical stature.

Many years later, this still haunted me, and this IA guy tried to screw me over when I left the United States police work to do government contracting (a.k.a. mercenary, hired guns or whatever you want to call it) work overseas. In order to get past the background checks, I had to get an IA clearance letter from each former government employer stating the results of any IA investigation(s), and that I was eligible for rehire, or that I left the agency in good standings. This IA investigator took Betty's complaint and said that I had a Conduct Unbecoming of a Police Officer Investigation on my record. This was serious sounding and slandered my name, despite the fact they could not point out a policy that I violated, or law that I broke.

What made this so bad was this Conduct Unbecoming of a Police Officer case never went past the letter recommending verbal counseling (shared below in this section). I never got called back in to IA to sign anything, nor was I disciplined for anything surrounding that investigation. As a matter of fact, I received the aforementioned Distinguished Service Medal and Commendation for my undercover work in that case and the overall operation. So, when I left the sheriff's office, I passed a federal background investigation and became a Special Agent with the DEA. This alleged Conduct Unbecoming of a Police Officer claim was not substantiated and was not in my personnel file. I know, because I asked for a copy of my entire file before I left the sheriff's office, and went to work with the federal government. In addition, I received letters from the Sheriff's office about my positive employment record while employed at the sheriff's office, and I received multiple levels of security clearances in other jobs after leaving that agency. Never before had this ever appeared during background investigations for more than a decade.

In 2012 the Sheriff wrote me a letter of recommendation to become Chief of Police, and in 2016 they gave a job verification letter stating I left the sheriff's office in good standings. A redacted copy of both letters is below for your reading pleasures and to corroborate my story. As you will see there is no mention of any negative employment or disciplinary actions taken against me during my time with the Sheriff's Office.

(BELOW) 1 of the 2 above described letters.

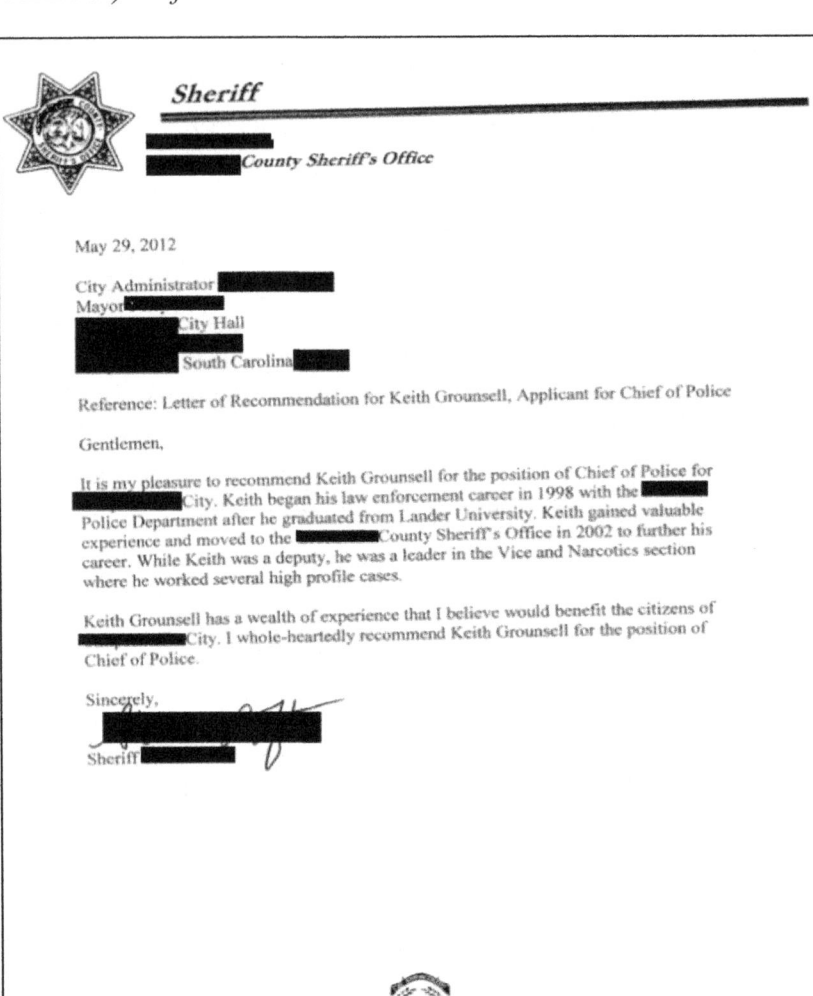

Sheriff

████████
████████ *County Sheriff's Office*

May 29, 2012

City Administrator ████████
Mayor ████
████ City Hall
████ South Carolina ████

Reference: Letter of Recommendation for Keith Grounsell, Applicant for Chief of Police

Gentlemen,

It is my pleasure to recommend Keith Grounsell for the position of Chief of Police for ████████ City. Keith began his law enforcement career in 1998 with the ████ Police Department after he graduated from Lander University. Keith gained valuable experience and moved to the ████ County Sheriff's Office in 2002 to further his career. While Keith was a deputy, he was a leader in the Vice and Narcotics section where he worked several high profile cases.

Keith Grounsell has a wealth of experience that I believe would benefit the citizens of ████████ City. I whole-heartedly recommend Keith Grounsell for the position of Chief of Police.

Sincerely,

Sheriff ████

An accredited law enforcement agency

(BELOW) The other of the 2 above described letters.

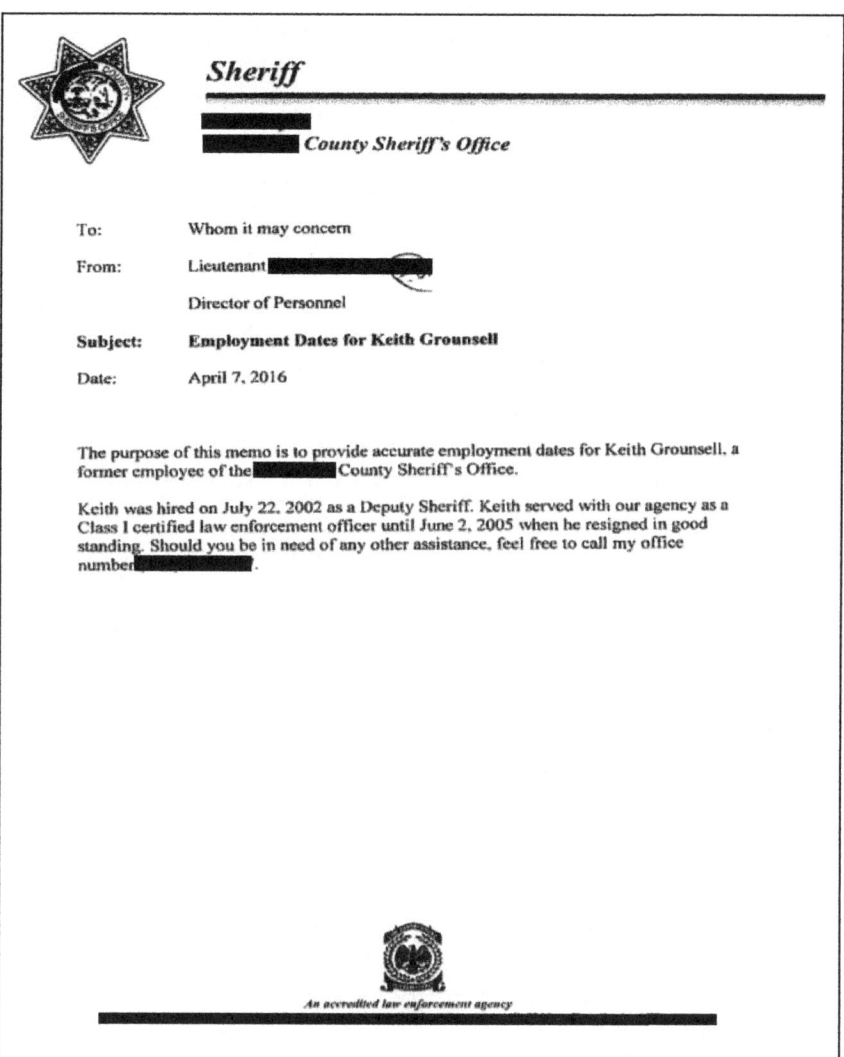

> ***Sheriff***
>
> *County Sheriff's Office*
>
> To: Whom it may concern
>
> From: Lieutenant
>
> Director of Personnel
>
> **Subject: Employment Dates for Keith Grounsell**
>
> Date: April 7, 2016
>
> The purpose of this memo is to provide accurate employment dates for Keith Grounsell, a former employee of the County Sheriff's Office.
>
> Keith was hired on July 22, 2002 as a Deputy Sheriff. Keith served with our agency as a Class I certified law enforcement officer until June 2, 2005 when he resigned in good standing. Should you be in need of any other assistance, feel free to call my office number.
>
> *An accredited law enforcement agency*

About a year and a half after receiving the 2016 employment verification letter, just after I announced I was interested in running for political office (i.e., Sheriff, after the current Sheriff was removed from office due to criminal indictments), all of a sudden, this report comes out that I had a

Conduct Unbecoming of a Police Officer IA investigation substantiated in my past. It was clear that someone at the sheriff's office was trying to tarnish my good name to hurt my political campaign and the probability of getting elected. Politics are a dirty game and built for dishonest people, so I really had no place running for political office. After the Sheriff was indicted, I knew that I could clean things up and professionalize the sheriff's office because I had a proven track record as Chief. My tenure of Chief was not very long, just under four years total, but was full of lots of craziness when I stood against unethical behavior and corruption. I was terminated and later reinstated. The Mayor, Chief of Police before me, and Lieutenant over investigations were all criminally indicted for charges ranging from Misconduct in Office to Destroying Evidence in a murder investigation. Despite all that going on, under my leadership, the city went from the #28 Safest City in SC to #1 Safest City in SC in about two years. These same people linked to indicted and convicted criminals, came after me to make sure I would not be elected Sheriff. They knew I was a threat because I could not be controlled or made to overlook violations, out of fear for losing my job. I became known for fighting corruption and standing against it. I ended up withdrawing from the political race for Sheriff because of the relentless attacks, and I was overseas and unable to come home to campaign.

Despite the attempts to tarnish my professional career, I have survived. Thankfully, a little investigating will show the lies are not true. All anyone had to do was look at the fact that after a two-year-long hiring process, including a one-year-long background investigation, I got a Top-Secret clearance with full polygraph as a federal agent, immediately after leaving the sheriff's office. This was after these outlandish allegations by Betty, which were totally made up to get her felony criminal charges dismissed. She was an addict and had no defense against her actions. I also had the two above mentioned letters readily available to show, if needed. I always kept important records in a fireproof safe and did not realize how vital it was until I tried to disprove what they were saying to discredit me as a political candidate.

Thank God I always keep all of my documentation, and I was also able to dig up a letter showing the recommendations to clear me of the investigation because there were no criminal wrongdoings or policy violations committed during the Betty drug deal with Pops. See the following copy of the letter, which cleared me and allowed me to become employed overseas again in late 2016.

(BELOW) While working at the sheriff's office, this was the last letter or correspondence I received pertaining to this matter. As far as I understood, I was given an oral counseling with no punishment and the matter was resolved without any misconduct allegations being substantiated from Betty's complaint.

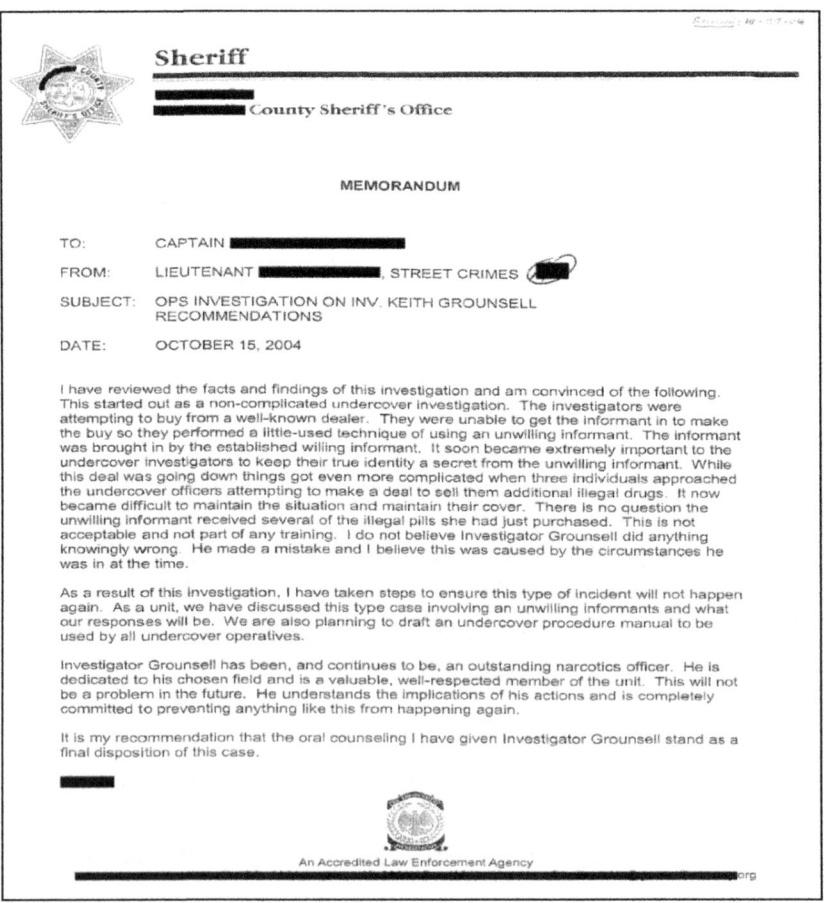

Sheriff

County Sheriff's Office

MEMORANDUM

TO: CAPTAIN

FROM: LIEUTENANT ████████████, STREET CRIMES

SUBJECT: OPS INVESTIGATION ON INV. KEITH GROUNSELL
           RECOMMENDATIONS

DATE: OCTOBER 15, 2004

I have reviewed the facts and findings of this investigation and am convinced of the following. This started out as a non-complicated undercover investigation. The investigators were attempting to buy from a well-known dealer. They were unable to get the informant in to make the buy so they performed a little-used technique of using an unwilling informant. The informant was brought in by the established willing informant. It soon became extremely important to the undercover investigators to keep their true identity a secret from the unwilling informant. While this deal was going down things got even more complicated when three individuals approached the undercover officers attempting to make a deal to sell them additional illegal drugs. It now became difficult to maintain the situation and maintain their cover. There is no question the unwilling informant received several of the illegal pills she had just purchased. This is not acceptable and not part of any training. I do not believe Investigator Grounsell did anything knowingly wrong. He made a mistake and I believe this was caused by the circumstances he was in at the time.

As a result of this investigation, I have taken steps to ensure this type of incident will not happen again. As a unit, we have discussed this type case involving an unwilling informants and what our responses will be. We are also planning to draft an undercover procedure manual to be used by all undercover operatives.

Investigator Grounsell has been, and continues to be, an outstanding narcotics officer. He is dedicated to his chosen field and is a valuable, well-respected member of the unit. This will not be a problem in the future. He understands the implications of his actions and is completely committed to preventing anything like this from happening again.

It is my recommendation that the oral counseling I have given Investigator Grounsell stand as a final disposition of this case.

An Accredited Law Enforcement Agency

It is amazing how something so small, such as a dope deal for prescription pills, can escalate into something that you have to explain the rest of your career, even though they admit that you violated no policies or laws. Having an overzealous IA investigator, who thought they needed to make an example out of an officer on the drop of a complaint, is not fair and impartial. This one IA investigator, who just so happened to be the supervisor at the time, should have taken a neutral approach, instead of trying to crucify me before I was even questioned, or given a chance to respond to the allegations of a drug addict. Of course, it went way beyond that situation and was personal to him, because I knew my rights and invoked them immediately. Instead of letting it go after it was done, many years later, this same person used this to attack me politically. There is no place for politics or unethical behavior in police work, most especially in a division where they are tasked to investigate this very thing that they themselves were doing.

Despite having all these letters of recommendation and proof all these attacks were politically motivated, I still almost lost a high-level job opportunity overseas because of this case (i.e. United States Contingent Commander on a U.S. federal government and United Nations police mission in Haiti). Below is the detailed explanation letter I had to write, in addition to the above letters being provided, in order to get hired on to do federal government contracting work over a decade after this incident. This letter went to the federal background investigators who would grant or deny my security clearance. Thankfully, after a thorough investigation, my security clearance was granted, and off to Haiti, I went.

"Attached is a copy of the memorandum that I received from my Supervisor (County sheriff's office) clearing me of the investigation (i.e. oral counseling/no intentional wrongdoing on my behalf and no policy or other violations committed) that you were asking me about. If for some reason you do not get this attachment I can rescan and resend it, or send it via FedEx. (It is saved as a Microsoft Office Document). I also have past letters of recommendation and

employment verifications from this same agency, written after this alleged Internal Affairs investigation, that do not mention anything about these allegations being substantiated and being found guilty of anything, much less conduct unbecoming of a police officer. Prior to my current position as Chief of Police, I never had any major disciplinary actions or punishment taken against me for any form of misconduct. I am willing to take a polygraph, if necessary, to clear my name and this matter. Thank you in advance for your attention to details in this matter."

To explain in further detail, this is what happened.

On 5-■-20■ I was working in an undercover capacity along with a second undercover (UC) Investigator and an established Confidential Informant (CI).

On this date, we drove out to pick up a subject named Betty. Betty was a known drug addict and dealer in the west Greenville area. Riding in the CI's vehicle, we drove out to Betty's residence and picked her up. Betty rode in the passenger front seat, myself and the other UC were in the back seat and the CI was driving. We drove out to a neighborhood where an older subject named "Pops" lived (I forget his real name). We had received information about Pops selling large quantities of Oxycontin and other prescription drugs to different people in the ▮▮▮▮ *City and* ▮▮▮▮ *County areas. We also had Intel that Pops had multiple guns and routinely answered the door with a sawed-off shotgun. (This was all corroborated when we executed a Search Warrant at Pops residence) On the ride over to Pops house Betty advised that since this was the first time that we are buying drugs through her (ref. to as an Unwitting Informant in attached Memo, but she turned into a suspect when she did all of the transactions herself) we were not permitted to enter the residence of Pops house. Betty advised that Pops would answer the door with a gun and would not be happy if she showed up with a new and unfamiliar face to buy drugs (fear we might be the Police).*

When we arrived at the house, we observed a group of approximately 3 male subjects playing basketball in the backyard/driveway area. As we pulled into the driveway, they opened up the gate and we pulled into the backyard area. The gate was immediately closed behind us and we were locked inside of the fenced in area until they reopened the gate for us to leave.

I handed Betty $120 in government funds to go inside and purchase some illegal prescription drugs from Pops. The drugs were to be brought back out and given to me. While Betty was inside the trailer with Pops, we started a drug conversation with the subjects playing basketball in the driveway, who also appeared to be doing access control and security for Pop's. We exchanged phone numbers with them and arranged for a multi-pound marijuana deal to take place in the near future.

After a few minutes, Betty came back to the car with a hand full of Hydrocodone and Alprazolam (Xanax) pills. As she was handing me the pills, she kept two for herself and handed me the rest. She immediately swallowed the pills without anything to drink. Almost simultaneously as she swallowed the pills,

Betty advised me that she took the pills as her payment for getting me the drugs that I wanted. I did not agree to this and it was totally unexpected. In the drug world it is common practice, for the middleman who facilitated the transaction to be compensated. Being a drug addict Betty decided (on her own) to take the pills before I tried to offer her something besides drugs as payment. Not wanting to reveal our undercover status and possibly jeopardize our lives, we did not come out of roll and arrest Betty in this long term undercover operation. In addition, it is an unwritten rule of undercover work and best practice not to get involved in an arrest of a subject who thinks that you are a bad guy. After the transaction we drove out of the area and dropped Betty back off at her residence. My reports were completed and documented just as I advised. Several months later Betty was arrested during a large round-up of drug dealers in the ▓▓▓▓▓ *County area.*

Four months after the transaction occurred, I was called into the office of Internal Affairs (IA), referred to as Office of Professional Standards (OPS) at that sheriff's office, and questioned as to whether or not I gave Betty the drugs. I advised that she took the pills and I did not stop her, but apparently, she told them a different story. My second UC could not help much in clearing up the situation because he and the CI were busy arranging the marijuana deal with the other subjects while this quick transaction occurred between myself and Betty. The sheriff's office thought I had violated a policy or General Order, but could not find a policy or General Order that I violated (as you will see in the attached memo). I did not come out of my UC role and make an arrest for several reasons:

The Golden Rule of UC work, the UC is never involved in the arrest. This is done to prevent the suspect, who thinks you're a bad guy, for inflicting injury to you because they thought they were being robbed and not arrested by the police. The suspect could have a legitimate argument in court if they kill the UC when they tried to arrest them, stating that they feared for their lives and thought they were getting robbed or going to die- so they acted out of self-defense.

We were locked inside of a gated area with no quick way to escape or get backup units inside to assist with the arrest.

I knew that Pops had multiple guns in the house and if we blew our cover and tried to arrest Betty we still had to deal with Pops and the 3 other male subjects or whoever else was inside the house. This would put us at a tactical disadvantage and the risk of making the arrest now versus later, does not outweigh the risk to the two undercover's and the CI that we were sworn to protect.

This would have jeopardized the covert nature of the CI's identity as a government agent. The CI had been a document CI for Federal and local law enforcement since 1976. Revealing the status of the CI as an informant would have potentially cost the CI his life.

This buy was part of a much larger investigation dubbed Operation Straight Shooter. This operation resulted in the arrest of over 115 different persons on over

250 Felony charges. The charges stemmed

from distribution of controlled substances

to solicitation of murder. Making this

arrest would have possibly jeopardized the

larger mission.

I could probably mention several

other reasons why I did what I did and

stood by my decision. The fact is I made a

split-second decision during a covert

undercover operation, and this was the

outcome.

As a result of this IA investigation,

the ███████ *County Sheriff's Office*

found out that they did not have any policy

and procedure in place for this undercover

situation. They felt that it was my duty to

take drugs off the street and not to allow

someone to take illegal prescription drugs

in front of a law enforcement officer,

especially not prescription drugs that were
purchased with government funds. It was
due to the complexity of the situation and
the fact that I did not do anything morally
or legally wrong that the investigation was
cleared with an oral counseling. I was
advised how to handle this situation if it
ever occurred again. If I could do it all
over again, I would have tried to have paid
her twice the amount, in money, that she
compensated herself with in pills. This
would have allowed us to give her money
and if she purchased pills with the money
then it was of her own free will and not
drugs belonging to or facilitated by the
government. I have been a paid instructor
to teach at an Undercover Narcotics
Investigation schools to local law
enforcement and this is one scenario that I
try to train the new undercover agents on.

I hope this clarifies some question

you may have had. If you have any further

questions, feel free to call or email me.

Thanks,

Keith Grounsell

Among other lessons learned, this situation goes to show that a police officer's word is no longer considered his bond. This was spoiled for us by a small group of corrupt cops over the years. The old *saying One bad apple spoils the whole bunch* is true in the eyes of the public, and as we all know, perception is a reality these days. This situation also proved to me that not all police officers on the job are good or honest people. I already knew this, but to have someone in IA that is not ethical was a double dose of messed up. I have forgiven this overzealous and jealous IA Investigator for what he did, but I will never forget, nor will I stand by when an injustice occurs. I spoke to many other police officers over the years who have told similar stories about how this same IA guy mistreated them. I do not know their individual circumstances, or if they were truly done wrong, but the one common denominator was that they felt like this IA guy talked down to them, and got personal during investigations. This condemnation and lack of professionalism are not appreciated or required in law enforcement, a career that already has a ton of stress and pressures, so we did not need one coming from inside the agency. Having an axe to grind against fellow officers who invoke their constitutional rights, and do not just roll over or bow to his scare tactics was evidence of some other deeper issues involving this IA Investigator.

Undercover 'Looks' During Operation Straight Shooter

Throughout my undercover career, I was constantly changing my look, which enabled me to work undercover in an assortment of different undercover operations. Also, it helped conceal my identity; if I was ever compromised in one deal, I could still work undercover in another area. It also helped to work in a jurisdiction covering over seven-hundred-fifty square miles. If someone found out I was a cop, they may send out a message, via word of mouth, who I was and what I looked like. If I constantly looked different, then it was to my benefit, and hard to pinpoint who I was (cop or criminal), which was one of the main reasons I did it. The majority of my time undercover was before social media was so popular, so it was a little easier to survive longer if you were ever compromised. Modern-day undercovers have it harder because anyone can snap a photo or video of someone, label them an undercover cop (without evidence), and blast it to thousands of people on different social media platforms in a matter of seconds. Thankfully, I did not have to deal with that issue.

Having the ability to look different all the time was not only good for undercover work, but it seemed to help my love life with my wife. If you have been married for any period of time, it can help spice up the marriage. My wife used to joke with me because I changed my look so often, saying it was almost like having multiple affairs without really doing it.

At one time, she said she used to like me with the long hair look. I liked long hair, but it was too much maintenance. I have a newfound respect for women that have long hair, which takes lots of upkeep and daily care. As I discussed earlier in this book, there are mental effects that come with these images that I was trying to personify. I often found myself mentally feeling like the character I had created for my undercover work. This can be unhealthy over time.

(BELOW) These are photos taken of me during Operations Straight Shooter. This kind of shows some of the different looks I had during a thirteen-month undercover operation.

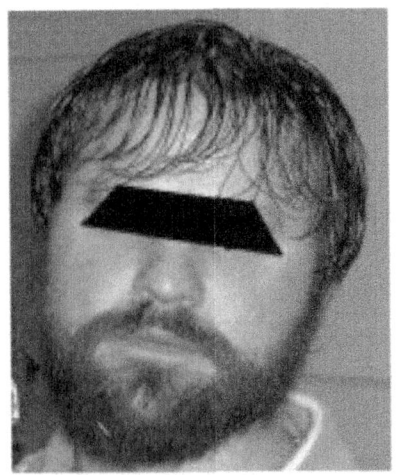 

*(**BELOW**) Continued: These are photos taken of me during Operations Straight Shooter. This kind of shows some of the different looks I had during a thirteen-month undercover operation.*

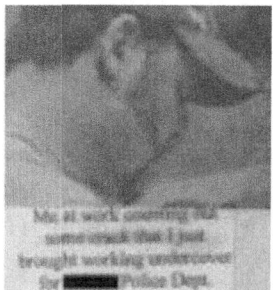

Final Results of Operation Straight Shooter

Operation Straight Shooter was named this because it started out focusing on street-level crack cocaine use, and a "straight shooter" pipe is the street name for drug paraphernalia commonly used to smoke crack cocaine. What started as a narrow-focused operation on one drug, and quickly escalated beyond street-level drug sales, because of the willingness of people to sell us larger quantities of an assortment of different drugs as long as you had the money. As a result of the thirteen-month undercover operation, over one hundred fifteen people were arrested on over two hundred and fifty felony charges. On the day of the roundup, we arrested eighty-two suspects in one day, and the others were picked up over the course of the next month or so. My undercover partner, Lyle, and I both received Distinguished Service Medals for this operation. This was one of the first times I was formally recognized for some of my long-term undercover work, and it felt really good. I do not do the job for the recognition, but it was nice to receive something like this when I did not expect it.

Below are press release/newspaper articles, and photos of our press conference room from Operation Straight Shooter. According to the sheriff's office, "no other operations in the history of the sheriff's office yielded more charges or suspects." As of the publication date of this book, no other "true undercover" operations have even come close. As part of the last of a dying breed of deep undercover officers, I take great pride in this accomplishment.

(BELOW) Photo of the layout of the Conference room at the sheriff's office just before the media entered & the Sheriff gave his press release speech. Notice pictures of some of the suspects, which were previous mugshots because most were repeat offenders.

(BELOW) Photo of 3 undercovers for this operation posing for a picture before the media arrived. We quickly left out the back door to avoid any media in this case, since we were working undercover still.

(BELOW) *Copy of the newspaper article discussing the results of this undercover operation.*

Big haul: Lt. [REDACTED] left, and Sgt. [REDACTED] display a small portion of the drugs seized during "Operation Straight Shooter" in [REDACTED]

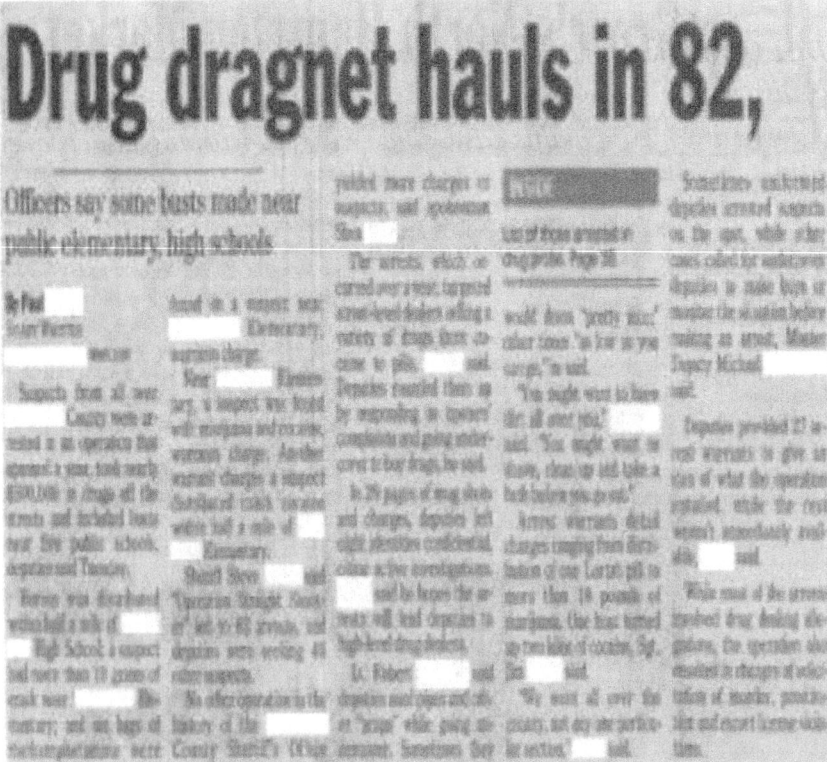

Drug dragnet hauls in 82,

Officers say some busts made near public elementary, high schools

By Paul [REDACTED]
Staff Writer

[REDACTED]

Suspects from all over [REDACTED] County were arrested in an operation that spanned a year, took nearly $500,000 in drugs off the streets and included busts near five public schools, deputies said Tuesday.

Teresy was distributed within half a mile of [REDACTED] High School. A suspect had more than 18 grams of crack near [REDACTED] Elementary, and six bags of methamphetamine were [REDACTED]

found in a vault near [REDACTED] Elementary, [REDACTED] supension charge.

Near [REDACTED] Elementary, a suspect was found with marijuana and cocaine, warrants charge. Another warrant charges a suspect distributed crack cocaine within half a mile of [REDACTED] Elementary.

Sheriff Steve [REDACTED] and "Operation Straight Shooter" led to 82 arrests, and deputies were seeking 41 other suspects.

No other operation in the history of the [REDACTED] County Sheriff's Office

yielded more charges or suspects, said spokesman Sgt. [REDACTED]

The arrests, which occurred over a year, targeted street-level dealers selling a variety of drugs from cocaine to pills, [REDACTED] said. Deputies treated them as by responding to tipsters' complaints and going undercover to buy drugs, he said.

In 29 pages of mug shots and charges, deputies left eight identities confidential, either active investigations [REDACTED] and he hopes the arrests will lead deputies to high-level drug dealers.

Lt. Robert [REDACTED] said deputies used open and oblique "snap" while going undercover. Sometimes they

(See [REDACTED], Page 38)

[REDACTED] list of those arrested in drug probe, Page 38

would dress "pretty nice," other times "as low as you can get," he said.

"You might want to have the all over you," [REDACTED] said. "You might want to dress, clean up and take a bath before you go out."

Arrest warrants detail charges ranging from distribution of one Lortab pill to more than 18 pounds of marijuana. One bust netted up two kilos of cocaine, Sgt. [REDACTED] said.

"We went all over the county, not any one particular section," [REDACTED] said.

Sometimes undercover deputies arrested suspects on the spot, while other cases called for undercover deputies to make buys or monitor the situation before making an arrest, Master Deputy Michael [REDACTED] said.

Deputies provided 23 arrest warrants to give an idea of what the operation entailed, while the rest weren't immediately available, [REDACTED] said.

While most of the arrests involved drug dealing allegations, the operation also resulted in charges of solicitation of murder, prostitution and escort license violations.

386

(BELOW) Copy of the distinguished service medal and certificate received for this operation   Also, an image of my UC partner (Lyle) and Myself at the annual awards banquet receiving this award.   We received a standing ovation from the crowd

What is Next?
(Vol. 3 Preview)

Operation Straight Shooter was a grand success, but there were still a ton of other unrelated undercover cases, and covert investigations conducted while working undercover for the sheriff's office. If you enjoyed what you read thus far, about my city (Volume 1) and county undercover experiences (Volume 2), please read about the continuation of my undercover experiences as a County Narcotics Investigator in Volume 3. You will see the continued growth in my abilities as an undercover to take cases to a higher level than what is seen by the average cop (i.e. multi-kilogram cocaine buys and posing as a hitman in a murder for hire, among many others), and learn more intricate details about undercover work behind the scenes (i.e. how I established my undercover identity, undercover props used, cover stories, why fitness was so important to a narc, undercover partners of the opposite sex, etc.). My county narc journey came to an end when I was selected to try-out and work undercover for the most preeminent drug enforcement agency in the world, the Drug Enforcement Administration, or DEA. This was achieved when I was hired on as a DEA Special Agent. I immediately took my undercover experiences to a different level with the feds, which you will learn all about in Volume 4 of A Narc's Tale.

Made in the USA
Middletown, DE
30 January 2023